P9-DGL-264

SCREWED

SCREWED

Laurie Plissner

F+W Media, Inc.

Published by Merit Press
an imprint of F+W Media, Inc.
10151 Carver Road, Suite 200
Blue Ash, Ohio 45242
www.meritpressbooks.com

ISBN 10: 1-4405-5710-1
ISBN 13: 978-1-4405-5710-1
eISBN 10: 1-4405-5711-X
eISBN 13: 978-1-4405-5711-8

Printed in the United States of America.

10 9 8 7 6 5 4 3 2 1

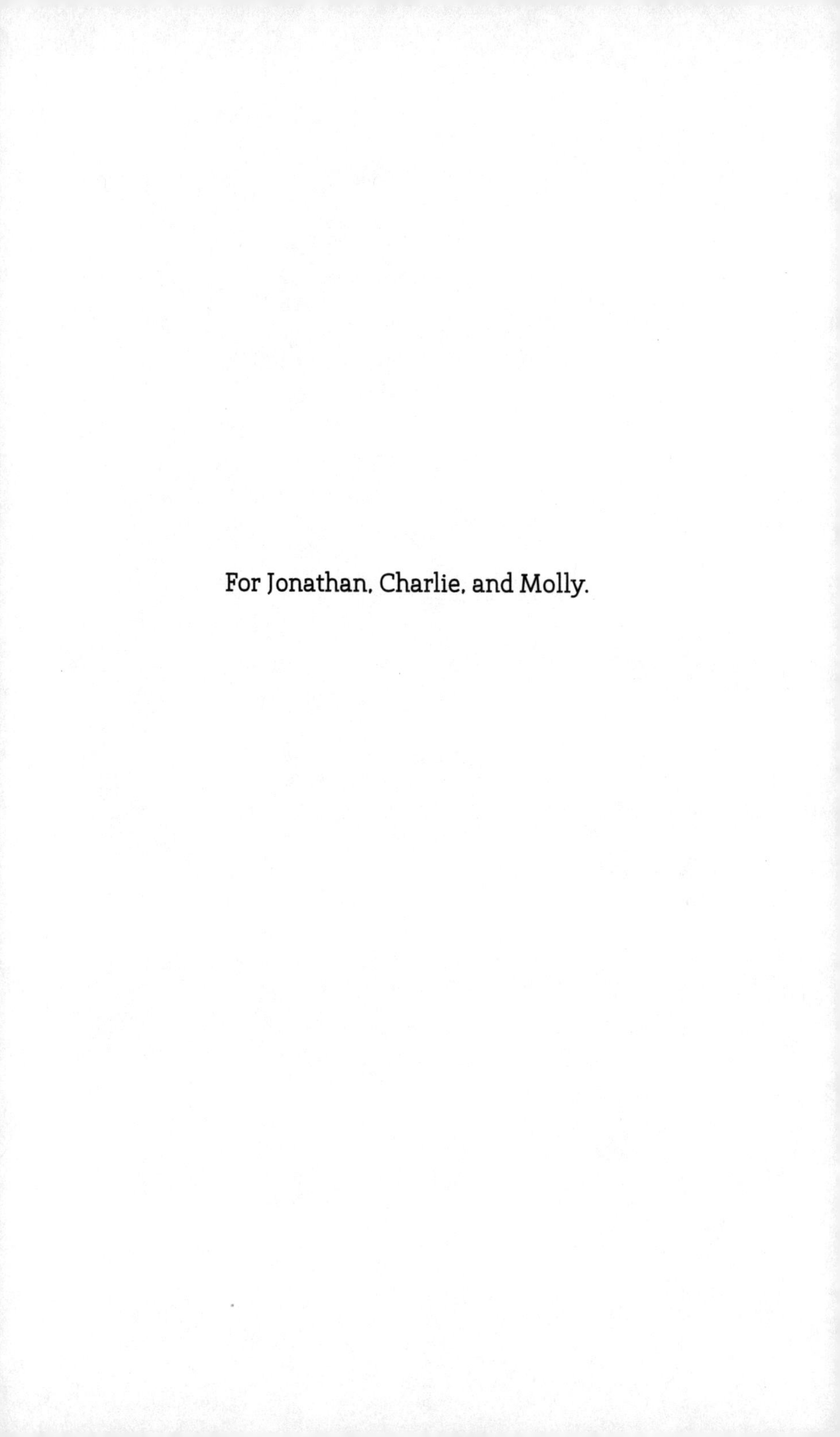

For Jonathan, Charlie, and Molly.

CHAPTER 1

Grace stared at the pale blue cross in the tiny oval window, willing it to disappear, wondering how anyone could call that a positive result. There was nothing positive about being seventeen and pregnant. If you were all grown up, then finding out you were about to have a baby would be the best news in the world, but Grace didn't even have a high school diploma yet, let alone a husband or a house or a job. Blinking back the tears, she continued to sit on the toilet, not sure where she was going to find the courage to leave her bathroom ever again. When she closed her eyes, she could see herself from above—a bird's-eye view of her own private train wreck. Stuff like this wasn't supposed to happen to girls like her.

Lined up like dead soldiers on the marble counter, the first six test sticks all displayed the same maddening plus sign. Three more pregnancy tests waited unopened in a brown bag under the counter, but Grace was beginning to realize that no matter how many times she took it, the results were going to be the same. Denial, though it had kept her from losing her mind for the past couple of weeks, was no longer a viable option. Finally Grace pulled up her pants and stood staring down at the evidence, her damp palms resting on the cool marble counter. Slowly and deliberately, she picked up each test stick and snapped it in two, as if physically destroying the messengers could somehow destroy the bad news itself.

Grace finally looked up and squinted at herself in the mirror. Deciding that she didn't look any different and almost convincing herself that all seven pluses had to be wrong, that it was just her irregular period being a little more irregular than usual, she was suddenly overwhelmed by nausea. She dove for the toilet and was just barely able to avoid puking all over the floor. Even after there was nothing left inside her, she continued retching, spasm after spasm, grateful there was no one home to hear her body turning inside out. Afterwards, Grace crawled into her bedroom and curled into the fetal position next to her bed, her cheek resting on the fluffy white rug as she stared blankly at a stray Q-tip that had missed the wastebasket. The smell of furniture polish and laundry detergent tickled the inside of her nose, threatening to bring on another bout of hurling. She wondered why it was called morning sickness. It was four o'clock in the afternoon.

Her cell phone rang repeatedly. On the third round she finally felt strong enough to reach up to her bed, where her phone lay, buzzing and vibrating relentlessly. "Hey," Grace whispered.

"What's wrong with you? Where have you been? You sound like death." Jennifer had never been one for small talk.

"I, um, have a problem. More like a disaster." As much as Grace didn't want to say it out loud—speaking the actual words would make it a historical fact—she didn't feel she could last another minute without talking to someone about it. Ready to collapse under a mountain of guilt and fear, she hoped telling Jennifer would somehow lighten her load. Maybe her best friend would have a solution, or maybe she could imagine a scenario in which seven plus signs didn't mean what Grace already knew they meant.

"Did you wreck your mom's Lexus? Your parents are going to go apeshit." Jennifer whistled into the phone. "Do you want to hide out over here for a few days until they cool down?"

"I didn't crash the car. I *wish* that were it." Grace longed for a problem that could be undone with a trip to the body shop and a fresh coat of paint.

"Well then, it can't be that bad. You always get straight As, so it can't be your report card. You gained a pound, and you're not size negative two anymore. Is that it?" Jennifer sighed impatiently into the phone, eager to hear what minor mishap Grace deemed so tragic that she could hardly speak. A chipped dinner plate from her mother's wedding set or a stain on the Oriental rug in the dining room was the worst Jennifer could imagine from Miss Goody Two-Shoes.

"I think I'm pregnant." Barely whispering the last word, Grace wasn't sure her voice had carried over the phone line.

There was a squeal followed by a thud as Jennifer dropped the phone. "What the . . . that's impossible. Only people who have sex can get pregnant. We had a pact—no hooking up till college. When did you change your mind? Who'd you do it with? Why didn't you tell me?"

"It's not always all about *you*, J."

"Whatever. Answer the fucking questions. Who was it?" Jennifer sounded like a hard-nosed cop trying to break down a suspect.

"It was Nick." Looking back, Grace herself could hardly wrap her head around it. Going all the way on the third date was so not in her playbook.

"Nick Salter, all-American? No way. He doesn't know people like us exist." *People like us* were kids who went to the school library to actually study, and who hoped to look back on high school as *not* the best years of their lives. "Who was it . . . really?"

"I knew you'd say that. That's why I didn't tell you we were going out."

"I don't believe you. Are you sure you didn't imagine this whole thing? Maybe you just dreamed you had sex with Nick. Maybe you're just bloated."

"I'm not imagining it. I took seven pregnancy tests."

"I still don't believe you. Are we talking about the same Nick Salter? Nick *Alexander* Salter, captain of the lacrosse team?"

"There's only one, Jennifer. The day after school let out he asked me if I wanted to go to the movies, and then we went out again, and on our third date it happened. It was my first time, and I got pregnant."

"Who the hell are *you*, and what did you do with my best friend?" shrieked Jennifer, certain Grace was the second-to-last person who would have the confidence to put out with an actual boy (Jennifer being the last), and the last one dumb enough to make a baby. "Best friends don't keep secrets, especially secrets the size of big, fat pregnant bellies."

"I didn't tell you because I'm embarrassed. It was such an idiotic thing to do, and I thought if I pretended it never happened, and I never told anybody, it would be like it hadn't." As Grace tried to explain her reasoning, she realized what a moron she was. This wasn't like pretending you hadn't refilled your Slurpee without paying for it at the 7-Eleven, or didn't have the answers written on your palm during a Spanish quiz. This was not the bad dream that would go away if she ignored it long enough.

"That's one way to deal, I guess, unless, of course, you get yourself knocked up. Didn't you make him use something? What were you thinking?" Jennifer was practically screaming into the phone.

Although she knew she should be more sensitive—it was too late for shoulda, coulda, woulda—Jennifer was so frustrated with her friend's foolishness, and the fact that she had been left out of the loop for so long, that she wanted to strangle her. Scolding her would have to do, for now. Teen pregnancy was for girls in the life skills program, not a girl with a perfect GPA who spent her spare time trying to solve the twin prime conjecture.

"I thought he did. He said he did. It was dark. I couldn't tell. Oh shit, I'm such an imbecile. What do I do now?"

Shutting her eyes tight, rocking back and forth as she gripped the phone in her suddenly sweaty hand, Grace prayed for a quick fix . . . or a painless death. She felt like she'd taken a long nap, and while she'd been sleeping, someone had ruined her life. Except that someone was herself, and this was no dream.

"Did you tell lover boy what happened? It's *his* responsibility. He has to step up." Jennifer was reeling, but she owed it to her friend to stay calm and help her figure out how to get through this. She made a silent vow to herself to stay a virgin until she was at least twenty, maybe thirty. No matter how great sex was supposed to feel, it couldn't be worth feeling the way Grace sounded over the phone.

"Nick's in Europe. When he took me home he said he was leaving the next day for a backpacking trip with his cousin, and he wasn't coming back until Labor Day."

On the one hand, Grace couldn't wait to tell him that she was pregnant with his baby. Would he say it had been love at first sight and he couldn't wait to marry her, take care of her? She floated off into fantasyland for a second, envisioning a bright future married to this budding professional athlete who looked like a model in a cologne ad. They would have a perfect child and a perfect life, just a little bit sooner than she had thought. But even as she daydreamed, she knew that wasn't how things worked out on MTV, or in real life. And truthfully, she was so humiliated by the whole thing that she couldn't imagine getting the words out if he was even around so that she could tell him, which was stupid, because what they'd done together in the back seat of his Jeep was way more embarrassing than talking about it, or at least it should have been.

"I hate to be the one to tell you, but either your babydaddy lied to you about his summer plans, or he has an evil twin, because I saw him out on the lake last weekend with a bunch of kids from school. Just because he looks like a movie star and all the girls want to jump him doesn't mean he's a good person—in fact, it's usually just the opposite. The hotter a guy is, the more likely he's going to be a total tool." As much as Jennifer liked being right, she hated having to tell her best friend that she'd made the worst mistake of her life with a guy who was nothing more than an empty box wrapped in fancy paper and tied with a shiny ribbon—take away his beautiful packaging and the only things left would be six feet of hair gel and half a bottle of Armani cologne. "Not that I'm saying I told you so. Not that I'm saying if you'd told me what was going on from the very beginning I could've saved you from fucking everything up, big time."

Unable to hold it in, Grace let loose a tidal wave of tears. In the back of her mind—well, really in the front of her mind—she knew that three dates with a boy didn't make a relationship, but she had let herself get tangled up in his adorably messy hair that he was always brushing off his forehead, and lost in his eyes, which, when they looked at her, made her feel like anything but a math troll. And it had all just been a setup, she realized way too late, so that Nick could add another name to his "I did her" list.

She knew that Nick Salter was way out of her league in every respect: a jock, captain of both the soccer and lacrosse teams, and winner of the junior class hot body contest at the spring picnic. When he asked her out, she was at once flattered and baffled. Able to choose from an array of more suitable candidates from the diving team and the cheerleading squad, what could he possibly see in her? She was a perennial benchwarmer on the junior varsity tennis team, whose major accomplishments were in the arena of mathletes, not athletes. It was so beauty and the beast, and she was the beast.

At first Grace thought maybe Nick was playing a joke on her, like one of those movies where a bunch of cool guys bet that one of them can't transform the class dweeb into a prom queen. But when he took her to the movies, he seemed genuinely interested in Grace as a person, just as she was, asking questions about her family and her future when she would have been perfectly content listening to him talk about himself, as long as she could stare at the perfect line of his jaw and the way he always looked like he almost—but not quite—needed a shave. On top of that, he had behaved like a gentleman, opening doors for her, ordering for her, never letting her pay for anything. Perhaps he was totally different from his public persona, and with her he could be his authentic, not-too-cool-for-school self. It had been too good to be true, and if she'd thought about it for more than a nanosecond she would have figured it out, but Grace had allowed herself to get caught up in the daydream.

Nick was a member of the high school elite, the ruling class in the microcosm of Silver Lake High School, and Grace, though not quite part of the peasant class, fell somewhere in the lower bourgeois rankings. Crossing class ranks happened rarely in friendship, and practically never in boy-girl relationships. It was an unwritten rule that the nobility didn't go slumming and the lower classes didn't try to raise their status by associating with those above them in the hierarchy. How could she forget the unbreakable laws of the high school jungle? How could she believe that the rules didn't apply to her? It was pure arrogance, she realized, and she was being punished for it, in a really big way.

It wasn't as if her features would turn people to stone if they looked at her. But they *would* probably offer her cookies and milk and ask her if she was lost. Sweet, freckled, innocent—definitely sneakers, not stilettos—appealing, but not exactly a guy magnet. Like someone's squeaky-clean little sister, she could still get into the movies for the under-twelve price, and when she went out to eat with her parents, the hostess handed her a children's menu and a box of crayons. What normal guy would be into that unless he was a burgeoning pedophile? That and the fact that she was scary smart placed her firmly on the geek side of the fence, and there were no geeks among Silver Lake royalty. But now she was questioning her intelligence. How could someone with a 2350 on the SAT end up naked in the back of some sleazebag's car, seduced by a few well-chosen words whispered in her inexperienced ears? Book smarts and street smarts were clearly two very different things. Looking back, Grace would have gladly traded a couple of hundred points on the test for some good old-fashioned common sense.

"So what do I do now?" Grace stuttered through her tears, trying to catch her breath. Having spent the first four weeks of summer at a Habitat for Humanity build upstate and the last two weeks panicking about the little construction project that was likely going on inside her uterus, Grace had been completely unaware that Nick was on the same continent. So his story about Europe had been nothing more than a kiss-off. Did the fact that he took the trouble to make up a white lie mean he was more or less of an asshole? She couldn't decide. Much too late, she realized that the fact that he hadn't given her his cell number or friended her on Facebook meant she wasn't even a footnote in his life. He had used her up, spit her out, and hadn't wanted any reminders that she had ever existed. All the road signs had been there, complete with bright flashing lights, but she had been too blinded by the glare of his shiny white teeth to read them.

"I'm so scared, Jennifer."

"It's simple. You're going to get rid of it. How many weeks did you say you were?" Jennifer asked.

Always practical, rarely emotional, when they were both eight and their pet goldfish died the same week, Jennifer had flushed hers down the toilet without a word, while Grace's fish had been treated to the piscine equivalent of a state funeral, buried in a Macanudo cigar box under the old oak tree in the backyard. For a week, Grace had worn a black armband to honor Goldie's memory, while Jennifer had simply gone to the mall and bought another fish. It shouldn't have surprised Grace that her friend's approach to this situation would be equally matter-of-fact.

"We did it on July second, so I'm about six weeks." This was exactly what Grace wanted from Jennifer, wasn't it—a take-charge, take-no-prisoners attitude? "You think I should get rid of it?" Grace couldn't yet bring herself to say the word *abortion.*

"Duh? What else were you planning on doing? Spending senior year puffing up like a balloon and popping out a mini-Nick next spring? How's that going to go over with Betsy and Brad? Something tells me they're not ready to be grandparents. It would make a hell of a college essay, though. What I did over summer vacation . . . ."

"I don't know. It's a baby, or it will be. It didn't do anything wrong. Some people think it's like murder to . . . to terminate a . . . you know."

Before this summer, Grace had never spent any time thinking about pregnancies, unwanted or otherwise. Pro-choice and pro-life were nothing more than slogans on bumper stickers. In a million years she couldn't imagine those words would matter to her. Babies were for married people, like monogrammed towels and mortgages—that's just how it was. She had never even held a baby before, and now she was going to have one. Her life was out of order; things couldn't get any worse.

"You're well within the first trimester, so it shouldn't be a big deal to take care of this. It's not a baby yet. It's just a bean." Jennifer wasn't totally sure she believed that, but under the circumstances, it seemed the most useful and helpful position to take.

When Jennifer put it that way, it didn't sound so terrible. Unsure how Jennifer had become an expert on pregnancy, Grace was nonetheless grateful that she was taking the lead.

"I don't know what to do. What are my parents going to say?" Grace's voice grew shrill as she thought about telling Betsy and Brad.

When she had gotten a B on the physics midterm, they had lectured her for two hours about how irresponsible she had been, how immature for not realizing how diligently she needed to study to get an A, the only acceptable grade. They didn't work as hard as they did for her to get mediocre grades and waste their money sending her to a second-tier college. The prospect of breaking the news to her parents was even more frightening than the tiny sea monkey that was growing somewhere deep inside of her. She would rather tell them she had flunked every subject including gym.

"What about them? Why would you rat yourself out to the chairwoman of SYFM? Then you'll be stuck with it forever." Jennifer was astonished by her friend's naiveté.

"I guess you're right, but they're my parents. Don't I *have* to tell them?"

SYFM stood for Save Yourself for Marriage, a teen support group advocating abstinence that Betsy had helped establish at their church. Grace's mother seemed convinced that monthly meetings in which she and the pastor talked about virginity being the ultimate gift of love to one's future spouse would be enough to keep a bunch of horny teenagers from gifting and regifting each other in the backs of cars and boats all around Silver Lake. Well intentioned but seemingly trapped in some 1950s health class film, Betsy actually believed that all twenty-six members of the group, boys and girls, were saving it for their wedding nights, when in fact only Grace, until six weeks ago at least, and four others, two of whom probably couldn't have gotten laid if they stood naked in the middle of Main Street, had actually taken the vow to heart.

"Exactly. They're your parents, the Super Christians, and they would never let you get rid of it. As much as they'd hate it, they'd make you keep it. So if you don't want to spend the next eighteen years staring at the five minutes of bad judgment that ruined your life, you'd better keep your baby news to yourself. We can handle this on our own, and then it will be like nothing ever happened. Betsy and Brad don't need to know everything that goes on in your life just because they're your parents." Jennifer found it hard to believe that as smart as Grace was when it came to calculus and chemistry, she was just that dumb when it came to real life.

"I'm not sure I can keep such a big secret from them. Besides, if I'm not going to tell *them*, then why would I tell Nick?"

If she and Jennifer could make this problem disappear without anyone else ever having to find out, then perhaps someday it *would* be like it had never really happened. To be able to erase this chapter from her life story was an incredibly appealing prospect.

Trying to keep her growing impatience out of her voice, Jennifer explained the situation. "Do you have a few hundred dollars for an abortion lying around? I'm broke since my parents started making me chip in for gas, and last time I checked, Habitat for Humanity was a volunteer job, so I'm guessing your pockets are empty, too. Nick has to know, because he's going to pay for the doctor. Get it? But nobody else needs to be in on your dirty little secret."

"You're right about the money—I've got nothing." Grace's parents didn't believe in giving their daughter an allowance when they already provided her with the necessities, and Grace hadn't been allowed to get a paying summer job because she needed to focus on college applications and volunteer work. "But what if Nick doesn't have the money, and what if he wants me to keep it?" She couldn't shake that white picket fence fantasy with Nick playing the doting husband and father, no matter how absurd she knew it was.

"Really? You believe a guy who thinks with his dick is suddenly going to turn into Father of the Year?" As harsh as she knew she sounded, Jennifer wanted to knock some sense into Grace before she fell too far down the rabbit hole.

"I guess, but I still think I have to tell my parents. They'll know something's wrong. It'll come out in the end, somehow, so I might as well get it over with."

Keeping a secret this major from her mother and father seemed impossible. Parents had the right to know everything about their children's lives, didn't they? Grace wanted to believe that in spite of her parents' strict, somewhat prehistoric views on premarital sex, their love for their only child would overcome their prejudices. She was *their* baby—their love for her was unconditional. Hate the sin but love the sinner, and all that. It had to be that way.

"Fine. It's your funeral, Grace. But consider yourself warned. Life isn't that simple, and parents are just regular people, full of flaws and prejudices and lots of good old righteous anger. So don't expect too much from them. Trust me: you'll be disappointed." Even as she pointed out the pitfalls that awaited, Jennifer hoped she wasn't right, but she had a bad feeling that her prediction was going to be directly on target.

"I hope you're wrong," Grace whispered, knowing in her heart that Jennifer was rarely wrong, and feeling even more alone and confused than she had before she'd spilled her dark secret.

"I hope so, too," Jennifer whispered back, wiping away the tears that were rolling down her own cheeks.

CHAPTER 2

Waking at 10:30 the following morning, Grace pressed her hand against her stomach, halfway expecting to feel her uninvited guest pushing back. Each day was one day closer to an ending she hadn't figured out yet, and this uncertainty about what to do next was a sensation she wasn't used to. Grace was the kind of person who always had everything all figured out.

She contemplated pulling the sheet over her head and going back to sleep for the rest of the day. As agitated as she was, she was also exhausted, and sleep was a welcome escape from her bulging new reality. In her dreams, Grace was still her old self, a zit on her nose being a major tragedy, breaking out in hives about a history exam even though she knew she was going to ace it. Life at seventeen had seemed so complicated before. The issue of what to wear to school or out to the movies, should she cut her hair or let it grow, red nail polish or purple. There had been so many decisions to make, decisions that seemed to matter: her happiness had actually hinged on picking the right pair of shoes. Now the easy perfection of her old life made Grace want to weep—pretty much everything made her want to weep—her life had been so ridiculously simple and she hadn't appreciated it for a second. Her world had collapsed, and there was no going back, no matter how hard she cried or how many times she threw up, and nothing would ever be simple again. In the last few weeks, she felt as if she'd lived three lifetimes.

The doorbell sound effect on her phone roused her from her miserable reverie. Maybe Nick was texting her to apologize. Maybe he had a good reason for blowing her off all summer. Maybe . . . not. It was Jennifer. MEET ME AT JOE'S.

"Two coffees, please, milk, no sugar, and two sesame seed bagels with nothing on them." Grace had been placing this same order for the past three years, since they'd entered high school and decided that they were too old to order chocolate milk.

"Make that one decaf and one regular," Jennifer corrected. "Caffeine's not good for the baby," she whispered in Grace's ear.

"But . . . ." Grace couldn't understand why Jennifer was suddenly worried about the bean's health when she was pushing Grace to get rid of it as soon as possible.

"Just in case," Jennifer said.

Not at all sure that Grace had it in her to go through with the quick and dirty solution to her little problem, Jennifer thought it didn't hurt to play it safe. There was a baby in there somewhere, or there almost was.

The two girls sat on a bench in the park, sipping coffee and gnawing on their breakfast, just as they had so many times before, but as with everything else, today was different. Everyone who walked by was pregnant, or pushing a stroller, or holding hands with a kid. There were little people everywhere, and they all seemed to be wailing, snot streaming out of their miniature noses. Grace wasn't sure whether she simply hadn't noticed those things before, or this was just the beginning of the vast karmic joke that had become her life, and all the ironies of her situation would now be displayed before her at every opportunity. A wave of nausea washed over her, and she took several deep breaths, clenching her teeth until it passed.

"So?" Jennifer prompted, facing Grace, sitting with her feet tucked under her, as if waiting to hear a bedtime story.

"So what?" Grace knew what Jennifer was asking, but she wasn't sure she was ready to put it on the record yet, to describe all the lame-brained things she had done that had led to this horrible place.

"Aren't you going to tell me how it happened?" Jennifer asked.

Her curiosity was eating away at her, and she assumed that Grace would want to talk about it. Wasn't catharsis supposed to be good for the soul? Besides, there had to be way more to this story than Grace suddenly deciding she wanted to live life in the fast lane.

"Well, the boy takes his boy part and puts it in the girl's girl part . . . ." Grace's closed lips smiled, just barely.

She really did want to tell Jennifer about that night, but she was sure her friend would lose all respect for her, maybe even want nothing to do with her for so casually abandoning her dignity. At this moment, Grace wanted nothing to do with *herself.*

"I'm glad you at least have the basics down. Now stop it. I want to know how he managed to cross the moat and storm the castle. You're not one of those dimwitted, insecure girls who gets talked out of her clothes by the first boy who says that she's pretty and that nobody else understands him." Jennifer was growing impatient. "What made you decide that July second was freaking opposite day?"

"It's really pretty simple. I was a moron, and I talked myself into having sex with him. That's how it happened." Even though Jennifer was her closest friend in the whole world who knew almost every secret Grace had ever carried, Grace still had enough pride to be ashamed. "I can't say it was his fault. He didn't hold me down or anything."

"You're not getting away with that. You need to talk about it. What made *him* so special? Besides the obvious."

Like an amateur detective, Jennifer was determined to figure out the mystery of the lost virgin. As hot as Nick was, it still didn't make sense that Grace would drop her knickers on the third date. Jennifer could never imagine being desperate enough to do naked gymnastics with some random guy in the back seat of a dark car, no matter how hot he was. Not that any guy had ever come close to asking.

Knowing that Jennifer had been out on exactly one date in high school, Grace never talked to her best friend about her own dating experiences. Jennifer was pretty, but there was something about her that sent guys screaming in the opposite direction. Maybe it was her mouth, which felt compelled to say whatever she was thinking, even if it was rude, or maybe it was because she had no patience for anyone who wasn't as smart as she was, which meant she was impatient with pretty much everyone.

"Somehow I just felt different that night, like I was the last virgin in our class, and that I was just tired of being the good girl who never did anything on a whim, who always researched everything and made thoughtful, mature decisions. I wanted to be young, instead of always being middle-aged and responsible. I thought he liked me, and I needed to do what he wanted so he would stay interested, and then my life would change. Blah, blah, blah." It didn't make much sense to Grace either, now. But at the time, it had felt perfectly logical and right.

"Your life changed, all right. But that kind of thinking is *so* not you." Jennifer placed her hand on Grace's forehead, feeling for a fever.

"I was tired of being a geek. Haven't you ever felt that way?" Grace assumed that Jennifer considered herself a card-carrying nerd as well—if you did really well in school and were lousy at sports, what other label was there?

"No, I've never felt that way. Just because we're co-captains of the math team doesn't mean we're geeks. I resent that." Jennifer crossed her arms defensively. Intelligence was a gift, not a curse, and Jennifer had the foresight to understand that in ten years the head cheerleader who studiously ignored her now would probably be answering the telephone and making copies at the law firm where Jennifer would be an up-and-coming young associate with a window office and a Porsche. High school was just a brief layover before real life started. "Someday you and I are going to be running the world while all those idiots who rule the school are going to be working for minimum wage and spending their weekends flipping through their yearbooks, dreaming about the good old days."

"I know you're right, but it's hard to think about life so far in the future. When he looked at me, I could see myself as important right now. It was a stupid reason to give it up, but it's the truth."

"But in your heart you knew it was a load of bullshit, because otherwise you would've told me about your pretend love affair the day he asked you out. He scammed you, and then you scammed yourself."

As much as Grace knew she deserved having Jennifer tear her a new one, it was hard to listen. "I guess so, but it didn't register when I was in the middle of it, when he was unhooking my bra."

Jennifer snorted. "That's ridiculous. A sudden attack of uncontrollable horniness? Isn't that a guy thing?"

"I know—it makes no sense. But what difference does it make why I did it, at this point? I've still got this bean inside of me, my parents will still hate me, and I still want to jump off a cliff."

"Because I think you'll feel better if you talk about it. Besides, I'm your best friend, and I need to know so I don't get talked into the same shit storm by some guy who knows exactly where to put his finger." Both Grace and Jennifer knew there was no danger of that happening anytime soon. Jennifer picked up Grace's hand and held it to her own chest, whispering, "And don't you say you want to die. Ever. You can't leave me alone to finish high school."

Thank goodness for Jennifer, thought Grace as she squeezed her eyes shut to push back the tears that were never too far from the surface. Was it just a side effect of her hormones working overtime, or was her whole life just so overwhelming? "All right. I'll talk about it. But no judging . . . out loud, at least. I've already sentenced myself to life without parole, so you don't need to remind me what a fuckup I am."

"Not a word. I'll keep all my rude comments to myself. I promise." Jennifer crossed her heart and blew Grace a kiss.

"Everything about him was completely normal and *so* nice. I really thought he liked me. I can see you rolling your eyes." Grace playfully punched Jennifer's arm, almost spilling her coffee. "He kissed me goodnight both times and that was all. He didn't try anything else." Grace paused and squinted at Jennifer who sat expressionless next to her. "Don't you have anything to say yet?"

"You just told me *not* to say anything. I was following orders," Jennifer said.

"It's not working for me. You always have something to say, and when you don't, it feels like you're not listening. Give me your comments so far." Grace braced herself for the inevitable lecture on falling for a cheesy line.

"Fine. It sounds like he was behaving himself . . . until he wasn't. Even sexual predators can have good manners. Did he kiss with tongue?" Jennifer wasn't kidding about getting all the details.

Grace blushed and made a face. "Not on the first date, but on the second. Is that significant? If I'd kept my lips together, maybe I wouldn't be in this fix?"

"No, don't be silly. I was just curious. I assume he was a good kisser." Anybody who looked like Nick had to be blessed with talented lips as well. It was usually a package deal.

"Unbelievable." Unconsciously she licked her lips as she remembered his tongue exploring her mouth. Her entire body had felt as if it were about to spontaneously combust. She had never known such a sensation existed, and now she was regretting that she had felt it with a guy like Nick. How amazing it would be to discover that kind of nirvana with a guy who thought of her as more than a place to park his junk for five minutes.

"That good, huh?" Not ever having experienced that sensation herself, Jennifer was still skeptical. It was nearly impossible to imagine how a little lump of flesh covered with tiny bumps could be that powerful. And in an elaborate rationalization to protect her own hulking ego from the lack of male interest, Jennifer had decided that all high school guys were drooling morons who didn't deserve to put their tongues anywhere near hers.

"Beyond. Anyway, that was it. Two dates, pretty much rated G, PG at most. I don't know why date number three went at warp speed." Grace worried that she had somehow unintentionally communicated to him that she wanted more, and he was simply accommodating her. Honestly, she could hardly remember the sequence of events on that fateful evening.

"They say the third time is a charm," Jennifer offered. "So, is he a turtleneck or a crewneck?"

"What are you talking about? He was wearing a T-shirt and jeans. Who wears a turtleneck in July?"

"I'm not talking about what he was *wearing*," Jennifer said slowly, tilting her head slightly.

"Then what . . . ."

"I'm talking about his other head. Is he a *turtleneck* or a *crew*?" Pulling the neck of her T-shirt up over her head and then down to illustrate, Jennifer burst out laughing. "Sorry, but it *is* kind of funny."

"Oh. That's disgusting. I don't know what he looks like down there. I didn't examine it or anything." After the third kiss, Grace had closed her eyes, not opening them until it was all over. His private parts could have been covered in red, white, and blue stripes for all Grace knew. "You're sick. Have *you* ever seen one up close?"

"It's called a penis, Grace. I think by this point you should be on a first name basis with it."

"You're avoiding the subject. Have *you* ever seen one, smart-ass?" It was time to give Jennifer a taste of her own medicine.

Barely able to keep a straight face, Jennifer said, "Sure, plenty of times."

"When? Who? Now *you're* holding out on *me*." Still waters apparently ran deep.

"My six-month-old cousin, every time I babysit and I change his diaper. By the way, he's a crewneck," Jennifer said between giggles.

"You're disgusting."

"Just trying to lighten the mood. I'm sorry I interrupted. Please continue your story." Jennifer took an imaginary key and locked her lips.

"Thank you. We went to Sal's Pizzeria and then we took a drive down that dirt road at the end of the lake. " It had started out so wholesome—Diet Coke and pizza. Even though she loved onions, Grace had ordered her pizza plain, hoping that there would be lots of kissing after dinner. Looking back, she probably should have gone for the onions—natural birth control.

"The only thing I know about Easton Road is that's where people go to have sex in their cars. It's common knowledge. I'd guess that was where you took a wrong turn . . . as it were." Again Jennifer looked skyward. She tried to control herself, but her eyes seemed to have a mind of their own. "Not that it's any excuse, but maybe Nick thought you knew where you were going and what you were doing."

"If you keep doing that, your eyeballs are going to get stuck. And *I* didn't know that was where everyone went to have sex. I mean, I knew that we were going to mess around, but I wasn't thinking of going all the way until we were in the middle of it.

How was I supposed to know that when Nick turned left by the lake, he thought I knew that he thought . . . shit."

"I'm closing my eyes so you won't see them rolling, but what kind of stupid are you? Are you telling me it was just a spur-of-the-moment decision, like chocolate, vanilla, or full-on sex, please? Really?"

"Stop being all judgy and preachy. It's not helping." Maybe all this therapeutic sharing wasn't such a good idea after all.

"Fine. I'm sorry. It's just that . . . ." Jennifer was finding it nearly impossible to keep her mouth and her eyes still, so she covered her face with her hands and nodded her head, followed by a muffled, "Go ahead."

"We parked and we started making out. He was kissing my lips, but I could feel it in my toes. You know?"

"No, I don't know, but don't let that stop you. Go on."

Maybe she shouldn't be so judgmental. Maybe if some guy stuck his gifted tongue down *her* throat, Jennifer would also unceremoniously part ways with seventeen years of common sense. Not that it was likely to be an issue any time soon. Her one and only make-out session had been courtesy of Alvin Kloster—his name said it all. It had been like burying her face in a plate of sushi. For the ten minutes, an eternity, that it had lasted, all she could think about was how soon she could escape to wash his saliva off of her skin. Comparing her own experience to Grace's was like comparing root canal to a day at the spa.

"He took off his shirt, and then he took off mine, and we kissed for a really long time, and then he slipped his hand in my pants, and I don't know what he did, but it was incredible. He said he wanted me."

In the end, Grace realized, it had been all about feeling wanted. How pitiful was that? Sipping her decaf, which tasted flat and bitter, Grace waited for Jennifer's harsh critique.

"Well, no one's ever kissed me like that, or touched my encyclopedia." At the age of two, Jennifer had informed the woman next in line at the Walmart that, "You're a girl like me, so we have vaginas." Mortified, her mother had arbitrarily renamed that part of the anatomy, and even now, more than fifteen years later, Jennifer still referred to it as her encyclopedia. "So I can't really speak to a situation where you're so incredibly turned on your brain stops functioning. Sex feels great. I get it. But you knew it was risky. And you certainly aren't, or I should say, *weren't* the only one who'd been missing out."

"Correction. The stuff before the sex felt great. The actual sex hurt. And as far as risk, I didn't think about condoms not being a hundred percent effective. They talk about having safe sex with condoms, but apparently that's not even remotely true."

"Didn't your mother's abstinence class explain all that? I don't remember what they told us in sex ed."

"Are you kidding? They never even use the word *sex* in SYFM." Grace wondered if Betsy really believed that if you didn't say it out loud, it couldn't happen. "And I don't remember a single thing from health class. It was a million years ago."

"What does your pastor call it? Fourth base? Home run?" Ready to launch into another harangue about euphemisms for sex, Jennifer bit her tongue to keep from laughing. "Sorry, I know it's not funny."

"They call it marital relations. Anyway, my mother and Reverend Halvert only talked about the spiritual side of it. Not all that relevant when a guy has his hand down your pants in the back seat of his car, and you've managed to convince yourself that hooking up is the key to happiness," Grace said.

"No, probably not. I'm sorry, sweetie. I had no idea you were that unhappy. Why didn't you tell me?" A little hurt by the knowledge that Grace had kept this from her, Jennifer resisted the urge to chastise her. The last thing Grace needed at this moment was more criticism.

"What could *you* do about it?"

Friends were supposed to share all their feelings, good and bad, but Grace had been embarrassed in her misery. Really, what did she have to be depressed about? Loving parents, no money worries, perfect grades, clear skin. *Now* she felt like she had every right to be despondent, but back then, she had felt guilty for being dissatisfied with her cushy life. Now she wished she had confided in Jennifer. Talking to someone who had been her best friend for more than a decade was way more comforting than nearly anonymous sex in the back of a Jeep that smelled vaguely like a cross between Old Spice and the inside of a gym bag.

"I don't know, but I'm sure I would have come up with something better, something that wouldn't end with you pushing a Volkswagen out of your encyclopedia in nine months," Jennifer said.

"Yuck, but you're right. I should have come to you first. Lesson learned . . . the hard way." Throwing her arms around Jennifer, Grace held her tight. "I love you, so much."

"Me too."

A double stroller rolled by, two babies screaming while the mother chattered away on a cell phone, ignoring the crisis taking place underneath the stroller's canopy. Even though Grace knew nothing about infants, she wanted to jump up and do something to make them stop crying, not that she had any idea what that something was.

"What am I going to do? I'm not ready for this," Grace moaned, her voice drowned out by the chorus of hungry, wet, needy human life.

CHAPTER 3

Jennifer's voice was loud over the phone. "Your little time bomb is ticking away in there. If you're going to tell them, you need to do it soon. It's been two weeks since you've known for sure, and it's not going to get any easier the longer you wait. Your options don't get any better as the bean gets bigger. You're eight weeks now."

It was easy for Jennifer to have all the answers. *Her* brain wasn't foggy with pregnancy hormones, and she wasn't the one who was stepping up to the guillotine.

"Thanks for the reminder. I'm going to tell them—but every time I open my mouth, it seems like the wrong moment." Not an hour went by that Grace didn't calculate how far along she was, and how much harder it was going to be to make a decision with every passing day.

"There isn't going to be a right moment, Grace, ever. You just have to get it out—it's like throwing up. You're an expert on that these days. Based on that alone, I'm surprised they haven't figured it out." Jennifer made a retching noise to illustrate.

"I've gotten to the point where I can barf silently, and you know my folks. They're pretty clueless. But you're right. I'm running out of time."

This is a disaster of biblical proportion, Grace thought, almost, but not quite, smiling at the irony. Her parents sat smugly in the front row of church on Sundays, tossing a hundred-dollar bill in the collection plate every week, running the canned food drive, spending Thanksgiving and Christmas mornings at the local soup kitchen. With one word, Grace was going to shatter their morally watertight little world. Could she get away with feigning total ignorance as to how she ended up in this condition? Was there any way Betsy and Brad would buy a twenty-first-century immaculate conception? Although she doubted it, Grace was just that desperate to resort to such a fraud. The alternative, to tell them the truth, was an act of bravery she didn't think she had the guts for.

"Are you okay? You look a little pale, honey." Grace's mother briefly rested her hand on Grace's forehead. "No, no temperature. I hope you're not coming down with something right before school starts."

"No, Mom, I'm not sick." If she didn't say something soon, Grace was sure her body would say it for her. There wasn't much room on her small frame to hide anything, and although she might have been imagining it, she was certain her stomach was starting to bulge. "But I do want to talk to you about something. Maybe tonight, after you get home from work."

"Sounds important. College stuff? Do you want to talk to Daddy, too?"

Having raised a good girl with values and plenty of fear thrown in for good measure, Betsy couldn't contemplate her only child getting into trouble. In her mind, a serious talk could only be about some academic decision, perhaps a change in the college list or a desire to take the SAT again, in pursuit of that elusive 2400. One more year, Betsy mused, and her only child would be off to college. The time had passed too quickly. As she climbed into her Lexus and drove off to show a house to a new client, she smiled to herself at how smoothly Grace's adolescence had gone, self-satisfied in her certainty that those parents who griped about the difficult teen years were obviously just doing it wrong.

After the last of the dinner dishes were dried and returned to the cupboard, Grace hung up the linen towel and retreated to her bedroom. In spite of her earlier determination to come clean to her parents, her nerve had once again failed her, and she decided to postpone her confession for yet another day . . . until the knock on her door.

"Grace, your mother said you wanted to talk about something?" Her father stood there, sipping from a steaming mug of coffee. "Do you want to go over your essay for the common app? Get your stuff and come out to the screened porch. It's a beautiful evening."

A beautiful evening . . . to slit my wrists, Grace moaned to herself. Before she could tell her father that she wanted to talk about something other than school stuff, he was gone. Essays? College had been the last thing on her mind the past few weeks. Not only did she have no 500-word, witty, sophisticated encapsulation of her personality to show them, but she was going to have to explain how she, the only child of two of the most morally irreproachable citizens in their quaint little Connecticut town, had managed not only to lose her priceless innocence to someone she barely knew, but had the audacity (they would never see it as just incredibly bad luck or a fleeting lapse of reason) to get pregnant. Heart thudding mercilessly against her ribcage, Grace shuffled toward the screened porch and the inquisition that awaited her. Perhaps the adrenaline that was flooding her system would bring on a miscarriage, or a heart attack. Either one would do. She stepped onto the cool slate floor of the Florida room. In the backyard, the green glow of fireflies appeared and disappeared, like tiny UFOs traveling through space. How Grace longed to be an insect at that moment.

"So, kiddo, what's up? Your mother and I know you've probably put together something good enough for the *New Yorker*." Her father smiled up at her eagerly. "Are you reciting from memory?" he asked, noting that Grace had brought no sheets of paper, no laptop. They had no idea that a meteor was about to crash land in their sinless little oasis.

"That's not what I wanted to talk to you about." Speaking slowly in an effort to control the quaver in her voice, Grace was sure she must sound drugged.

Crickets chirped rhythmically, and a dog barked in the distance. Wishing she had rehearsed exactly what she was going to say, Grace didn't think she could actually get the words out. Other than the abstinence meetings and Betsy's admonition that a boy would never buy the cow if he could get the milk for free, Grace's parents had never discussed sex with her, convinced that ignorance was bliss and that their child was not one of those girls who would ever be stupid enough or reckless enough to get pregnant. They were churchgoing people, and they had raised her with principles. Kissing, maybe, but not much beyond that, they were certain. Not *their* daughter. *Their* daughter knew better.

"What's up?" her mother asked. "Are you *sure* you're not ill? You're acting kind of strangely."

Planting her feet firmly, Grace took a deep breath. Uncertain what was going to come out of her mouth, she would either tell them she was pregnant or vomit all over their shoes. "Mom, Daddy, I did something bad, and I don't know what I was thinking, and I'm so sorry, but please . . . ." Stars danced in front of her eyes and she sank to the floor. The cold stone felt good on her clammy skin. Slow, deep breaths of the cool night air, and the stars began to recede.

"What did you do?" The way her mother asked, Grace knew that she had already figured it out, but her father was bewildered, looking first at his daughter and then at his wife, eyes wide. Men were so clueless.

"I'm pregnant." She had done it, and the word hadn't caught in her throat as she had feared. It had been surprisingly easy in the end.

A single gasp from her mother and the crash of her father's cup shattering on the stone floor. Grace's arms stung as shards of pottery glanced off her skin. Had he accidentally knocked it off the table, or had he thrown it to the floor?

"You're what? That's impossible!" Her father sounded just like Jennifer had. Apparently you didn't look any different after you lost your virginity, because her father was clearly stunned by the news. Perhaps Grace could go with the Virgin Mary argument after all, like a Hail Mary pass in the fourth quarter, as her parents—or at least her father—could not imagine his seventeen-year-old daughter doing the nasty with some filthy boy.

But Grace's mother was less trusting. Her voice was like steel—all business. She was already in damage control mode. "How far along are you?"

"Eight weeks," Grace whispered, chin down, not wanting to see the disappointment in her mother's eyes.

"Eight weeks," her mother echoed. "Nice of you to share this little tidbit with us. What were you waiting for? The three wise men?" There went the Virgin Mary excuse.

Now that she had told them the worst, she could be honest with them. Looking up at her parents, her eyes glistening with tears, Grace blinked twice and said simply, "I was afraid."

"Afraid? You should have been afraid eight weeks ago, before you let some boy . . . ." Brad couldn't bring himself to finish the sentence. "What the fuck were you thinking?" Grace gulped. She had never heard her father say *fuck* before.

"I know. I was afraid then, too, but I just, and he . . . ." There were no words to explain to her parents the feeling that washed over her body when Nick had touched her and whispered in her ear how he'd never met anyone like her, how perfect they were for each other. Every time she closed her eyes, she could see his face hovering above hers. And even if she could somehow describe the situation, it wouldn't matter now.

"So who is this *he*? How the fuck could you let some reprobate anywhere near you when you know how we feel about such things?" Now that her father had discovered his new word, he seemed to enjoy it, how the hard *k* sound made Betsy wince.

"Brad, I don't think we need to wade in the gutter just because our daughter has chosen to go for a swim there. That language is completely unnecessary . . . and beneath you." Betsy's lips were pursed, and she looked down her nose at Grace if she were a cockroach. "But it *would* be nice to know what kind of garbage you've been consorting with, Grace."

"His name is Nick Salter. We only went out a few times. We just did it once. I thought we were being careful. I don't know what happened. He used a condom, but . . . ."

The words tumbled out of Grace's mouth, her face turning red in the dark as she said the word *condom* in front of her parents. She realized as the words petered out that no explanation on earth would suffice. Her parents were likely aware that condoms were only about ninety percent effective, a statistic that had been far from her consciousness when Nick slipped his hand inside her jeans in the back of his Cherokee.

Sounding like one of the famous abstinence lectures, her father said, "The only way to be careful is not to let some teenage Lothario climb all over you. *Where* did this happen? Not in this house, I hope." Brad raised his hand and Grace flinched, afraid he was going to hit her, but instead he swatted at a bug only he could see. If he had slapped her, she would not have been at all surprised—he was that angry. "Like two animals."

"We did it in the back of his car, down by the lake."

Doing it in the back of a car was both skanky *and* clichéd. But as horrible as it was to regurgitate all of these details for her parents, Grace thought that by confessing she could somehow repair a tiny bit of the trust she had shredded. If she came clean, she could prove she was worthy of being their daughter again. Just because they weren't Catholic didn't mean she couldn't tap into the power of the confessional.

"For such a smart girl, you certainly are proving to be pretty stupid when it comes to life. This is not how I raised you. I expected a lot more from *my* daughter."

Her father's voice was suddenly detached, as if he were talking to one of his clients at his law firm, explaining why the case was a loser and he wouldn't take it to court. As her father, Brad knew he had no responsibility here. Educating a daughter about the hazards of dating and premarital sex fell squarely under the purview of maternal responsibility. Fathers brought home a regular paycheck, killed spiders, and took out the garbage. The other stuff was for women to handle.

His rage cut through her, splitting her heart in two. "I know, Daddy, and I don't know what I was thinking." That wasn't true. She remembered exactly what she'd been thinking as Nick slipped his hand inside her panties. *I don't know him well enough to be doing this, but it feels so good, and everybody else is already doing it, and if we're careful, nothing will happen, and if I don't do this, he won't like me anymore, but if I do it with him, he'll be my boyfriend and he'll love me, and I won't be a weirdo anymore.*

"And what do you and this Nick person propose to do about it?" Her parents were taking turns interrogating her, but neither offered up even a modicum of sympathy or understanding. They weren't doing the good cop/bad cop thing; they were both bad cops.

"I haven't told him yet. I thought he was away for the summer, but he's here. I'm going to tell him tomorrow. I wanted to tell you first. I don't know what to do next." That was the truth, and that was why she had wanted to tell her parents. They would know how to handle this. They would make it all right again—that was what parents were supposed to do. "I want you to help me figure out what to do. Please?"

Her father grunted, and Grace could just barely make out his face in the dim light of the candles flickering on the glass-topped table next to his chair. His lips were clamped tight shut, almost disappearing inside his mouth, and his fists were clenched in his lap. Turning to her mother, he said in a monotone, "Betsy, I'm done. Take care of this. I don't want to hear another word about it." Saying nothing to Grace, avoiding her eyes, brushing past her hand as she reached out to touch him, he stormed back into the house, his shoes crunching on the pieces of broken pottery. The door slammed behind him, and the glass panes rattled.

"Mom, I'm sorry. I know it was stupid. I made a terrible mistake. Please forgive me," Grace whimpered as she crawled across the floor, not caring that pieces of the broken cup were cutting her palms, to where her mother sat on the old wicker settee.

Craving some sign that although she may not be forgiven—Grace knew that would probably take years—she was still loved, Grace reached for her mother's hand, tried to rest her head on her mother's lap. But Betsy pulled her hand away, crossed her legs, and stared out into the dark yard.

"Mommy, please, I need you." Grace was begging for what she felt in her heart was her right, in spite of what she'd done, but it was no use. A wall had been erected between them, and no amount of pleading would be enough to tear it down, or carve even a tiny doorway. Although her mother was less than a foot away from her, Grace had never felt more alone.

"You should have thought of that before. After all we've sacrificed for you, you behave like a common piece of trash. What will people think of us when they find out what you've done? Your father and I have a spotless reputation in this town, and with one careless act, you've managed to destroy that, you selfish ingrate. If I'd known this was how it was going to turn out, I never would've had a child in the first place."

Betsy's voice was stiff and distant, as if she were speaking to a stranger who had bumped into her on the subway. The words burned Grace like acid. She had expected her parents to be angry, but she hadn't anticipated total rejection, a total denunciation of her entire life up to this point. When she looked up at Betsy, it was not disappointment that she saw in her eyes, but stone-cold hate. Jennifer had been right all along about not telling them, but there was no way to unring this bell. Now her mother regretted Grace's very existence. As furious as Betsy was, Grace didn't want to believe that their relationship was really that fragile.

"Is he that good-looking boy with the hair and the eyes you went out with a couple of times at the beginning of the summer?" asked Betsy as she rubbed at her throbbing temples in vain.

She looked down on her friends who talked about how much they needed their evening glass of wine, grape-flavored grownup medicine for women who needed to dull the aches and pains of having it all. But right now she would have given her left arm to be on her second glass of Chardonnay. Condescending magazine articles sneered at avoiding your problems by self-medicating, but now Betsy understood: whatever it took to get through the night.

"Yes."

A woman would have to be blind not to notice all of Nick's outstanding qualities. Even her mother, seething with anger at what she saw as adolescent defiance, could recall the extraordinary features of Grace's fellow gutter rat. Had Nick been less physically attractive, less magnetic, would she be in this situation now? Probably not, Grace reluctantly acknowledged. The depth of her own shallowness shocked her. What more was there to say? Her grandmother, who had died the year before, used to say something about being careful not to fall for a sharp haircut. At the time, Grace had just nodded at yet another of her grandma's outdated aphorisms, which had made no sense, like cat's meow and giggle water. Now Grandma's warning words echoed in her ears. Nick, in all his Abercrombie & Fitch poster glory, was nothing more than a sharp haircut.

CHAPTER 4

Each hour seemed to simultaneously drag on forever and pass in the blink of an eye. If only Grace could stop time or speed it up, or, better yet, go back to that moment in the back seat, right before Nick unzipped his jeans and Grace's brain ceded control to her body. Standing naked in the bathroom, staring at her stomach in the mirror, wrapping a tape measure around her waist to see if she had started to puff up yet was a total waste of time, but she couldn't stop herself.

Now that she knew Nick wasn't trekking across Italy, Grace had no excuse not to tell him about the little souvenir from their third and last date. How would she tell this guy she hardly knew that ten minutes of fumbling in the back of his Jeep had resulted in a potential lifelong connection between them? There were no words.

Jennifer's text was informative, and unwelcome. HE'S ON THE LAKE WITH SOME CHICK, ON ONE OF THE FLOATING DOCKS. GO GET HIM.

NOW? HOW DO I GET HIM ALONE? WHAT DO I SAY? Grace texted back.

Thanks to Jennifer, Grace didn't have the coward's luxury of claiming she didn't know where he was. In the eight weeks since she'd last seen him, Nick had become like someone from another planet—the popular planet—and Grace couldn't imagine how she could speak to him, let alone tell him what she needed to tell him.

TELL HIM YOU'VE GOT A BABY ON BOARD AND YOU NEED $500 FOR THE DR.

Grace knew that Nick had a right to know about the thing, the baby. Maybe he had intended to go to Europe, but somehow his plans fell through. Maybe he wasn't the skeevy guy she now thought he was. Maybe he hadn't called her because he'd lost her number, or he was too busy working at the local homeless shelter, which was nowhere near the lake where Jennifer kept spotting him, but still. Maybe he would be gentle and supportive, would help her through this, whatever she ended up doing. Maybe it would all work out for her. Maybe he was secretly in love with her. Maybe the chick on the lake with him was his cousin. Maybe he would propose on the floating dock in the middle of Silver Lake. And maybe pigs could fly.

$500?? Grace texted.

THAT'S HOW MUCH IT COSTS ON AVERAGE. Not one to leave anything to chance, Jennifer had researched the whole abortion process on the Internet. With the widespread availability of the procedure, in spite of all the well-publicized opposition, it was clear that Grace was not alone in her moment of weakness.

I THINK I'M GOING TO PUKE. I CAN'T DO IT, Grace's fingers clumsily texted back.

MAN UP, WOMAN!! I'LL MEET YOU AT THE SOUTH LANDING IN FIFTEEN MINUTES. WEAR YOUR BATHING SUIT.

Jennifer realized her friend needed to be held up and pushed forward, and there was no one else to do it. In the forty hours since Grace had broken the news to her parents, they had not spoken a single word to her. Jennifer had predicted Betsy and Brad would react badly—what else could you expect from the Cheerleaders for Chastity Belts—but even she wouldn't have guessed that they would be so coldhearted that they would shut Grace out with a total silent treatment right when she needed them most. So much for Christian charity and the Golden Rule. Jennifer had always known they were full of shit, and it only confirmed her suspicion of religion and religious types in general.

BATHING SUIT!? DON'T MAKE IT WORSE.

HE'S IN THE WATER. YOU'RE GOING TO HAVE TO SWIM FOR IT. DON'T WORRY. YOU DON'T SHOW YET.

After she put her phone back in her bag, Jennifer floated in the water, keeping an eye on her quarry. There was no way she was going to let Nick Salter, a.k.a. Scum of the Earth, get away with this. If Grace couldn't talk Nick into doing the right thing, and paying for it, Jennifer was ready to castrate him with the pocketknife hanging from her key chain. Looking at her watch, she swam back to shore to meet Grace and give her a last-minute pep talk. Grace's car was already there, under a tree at one end of the lot. When Jennifer walked up to the parked car, Grace's forehead was resting on the steering wheel. The windows were all closed in spite of the August heat, and for a second Jennifer wondered if Grace was breathing. Frightened, she tapped frantically on the glass, and Grace lifted her head with a start.

Opening the car door, Grace said, "I'm sorry. I was trying to psych myself up. But I think I just ended up hyperventilating."

"You'll be fine once you confront him." Jennifer didn't believe that for a second, but what else could she say? Telling Grace this was only the beginning of her nightmare might be a more accurate assessment, but it would definitely not encourage her friend to march into the water. At the moment, Grace needed all the help she could get, which included lying.

"I haven't seen him since the night we . . . ." Grace's voice trailed off.

"Don't think about that. Just give him the facts. Try not to cry. Ask him for the money. Arrange a time to get it from him, and let's move on. The sooner you talk to him, the sooner you can get him, every little piece of him, out of your life." At the moment, the only thing Jennifer had to offer was a confident voice and her anal-retentive organizational skills.

"If you see me flailing around on my way out to the dock, promise me you'll let me drown." Grace was only half-joking.

"As your best friend in the whole world, I promise to let you go to a watery grave." Jennifer held out her hand, and the two girls sealed their pledge with a pinky swear. After giving Grace a light kiss on the forehead, Jennifer gently swatted her butt. "Now scoot. Get it over with."

Silver Lake had been Grace's favorite place to spend summer afternoons since before she could swim, but after today she wondered if she would ever want to come back. Now the late summer sun glinting off the water was like a spotlight highlighting her mortification. There was no place to hide, and she felt certain that all the kids sunning themselves on the patch of rocky beach could see inside her to that tiny bean that was growing larger every minute, every hour. Feeling vulnerable and fat in her skin-tight Speedo, Grace waded into the cool, clear water. No breeze ruffled the lake, leaving the surface like a sheet of smoky glass, and Grace cut cleanly through it as she swam toward the floating dock, wishing lakes had sharks and that one would appear and bite her in half—anything to avoid what came next, which she knew was ridiculous, because how could she be afraid to talk to someone who had already seen her naked, been inside her, and how could she be afraid when the scariest thing in the world had already happened?

Five yards short of the floating dock Grace treaded water, watching Nick and some girl wearing a bikini that consisted of a few strings and four impossibly tiny triangles of fabric. They were passing a joint back and forth. Nick inhaled deeply, and then leaned over the girl, blowing the smoke directly into her mouth. They both burst out laughing, collapsing on each other, as if shot-gunning were the funniest thing in the world.

Suddenly Grace could easily see through the sparkling shell that had shone so brightly two months ago, obscuring her ability to see who he really was. Disaster had given her clarity, and now she marveled at how she could have been so into him. Yes, he did have the most incredible body, every muscle perfectly outlined under flawless skin, and his face belonged on the cover of a magazine, but was Grace really so one-dimensional that she would mortgage her entire future just to get next to that? She would never have thought so—she still didn't think so, but what other explanation was there? But this wasn't the moment for serious introspection; Grace's legs were getting tired, and there was no time for cold feet. The countdown clock was ticking, and there were no timeouts in this particular game. Putting her head down, Grace propelled herself the last few feet and grabbed the slippery wood, pulling herself up so that her head was visible over the edge.

"Hey, Nick," she called out, sucking in her stomach even though it was still under water.

"You want some?" Nick looked in her general direction and flashed his even white teeth, holding out a half-smoked joint. For a second he wasn't sure who it was, his pot-fuzzy brain moving in slow motion, trying to remember. Oh yeah, Girl Number Seventeen, Grace, who reminded him of the little wooden angel his mother always put on top of the Christmas tree. So cute, so young. Like a warm peach, she had been so fresh, so ripe, so ready to be devoured. And those jeans, painted on—she was asking for it, and he had simply obliged. *What the fuck does she want with me now?* he wondered. Maybe he could convince her to do a three-way, but even as the fantasy started to take shape in his mind, he realized it could never happen—she was too much of a prude.

Grace was his seventeenth. If he kept up this pace, he would easily reach his arbitrarily chosen goal number of twenty-one before he graduated. He knew his square jaw and perfect proportion were the result of a lucky draw from the gene pool, but his way with the ladies wasn't only attributable to his physical beauty. It was hard work; it took skill and patience. Coasting on natural ability was egotistical and didn't guarantee success. Piles of books had been published on the subject: how to touch a girl in just the right place in just the right way to make her beg for it. Like teaching himself to place the ball in the corner of the soccer net—not too hard, not too soft, right between the goalie's outstretched hands—after lots of study and plenty of practice, he had it down. Banging a girl was no different. Most teenage guys would probably admit to wanting to screw as many girls as possible, and who cared whether *they* enjoyed it—coming was for guys. He knew he was unique in his desire to make the girl think it was her idea as much as his. For this talent and dedication, his friends had dubbed him the Pussy Whisperer.

Through his pot fog, Nick thought back to the moment when he'd first slipped his hand inside Grace's jeans, wiggling his index finger just the right way, feeling how warm and wet and ready she was. That moment, right before they did it, when he could feel how much she wanted him—that part was almost better than the actual fucking . . . almost, but not quite. Maybe he could convince Grace to let him back in; the second time would be way better for her than the first. She'd been so uptight, and he had to admit he'd been too focused on his own enjoyment. This time he would make sure she came.

"What? No, I don't want any." Grace's clipped voice jarred him back into the present. No, she clearly wasn't going to be up for any water aerobics.

"Okay. Whatever," he replied, taking another drag. Maybe if he inhaled hard enough, and held his breath long enough, she would just disappear, and he could get back to, um, whatshername . . . Amy, that was it. Grace was a pain in the ass anyway. She was the kind of girl who wanted to make love, when all he wanted to do was fuck.

Okay? Grace was surprised that was all he had to say. He must be so baked that he was simply incapable of registering any surprise, or discomfort, at seeing the girl he had screwed barely two months ago and never bothered to call. As he delicately pinched the tiny white cigarette, which was now so short it threatened to burn his fingers, he started to laugh again.

Bikini Girl, known to the rest of the world as Amy, put her hand proprietarily on Nick's tanned, ripped stomach and glared at the interloper. "Can't you see we're kind of busy?" she fumed. Nick had just been whispering in her ear all the wicked things he was going to do to her, right here in the middle of this lake, and there was nothing better than messing around high.

Grace shook her head and breathed through her mouth. The sickly sweet smell of the pot made her queasy. She prayed she wouldn't throw up. Ignoring the unbelievably hot girl whose hand had slid from Nick's stomach down to his bulging crotch, Grace said to Nick, "We need to talk . . . now."

"Why so serious? We're seniors. It's summer vacation. Come on, have a hit. It's really good shit. Whatever's bugging you, it'll go away like that." Nick snapped his fingers unsuccessfully, giggling at his own ineptitude.

"About that. You told me you were going to be away all summer. Why did you lie to me? Jennifer told me you've been here the whole time."

Fearing she sounded like a jealous girlfriend, Grace bit her lip and stopped talking. There were way more important things to talk about than some stupid fib about a backpacking trip. It wasn't like she was trying to get him back, to salvage a relationship that had existed only in her Disney Princess imagination. This was a business meeting—she needed a financial backer—and nothing more.

Nick hesitated. Clearly he hadn't expected someone as timid as he believed Grace to be to call him out. "It fell through last minute, that's all. You sure you don't want some? It's really good weed. From California." Nick wished this girl would just chill. When he didn't call, he'd been sending the message loud and clear that it was just a summer thing, a pre-summer thing, really, and she needed to move on.

"No, thank you."

Even in moments of extreme stress, Grace's manners never wavered. Manners. If only she had remembered the etiquette book's advice to keep her legs crossed at the ankles at all times. On her thirteenth birthday, Grace's mother had given her the *Guide to Manners and Dating for the Proper Young Lady*. It had been published sometime in the 1960s, but according to Betsy, breeding and social skills were timeless. If Grace read this book, Betsy was sure she would be prepared for anything. Not entirely true, although if her petticoat tore, her bouffant frizzed, or she got frosted lipstick on her Peter Pan collar, Grace would know exactly how to handle it. Unfortunately, the book hadn't offered any advice about what to do when the hottest guy in school had his tongue down your throat and his hand inside your panties.

"By the way, this is Amy. Amy, this is Grace."

Now Amy was no babe in the woods. She wasn't the kind of girl you took home to Mother—he actually thought about stuff like that, though he wouldn't admit it. Grace was the kind of girl you took to Sunday night dinner: good grades, perfect manners, kind of preppy. Amy, on the other hand, was the kind of girl you had fun with. She knew as well as he did that this wasn't going anywhere serious, and she was fine with that. When she slipped her hand inside his bathing suit, it was because she wanted to, because she liked the way his cock felt, not because she thought *he* would like it and she was doing it just to please him. That made all the difference for Nick.

Grace, on the other hand, was complicated. She was someone who needed attention, who wanted a boyfriend, someone to talk to and someone to listen to her. It wasn't all about living in the moment for a girl like Grace. In her mind, every guy was potential husband material. Not what he was looking for the year before he went to college. Amy just wanted to smoke pot and get naked. It was no contest. He probably should have thought about that a little more before he worked his charm on Grace. It had been too easy, like trapping a helpless little bunny, and now, looking at her, a mass of dripping wet hair and chattering teeth, he kind of regretted taking advantage of her. Somehow she had been more virginal, and vulnerable, than most virgins, and he should have hit the brakes. Now she was coming to tell him off. It had probably taken her the whole summer to work up the nerve to come tell him, in perfectly grammatical English, what she thought of him. Well, he guessed Amy could wait a little. If she was as horny as he was, a quick swim while he listened to Grace vent for a few minutes (he knew he owed her that, after what he'd taken from her) wouldn't be enough to take the edge off.

"Could we have a minute alone?" Grace said to Bikini Girl as she pulled herself onto the dock, still sucking in her stomach, feeling extremely self-conscious next to this waif in the handkerchief that passed for a bathing suit. She was so thin, her stomach was practically concave. Grace wondered where she kept her internal organs.

"Who *is* this toad?" Amy asked, furious that an otherwise perfect afternoon was being interrupted by some doofus in an old-fashioned one-piece who looked like she'd escaped from the day camp at the YMCA. The fact that Amy didn't recognize Grace, even though they'd gone to the same high school for three years, and the same middle school for three years before that, confirmed to Grace everything she already knew, and everything Jennifer had reiterated: the kids who sat in the cool section of the cafeteria were completely unaware of those who sat in the social ghetto next to the kitchen.

"She's nobody. Give me a minute, and I'll get rid of her." Nick ran his hand across Amy's chest and she shivered with pleasure. "Don't go too far."

Nick was definitely worth the wait, so she shrugged, and said, "Fine, but you'd better have more pot." Giving Grace a withering look, she executed a flawless dive and disappeared under the water, surfacing about ten yards away. She swam effortlessly towards shore.

At Nick's characterization of her as a "nobody," Grace's heart fell to somewhere down by her feet. While she hadn't expected a kiss and an apology, she hadn't been prepared for such a royal dis, and she wished with all her might that she were anywhere else, anybody else.

"So, what do you want?"

Nick waited. He figured he knew what was coming, and although he didn't understand why Grace needed to swim out to the middle of Silver Lake to scold him for not calling her all summer and lying about going to Europe, he could understand how she must feel. Getting dumped sucked, even when in his mind they'd never really been together. Nice girls required too much effort. He made a vow, which he already knew he probably wouldn't be keeping, to avoid such complications in the future. Definitely not worth having to stare into those puppy dog eyes after all was said and done, and he knew there was no way she would ever go down on him.

Taking a deep breath and looking him square in those clear blue eyes, which, even after all that had happened, made her heart pause, Grace stammered, "I'm . . . I'm pregnant."

The warm sun, the deliciously wooly dizziness, the anticipatory throbbing between his legs—all gone in an instant as his blood turned to ice, seemed to stop flowing through his veins. Inside his bathing suit, his hard-on, courtesy of Amy's practiced hand, wilted.

"What did you say?" Nick had heard exactly what she'd said, but he needed time to let it seep into his brain.

"I'm going to have a baby, your baby. I'm almost eight weeks pregnant."

This wasn't nearly as bad as telling her parents had been. Nick had no moral authority over her. Her only fear had been that he didn't care about her, but she already knew that he didn't, that she had just been one of many back seat conquests—definitely not the first, and certainly not the last. Her shoulders fell as the tension left her body and her breathing returned to normal.

When he felt he could speak without his voice shaking, Nick said, "It can't be mine. I used a condom. I was careful." He didn't doubt for a second that it was his—until he got to her, she'd been convent material. It was a knee-jerk reaction. That's what guys were supposed to do. Deny, deny, deny.

"That was my first . . . and last time. Apparently condoms don't work all that well. It must have been defective, or you put it on wrong."

Although Grace had vowed not to lay any blame, since she had willingly gone along with the program, he *had* been the one wearing the condom. Closing her eyes for a second, she waited for him to reach out to her, to wrap his arms around her and tell her everything would be okay, that they would figure this mess out together. But she wasn't in charge of his feelings, and Nick just sat there, mouth hanging open, his hands balled up in fists, glaring at her with anger and frustration.

This couldn't be happening to him. "What are you going to do about it?"

Nick wanted to grab her by the hair and drag her to the nearest clinic, but he knew that ultimately it wasn't his choice. He could see his whole life slipping away through what must have been a microscopic hole in the fucking condom, like sand sliding through that tiny opening in the center of an hourglass. Since he was fifteen, he'd been a loyal Warrior Condoms customer, buying the giant box at PriceSaver, coasting on their reputation as the protection you can depend on when you march into battle. There was no way he had put it on wrong—he could unwrap it and get it on in the dark in under ten seconds, including blowing into it to check for any holes. But in spite of that extra step, the Warrior Corporation had failed him. He wondered if he could sue them for wrecking his life. The way he saw it, Warrior should have to pay for the abortion, or the baby, or the hit man.

"I don't know."

She noted that he hadn't asked what *we* were going to do about it. Whatever happened, she was going to have to handle this on her own. But she wished he would at least ask her how she was feeling, if she had morning sickness or if she was scared. It wouldn't have cost him anything to show a little sympathy.

"Did you tell your parents?"

Nick's family, although not nearly as devout as Grace's, belonged to the same church as the Warrens. He was well acquainted with their very public abstinence outreach program and their prim, first-pew sensibility. In fact, although now he felt embarrassed to admit it, that had been a large part of her appeal. Nailing Grace had been like winning the Heisman Trophy of sexual conquest. She wasn't just your run-of-the-mill virgin—she was an *über* virgin. Sticking it to her was an ego boost for an ego that needed very little boosting.

Bile rose in his throat as his new reality took shape. If Grace's parents knew about the baby, Nick was sure he was doomed to become a father. Panic engulfed his body as he thought about the lacrosse scholarship that had been a certainty until this second. He didn't know anything about becoming a father—could he still go to college, or would he have to get a job to support Grace and her kid? His mind spun out of control as he started adding up the cost of diapers and formula and rent. For a second he hated being a guy, because being the guy meant he had all of the responsibility (except for carrying the thing for nine months and pushing it out and taking care of it), and none of the rights.

"I did. They're not speaking to me." Just thinking about that made the tears well up and Grace wondered if she would ever be able to stop crying, or whether the baby had turned her into a blubbering mass of blubber.

"I bet. Fuck." Although he was furious with Grace for not telling him first, letting him have some say in what came next, Nick felt a little bit sorry for her. The Warrens's numerous high-profile good works had made them minor celebrities in Silver Lake, and Grace's little foray to the dark side in the back of his Jeep was likely an unforgivable crime. Based on his limited knowledge of them, it wouldn't surprise Nick if they never spoke to their daughter again. That last night with Grace, the night they had apparently made a baby, Grace's main worry had been getting home before curfew, because she didn't want to get in trouble with her parents. "What about me? Did you tell them I was the father?" Not that he was scared—no one was going to force him to do anything—but it would be nice to know if Grace's dad was going to show up at his house with a shotgun and a marriage license. And what would Nick's parents have to say about this? If he had to give up his scholarship, his parents would likely cut him off as well. He could hardly comprehend how a perfect day could fall apart so fast.

"I told them I was pregnant, they said some mean, horrible things to me, and now they're giving me the silent treatment. That's pretty much it. My mom knows it was you, but I don't think she cares —it's the fact that I did it at all. I'm the one who's related to her, and I'm the one who's going to have the evidence under my shirt for the world to see. I've humiliated her and my dad. Apparently that's an unpardonable sin." As miserable as she was, Grace felt slightly better talking it out with Nick. Not that he was saying anything kind or comforting, but as her accomplice, he had to have some empathy, even though he was doing a good job of hiding any feeling at all. How she wished she'd seen this side of him before her panties came off.

"So why didn't you just have an abortion and leave them out of it? They didn't need to know what happened. You should have come to me right away, and we could have taken care of everything ourselves. What did you think was going to happen when you told your fucking parents?"

"I don't know," Grace said quietly. She didn't want to admit that she'd stupidly thought that telling her parents would make it better.

"Now that you've dragged the moral majority into this shit show, my future's about to drive off a cliff, and for no good reason. It could've been a dented fender, and now it's going to be a fucking ten-car pileup," Nick seethed.

"That's what Jennifer said, but how could I keep it from them? They would figure it out. Besides, I thought you were on the other side of the Atlantic, and I don't have five hundred dollars for an abortion." Grace was already regretting her decision to own up to her sin to Betsy and Brad. Jennifer had vigorously advised against it, and now Nick was raking her over the coals.

"They wouldn't have figured it out if you'd gotten rid of it right away." Calling the baby, or fetus, or whatever it was, *it*, felt wrong somehow, but it was much easier to distance himself from an 'it' than from the soft, round, blue-eyed baby that 'it' would become in a matter of months. "Fucking idiot," he muttered to himself. "So your friend Jennifer knows. You haven't told anyone else, have you? You saw what happened when you told your stupid-ass parents. This mess is nobody's business." If word got out that he'd knocked up the poster child for the purity pioneers, his life would be over.

Frustrated by Nick's failure to focus on the actual problem of what to do right now, Grace let out a small shriek of exasperation. Although his reaction was not surprising, she had hoped for something different. But she could be tough if that's what was called for. "Don't worry, I won't tell another soul you're the father. I'd sooner die than have anyone know what I let you do to me in the back of your shitty car. But right now, we've got bigger worries than who's privy to our dirty little secret. We both screwed up in a big way eight weeks ago, and I need to figure out what to do *today*. You need to help me. It's *your* baby, too."

Nick flinched at the words "your baby." He lay back on the warm, wet wood and stared directly into the sun. The white light burned his retinas, but he refused to blink. Athletic scholarships and hot girls who spread their legs when he smiled at them were no longer a given. This was really happening, and for the first time in his life, Nick Salter felt like a total loser.

CHAPTER 5

It was still dark outside when Grace's mother shook her awake on the Friday before Labor Day weekend. "Get up. Get dressed." Her voice was stern, but at least Betsy was speaking to her. Those were the first four words either of her parents had addressed directly to her since the night she'd confessed to her terrible crime.

"Mom? What's going on?"

The strain of her parents' hostility and the needs of the baby growing inside of her were a draining combination, and sleep was Grace's only escape. If the sound of a car backfiring or a door slamming didn't wake her, she could sleep fifteen hours at a stretch. At four in the morning, she was nowhere near ready to face the day.

Not providing any information, just standing in the doorway watching as Grace dressed quickly and quietly, Betsy yawned and looked at her watch. Wherever they were going, Grace thought, her mother was in a hurry. Betsy examined Grace's profile in the light from the hall, trying to see if her belly was starting to stick out. It was hard to believe there was really a baby in there: her own flesh and blood, her grandchild. Nausea gripped her, and she turned away.

In the car, Betsy flipped to a new radio station and turned it up loud. Silence invited conversation, and Betsy had nothing to say to the person sitting next to her. In the few seconds it had taken for Grace to tell her parents what she had done, she had become a stranger in her mother's eyes. It was a surprise even to Betsy that she could so easily relinquish her maternal instinct. The bond between mother and child should have been much stronger than that, but Betsy had no control over what she was feeling. As much as she longed to feel loving and protective toward Grace, who was curled up in a ball in the front seat, practically glued to the passenger door, instead she felt only rage and betrayal. It was clear that the daughter was afraid of the mother, and though Betsy was sorry her daughter felt that way, she couldn't bring herself to reach across the front seat and still her daughter's shivering shoulders. It would have been like reaching across the Grand Canyon.

For three hours they drove, across the Connecticut state line and into the heart of Massachusetts. If not for the annoyingly enthusiastic deejays on an endlessly changing stream of radio stations, Grace would have had no idea where they were, as she had not opened her eyes once since the mystery road trip had begun. The car sped along, and the only thing Grace knew was that she was being taken farther and farther away from anything familiar. Afraid that her mother was going to drop her off at some home for unwed mothers, Grace wept silently. As terrible as it was living with the disapproving stares and deafening silence at 78 Hill Road, the thought of being abandoned at some orphanage for wayward teens was much worse. She hadn't seen a suitcase, but maybe Betsy had hidden it in the trunk. And if Betsy left her someplace, she wondered if she would pick her up afterwards, if life could ever go back to the way it was before. A dozen unanswered questions raced in circles through Grace's mind.

In the midst of imagining a series of asylums her mother could be taking her to, Grace fell asleep again, the hum of the air conditioner and the engine too hypnotic to resist. Only when the car was parked did Grace wake up, slowly swimming up through her muddy brain into consciousness. When she awoke, for just a second, life was as it had been before. But then there was the jolt of her new reality, and that heavy feeling, like a cold, hard rock in her stomach, returned.

"Grace, wake up. We're here," Betsy said tersely, poking Grace's shoulder with her index finger, making as little physical contact as possible.

At her mother's touch, Grace sat bolt upright. Thus far, the top-secret mother-daughter outing had not prompted much of a thaw in family relations, but at least her mother was still talking to her.

"Where's here?" Grace sat up and stretched, looking out the car window at a large mirrored glass office building. The landscape was completely unfamiliar to her.

Ignoring Grace's question, Betsy got out, slammed the car door behind her, and marched across the parking lot toward the glass cube. Running to catch up with her mother, Grace considered the possibilities. Perhaps Betsy was taking her to a doctor before she took her to the home for unwed mothers. Or maybe there was an adoption agency in this building. It was no use asking. Betsy was clearly still not speaking to her unless absolutely necessary, and Grace would find out soon enough.

Two minutes later they were in the waiting room of a place called the Women's Health Center of Massachusetts. Grace could understand that Betsy wanted to avoid the local obstetrician, but had it really been necessary to drive all the way to Massachusetts to get a prenatal exam? Taking a seat at one end of a worn leather sofa, Grace picked up a parenting magazine and pretended to read. Across from her, a blond girl who looked about her age gnawed nervously on her fingernails and stared at her feet. In another chair sat a forty-something woman, clearly the biter's mother, flipping violently through an old issue of *National Geographic*.

"Grace Warren. We have an appointment," her mother whispered to the woman at the front desk.

"Please fill out these forms. The doctor will be with you shortly." The receptionist tried to hand Betsy a clipboard, but Betsy pushed it back across the counter.

"I'd rather not. If I'm paying cash, why do I need to give you any information?" Betsy took out her wallet and withdrew a wad of bills. "I'm not submitting anything to insurance, and I'd like to maintain my privacy."

"It doesn't matter what form of payment you use, ma'am, you still have to fill out the paperwork. Those are the rules. And you don't pay until after the doctor does the initial examination, just in case." Once again, the receptionist placed the clipboard on the counter, the attached pen dangling from a silver chain.

"Just in case what? That's outrageous." Certain that if she didn't back down, she would get her way, Betsy stared venomously at the woman in the pink and blue polka dot smock who was at that moment dreading her decision to take the extra shift that morning.

"No paperwork, no procedure," said the receptionist, glaring up at Betsy and turning back to her computer, ending the conversation, silently cursing all the spoiled, self-centered bitches who were such crappy mothers that it was no wonder their daughters ended up pregnant.

Nostrils flaring, Betsy stuffed her wallet back into her enormous designer handbag and flounced, clipboard in hand, over to the couch where Grace cowered, wishing that whatever was going to happen next would hurry up and happen. A doctor's visit couldn't be worse than the waiting, imagining her legs splayed open, some stranger touching her, looking inside her. While she knew that she deserved whatever humiliation she was about to suffer, and she had better get used to it, as there were likely plenty of doctors' visits in her future—hopefully not all three hours away from home—she had hoped that her mother would begin to relax, but Betsy remained as cold and hard as a block of ice. As terrible as this ordeal was, it was so much worse because Grace had no shoulder to lean on. Jennifer was doing her best, but she was a kid herself, and no matter how gently she patted Grace's back, or murmured comforting words in her ear, or tried to make Grace laugh, it just wasn't enough.

A woman dressed in pale pink scrubs and holding a pink file folder opened the door to the rest of the office. "Grace?"

Betsy and Grace stood simultaneously. "Just Grace, please." The nurse smiled warmly and held the door open for Grace, while Betsy returned to the sofa, teeth clenched, shoulders up by her ears.

"Okay, Grace, take everything off and put this on, open to the front." She handed Grace a pink paper robe and left her alone in the examining room. Arctic air blew out of the ceiling vents, and Grace huddled on the paper-covered table, arms crossed, trying to keep her teeth from chattering in the chill room. The fact that everything in the office was pink did nothing to take the edge off her nerves.

The door opened again. "Hi, Grace, I'm Dr. Ryder, and I'll be taking care of you today." Thankfully, Dr. Ryder was a woman. If a man had walked in and asked her to spread her legs, she probably would have passed out.

"So, you think you're about eight weeks or so?" Dr. Ryder asked, scanning the piece of paper in the folder.

"I think so. I only did it once, on July second." This was beyond embarrassing, and Grace was grateful that the nurse hadn't allowed her mother to accompany her beyond the waiting room.

"Were you using birth control?" As sophisticated as young people were today, the myth persisted that you couldn't get pregnant the first time.

"Yes, he wore a condom, but I guess it leaked."

"And you took a pregnancy test?"

"Seven." After all that had happened, Grace couldn't believe she'd been stupid enough to believe that if she peed on enough sticks, she would eventually get the result she wanted.

"You took seven?" The doctor tried to suppress a smile. "Sometimes it's hard to accept, isn't it?" She patted Grace's knee. "Well let's take a look. Have you ever had a gynecological exam before?"

"No, ma'am."

"It's not as horrible as you think it's going to be. Just lie back on the table and scoot your bum down to the edge. That's a good girl. Now put your feet in here." She guided Grace's feet into the stirrups. "Just relax your legs and let your knees come apart. I'm just going to look inside. Close your eyes, take a deep breath, and relax."

Grace felt the doctor's latex-covered fingers, and although she tried to do as the doctor said, every muscle in her body contracted.

"I know this is scary, but you need to unclench." The doctor held up a piece of metal that looked like a cross between a duck's bill and a medieval torture device. "This is called a speculum, and I'm going to slip this part inside of you so I can see your cervix. I promise it won't hurt, as long as your muscles are relaxed."

"Okay," Grace whispered, as tears dribbled silently over her cheeks and into her ears.

"You poor thing. Don't worry. The worst part is almost over, and then we'll talk about what comes next," the doctor said softly.

Grace nodded as the cold metal slid inside her, and she could feel the metal pieces spreading apart, stretching her insides. She didn't trust her voice, afraid that if she tried to speak, she would start crying hysterically, and she wasn't sure she would ever be able to stop. It really didn't hurt much, although she couldn't imagine how a baby's head could ever fit through that part of her body. She would surely split in two if it came to that.

Dr. Ryder withdrew the speculum and placed it on the paper-covered tray next to her. "Okay, now I'm going to do an ultrasound to check the fetal heartbeat. Because you're barely eight weeks, I'm going to do it internally, but I promise it will be less uncomfortable than the exam I just did. Also, we'll need to do a blood test to check for STDs. I know this is an awful lot to take in, and the odds are low that you picked up something, but we have to make sure." As much as she hated piling on the bad news when this kid's plate was already overflowing, Dr. Ryder had no choice but to do her job, no matter how unpleasant.

Not knowing what else to say, and wondering what other indignities she would have to suffer before this ended, Grace merely murmured, "Okay." The bean was bad enough, but a sexually transmitted disease would be the shit cherry on top of her crap sundae. If Nick had given her AIDS or herpes on top of this baby, she would definitely do herself in. Well, first she'd kill Nick, and then she'd do herself in.

As the doctor pressed buttons on the machine, typing in Grace's vital information, she said, "Have you made a decision about the pregnancy? There's no objectively right answer, you know. It all depends on your situation."

"I just want to wake up and be me again. But my parents would never let me have an abortion—they think abortion's murder. So I guess I'm going to have it, and maybe put it up for adoption." Until that moment, Grace hadn't actually thought about what *she* wanted to do. She had assumed she didn't have a choice once she owned up to Betsy and Brad.

Dr. Ryder paused. "That's weird. We have you down for a D & C this morning."

"A what?" There was so much Grace didn't know, didn't want to know, but she realized she had no choice but to get educated, and fast.

"D & C stands for dilation and curettage. We insert an instrument in the uterus and scrape it out." Dr. Ryder spoke without emotion. She felt sorry for the poor, trembling girl lying on the table in front of her, but if she was old enough to go all the way, then she was old enough to hear all the facts.

Grace gasped. That sounded horrible—cruel and painful. Placing her hand on Grace's shoulder, Dr. Ryder said, "Don't worry, you'll be asleep, so you won't feel a thing."

Recovering slightly, Grace said, "That can't be possible. My parents would never let me have that done."

"Well, let's look into this." Dr. Ryder picked up the phone on the wall and spoke quietly into it. A minute later there was a knock at the door. "Come in."

In walked Betsy, her purse tucked tightly under her arm. "Is everything all right?" She looked suspiciously from Grace to the doctor.

"Everything's fine. Grace is definitely pregnant, based on a cursory examination of her cervix and uterus. I was about to do an ultrasound, just to confirm and make sure everything looks normal before we proceed."

Betsy nodded but said nothing.

"We have Grace down for a D & C, but she says that must be a mistake. We haven't discussed all of Grace's options yet, but it would be helpful to know if an abortion is a possible alternative. Perhaps you can help clear things up, Mrs. Warren." Turning back to Grace, she said, "Ultimately, of course, Grace, it is *your* choice. Have you had a frank discussion with the father? Does he have an opinion?"

At the mention of Grace's co-conspirator, Betsy found her voice. "The father is of no consequence in this. And while I am opposed to abortion in principle, I feel that under the circumstances, an exception must be made. We live in a small town, and we are very active in our church. A baby out of wedlock would destroy us." Betsy was breathing hard and her face had broken out in red splotches. "We cannot have Grace flouting our values in front of everyone."

"Mrs. Warren, while I appreciate your discomfort, I think there are many more important things to consider than whether a few people might look askance at your daughter's unfortunate situation. She is neither the first nor the last teenager to face such a decision, and whether or not the folks at your country club will judge you harshly based on the fact that your daughter engaged in premarital sex and got pregnant is, I think, irrelevant at this moment." Dr. Ryder thought but did not say that having an abortion merely to save face was pretty much the ultimate in flouting one's values.

Dozens of furious mothers had passed through the clinic, but there was a wild look in Mrs. Warren's eyes that was disturbing. Praying Mrs. Warren wasn't carrying a weapon in her oversized handbag, Dr. Ryder waited for the inevitable firestorm response, one hand resting protectively on Grace's shoulder.

"I brought my daughter to this clinic for a simple medical procedure, not a counseling session, so I would appreciate it if you would keep your words of wisdom to yourself. You know nothing about my life, and I don't need a graduate of some low-end medical school who can't be more than thirty, with no children of her own, telling me how I should deal with *my* daughter."

Out of all the clinics she could have chosen, Betsy wondered how she had the bad luck to choose the one occupied by a big-mouthed, know-it-all busybody. All she wanted to do was undo Grace's misstep and never speak of it again.

Willing herself to remain calm, Dr. Ryder spoke quietly but firmly. "Part of the process is to explore the patient's options, and I am merely trying to provide a neutral perspective in what I know is an emotionally charged situation. Ultimately the decision belongs to Grace, and I am simply doing my job by providing her with as much information as I can." She paused and took a breath. "By the way, for your information, I am thirty-four years old, I have a six-month-old daughter, and if you consider Harvard Medical School low end, well, so be it."

Turning to Grace, Betsy spoke through gritted teeth. "Grace, you have conducted yourself in an appalling manner. Your father and I are devastated that you would do this to us. At this point, your only concern should be to make this go away before all of our lives are ruined. There is really nothing to discuss. Do you understand me?" Betsy took a step towards the examination table and Grace recoiled, the tissue paper crackling loudly.

Genuinely afraid for Grace's safety once she and her mother left the clinic, Dr. Ryder wondered whether she should be calling social services about this woman. "Mrs. Warren, if you would please return to the waiting room. I need to finish Grace's exam, and this conversation isn't getting us anywhere."

Without a word, Betsy stormed out of the room, slamming the door so hard that the framed diplomas on the wall shook. "I'm so sorry, Dr. Ryder. She's just really mad at me, and . . . ."

Dr. Ryder held up one hand. "You don't need to apologize for your mother. You have no control over her behavior. *I'm* so sorry that you're facing all of this with no support system. Do you have anyone to talk to about this? Going through a crisis like this alone is not a good idea."

"I have a best friend, Jennifer, who knows everything, and she's been great. She told me to get an abortion without telling my family. I should have taken her advice." Grace smiled sadly. Jennifer's prediction was proving itself correct at every turn.

Sometimes this job was so difficult. The actual practice of medicine was the easy part. When she was dissecting cadavers in medical school, Emma Ryder never imagined that she would end up being a social worker as well as a doctor. "It's a big decision, one that you'll carry with you for the rest of your life, whether or not you ever *choose* to have children someday. Not a decision to be made lightly or out of fear, because you're the one who has to live with whatever you end up doing—not your parents, not your best friend, just you."

"I don't know what to do." The tears cascaded down her cheeks, again.

"It's not easy. There's so much to think about. You don't have any adults in your life to talk to? Right now you really need someone to take care of *you*, make you feel safe, whatever you decide."

Grace shook her head.

"No aunts, grandmothers?" As she spoke, Dr. Ryder turned a dial on the ultrasound machine and held up the internal probe, a plastic cucumber in a latex sheath. "Now relax, and let's take a look at you from the inside."

"Nobody," whispered Grace as she tried to relax her pelvic muscles, silently vowing that she would never let anything or anyone inside her ever again.

"There's the baby, or the fetus," Dr. Ryder said, pointing at a spot on the computer screen. "It's about an inch across, but it starts growing pretty rapidly at this point. So if you do decide to terminate your pregnancy, it's best if you take care of it within the next few weeks. It gets harder after that, both psychologically and technically."

"That's my baby," Grace whispered, dumbfounded by the fact that she and Nick had in the course of rolling around in his Jeep actually created a human life. It shouldn't be that easy to make a baby. It should be complicated and time-consuming, like knitting a sweater or building a house. Looking at the pulsating shape on the screen, Grace could now imagine the bean as a baby, and she was scared about what that meant. *It* was no longer just an *it*.

After Dr. Ryder had finished spelunking in Grace's insides, she helped her sit up. "There you go. Your options are these. A termination, today or in the next couple of weeks, which we can perform here, or I can recommend a clinic closer to your home." When Dr. Ryder first looked at Grace's folder, she had wondered why they had come all the way to Massachusetts from Connecticut, but now she knew all too well. "If you choose to carry the baby to term, and you decide not to keep it, there are many couples who would love to adopt your baby. And there are many different kinds of adoption, which you can learn about if you decide to go that route. I'll give you some brochures that explain the basics."

Grace still felt shaky, but something had changed. This wasn't just about her, or Nick, or her parents, anymore. There was a strawberry-sized person growing inside of her. Not exactly in a position to take a moral stance, Grace still didn't feel like abortion was murder, like those religious fanatics she sometimes saw on the news. But she did worry that if and when she ever had children on purpose, she would be unable to look at them without reliving the moment when she eradicated what would have been an older sister or brother. Could she handle that kind of *what if*?

Even so early on, the fetus was recognizable as a person, with sort-of fingers and toes and ears. Grace was regretting having gone to see *Bodies . . . The Exhibition* in New York City, which had perfectly preserved fetuses at every stage of development on display. How could she get rid of what looked like a miniature baby, even if she wasn't sure that a tiny creature that had no ability to survive on its own outside of her body was actually a baby? It was way too complicated an issue to tackle, especially in her current condition, with her hormones raging and her parents fuming. But she didn't feel certain enough to take what on some level was a human life into her own hands.

"I think I've decided. I'm going to have it." Saying it out loud confirmed her feelings, at least for the moment, or until her mother returned and started screeching at her.

Dr. Ryder sighed deeply. Grateful that she had never had to make such a decision, she had no firm opinion as to what was the right thing to do in this type of situation. "Okay. I don't think your mother is going to be too happy—probably the understatement of the year—but remember, it's your life, and you have to do what's right for you. Let me give you some literature about what comes next. You don't need to decide about adoption right now, but you will need to find a doctor close to home, take prenatal vitamins, and get lots of sleep. And of course, no caffeine or alcohol. I'll leave you to get dressed while I get the brochures." Dr. Ryder hesitated and then added, "And don't forget, if you change your mind in the next few weeks, you can still terminate your pregnancy."

Slowly Grace got dressed, wondering how her mother would handle her decision. Would she hit her? Leave her by the side of the road? Although her parents had never even spanked her when she was growing up—she had never given them any reason to lay a hand on her in anger—she could imagine Betsy slapping her hard across the face. Grace's transgression had cracked the perfect veneer encasing her family, revealing a rough, primitive core that Grace could easily imagine included physical violence.

Dr. Ryder returned with a folder and handed it to Grace. "Good luck. The next year is going to be really hard, but I know you can handle it. You're a very strong person." She hugged Grace, and Grace rested her head briefly on the doctor's compassionate shoulder. "I put my card in there. If you need someone to talk to, I want you to call me. My home number and my cell are on the back. Who knows? Maybe your parents will surprise you."

Grace shrugged. "Maybe." But the possibility that Betsy and Brad would change their minds and suddenly throw their arms around her seemed less likely than Nick suddenly declaring his undying love for her and proposing on one knee.

Grace walked into the waiting room, where the nail biter had been replaced by a visibly pregnant Goth girl with raccoon-eye makeup, black motorcycle boots, and no mother hovering nearby. It had been less than an hour since she first put on the paper gown, but she felt like a completely different person.

Betsy jumped up, dropping the magazine that had been sitting unopened in her lap. "That was quick. Do you have extra pads? It's a long ride home." Now things could get back to normal. No one would ever have to know—no judgmental stares at the club, at church, at the farmers' market. Betsy made a mental note to have a little chat with Jennifer about the value of discretion. The tiny miners who had been swinging their pick axes inside her skull since Grace broke the news started to pack up their tools.

"I didn't do it." Grace's voice was loud in the library-quiet waiting room.

Grabbing Grace by the arm, her nails digging in, Betsy practically dragged her out of the office. The receptionist started to call out to Mrs. Warren, as she hadn't paid for the pelvic exam, but she thought better of it. She would sooner pay the hundred dollars out of her own pocket than risk a black eye from that crazy witch. Pounding the computer keys in frustration, she thought for the hundredth time about quitting this freak-show job with its lunatic right-to-lifers waving their picket signs dripping fake blood, and the outraged mothers who refused to believe that their teenage daughters were having sex until it was too late.

"What are you talking about?" Betsy hissed at Grace as they stood in the hallway waiting for the elevator.

"I couldn't do it, and I'm the one who has to live with the decision for the rest of my life." Echoing Dr. Ryder's words, Grace sounded way braver than she felt. On the ride down, Grace pressed herself into the back corner of the elevator, as far from her mother as she could get. There was someone else in the elevator, so Betsy just stared straight ahead, white-knuckled hands clinging to her purse as if it were a life preserver.

As the glass door of the office building closed behind them, Betsy again grabbed Grace by the arm and picked up right where she'd left off. "About that you're mistaken, young lady. We *all* have to live with your so-called decision. What right do you have to behave this way? I don't know you anymore."

"But Mom, Reverend Halvert says every life is precious, even the lives of the unborn, and he's the leader of our church." Maybe the stress had made Betsy forget about the bigger picture.

Betsy laughed—a short, inappropriate chortle. "Reverend Halvert never had a pregnant teenage daughter."

"You always taught me that God created life. How can we destroy something that God created?" Grace was grasping at straws, trying to remember something she had learned in Sunday school that might remind Betsy what really mattered.

"An accident in the back seat of a car is *not* God's creation."

Grace gasped at her mother's icy tone. With thirteen little words, Betsy renounced everything she had ever taught Grace.

Letting go of Grace's arm long enough to find her keys, Betsy suddenly stopped in the middle of the parking lot, oblivious to the car that almost hit her from behind. She looked up at the sky and let out a shriek, a combination of anger, frustration, and maybe even a little fear. Grace watched, transfixed, as her mother appeared to vent her wrath at God. Then taking a deep breath, Betsy adjusted her sunglasses, looked around to see if anyone had witnessed her manic moment, and marched toward the car. Before Grace was safely in her seat, Betsy had started the engine and shifted into reverse. Grace slammed the door, just missing the car parked next to theirs as Betsy lurched out of the parking space and tore out of the lot. Perhaps, Grace thought, they would be in a terrible car accident on the way home, and then the only urgent decision would be left to her father: open or closed casket.

Simultaneously merging onto the highway and dialing her phone, Betsy was oblivious to the cars speeding past. "Brad, it's me."

"How did it go?"

Brad really didn't want to know any of the particulars, but he felt compelled to ask, as long as his wife was stuck with taking care of all the minutiae of this unpleasant business. He couldn't even say the word *abortion* out loud, and the thought of blood and scalpels and DNA belonging to some random guy who had done heaven knows what with his daughter made him physically ill. On some level, he could identify with those crazy people on the other side of the world who carried out honor killings. How did a father ever recover from something like this? It would have been so much easier if she'd been caught with a bottle of his Valium or a fifth of Jack Daniels in her locker. A blurb in the Police Blotter, with not even her name mentioned because she was underage, and that would be the end of it. But being pregnant was like wearing a sandwich board for nine months that said I'm a Teenage Tramp.

"It didn't," Betsy hissed into the phone.

"What are you talking about?" Brad asked.

"She wouldn't do it."

"*Wouldn't do it?* Why didn't you *make* her do it? You're her *mother*." Now Brad regretted not having gone along to make sure things were done properly. He knew a woman couldn't be depended on to take care of business when there were emotions involved.

"What was I supposed to do? Hold her down? That's not how it works in this country, I'm afraid. Parents have all of the responsibilities and none of the rights."

Betsy was determined not to take the blame for this one. Her husband, who thought like a lawyer even when he wasn't at work, always needed to find someone to point the finger at when things went wrong. There was always a guilty party, and Betsy wanted to make sure the blame that resided firmly with Grace didn't get transferred to her. With a memory like an elephant,

Brad would remind her at every opportunity for the next twenty years how she screwed up what should have been a simple task and ruined everything.

"So, Bets, what do we do now?" Furious with his wife for making it more complicated than it needed to be, Brad did have the wisdom to realize that lashing out at her wasn't going to solve the problem, even if it did make him feel better temporarily.

"I think we have to go to Plan B," Betsy said.

"There's a Plan B?"

Brad wondered if his wife was starting to lose it under all the stress, not that she wasn't entitled to be a little nutty. Now she was sounding like a secret agent planning to infiltrate enemy headquarters. Up until the last few days, their life had been relatively simple, straightforward, and sanitary. Their little family had always functioned like a well-oiled machine, each member knowing his or her jobs and performing them perfectly. An unwanted child, an unwed mother—Grace had thrown a major wrench in the works. Neither he nor Betsy had the tools to deal with such a catastrophe. It was not part of their world, and he had no interest in figuring it out. An economics degree from Yale and a law degree from Columbia had not prepared him for an adolescent girl who, without warning, decided to go off the rails.

"There has to be. We can't just leave it like this, can we? I don't know what to do."

As furious as Betsy was, somewhere, in a part of her brain she rarely accessed, she felt a maddeningly maternal tug that she fought to bury deeper. The internal conflict was making deep furrows in her forehead, in spite of the five hundred dollars' worth of Botox Dr. Rick had just shot in there. If Brad loosened his grip on his anger, even a little bit, she could almost see getting through this as a family. If Brad could ease up, that could be their Plan B. Other people had daughters who got pregnant, even though they didn't know any of them personally, and their families managed not to implode. Maybe it didn't have to be the end of the world. Maybe they could figure this out as a family.

"Well, the way I see it, the one thing we *cannot* do is just leave it. Grace needs to understand that her behavior will not be tolerated. Let me take care of it. I have an idea. Come straight home." Slamming down the phone, his self-righteous anger renewed by Grace's latest act of disobedience, Brad stomped down the stairs to the basement.

Betsy was a very bright woman. Part of Brad's reason for marrying her was to ensure he would have intelligent children—he couldn't imagine being married to some bubblehead with an honorary degree from Neiman Marcus who would spend all his money and saddle him with a brood of helpless morons. But like all women, Betsy was too emotional, and that was a crippling weakness. In Brad's mind, life was simple if you didn't get tangled up in all that touchy-feely crap—such a waste of valuable time. He was certain that dealing with Grace was all about teaching her a lesson, making her realize on a cellular level how badly she had behaved, how she had violated the family code. A good spanking would do the trick, but unfortunately, the days when corporal punishment was synonymous with no-nonsense parenting were long over. Although she had already begged for forgiveness repeatedly, words were cheap. Grace needed to show by her deed—namely, getting rid of this egregious error—that she was truly contrite.

In law school, the professors had taught him, or he had chosen to learn, that somebody was always right, and somebody was always wrong. Even when a case settled for nuisance value, with no one admitting culpability, the guy who got the check was the clear winner. And of course, he got paid no matter what, so he was *always* the winner. In their current dilemma, while Grace was the clear loser, she was threatening to drag her parents into the ditch with her. Having done nothing wrong, Brad wasn't going to let that happen. It was all about accountability.

"Bye," Betsy said, knowing her husband was already long gone.

It didn't sound like Brad was ready to let go, to let this play out according to a scenario he hadn't designed. She could almost hear the steam coming out of his ears, right through the phone. But as long as her husband was willing to take charge of the situation, Betsy decided to step aside and let him have a turn. Initially he had passed the buck to her, and she was relieved that he now wanted to participate in this horrible moment in their life. Hopefully, whatever he had in mind would be more effective than what she had set out to do.

Thinking back to the other night when she had arrogantly recalled how simple raising Grace had been, she realized she was now being punished for thinking she was better than everybody else. If only she'd been paying more attention when Grace started dating, not that she went out much. And she'd thought Grace was so smart—shouldn't a kid who got a five on the AP Biology test have been way more savvy when it came to sexual reproduction? Wondering how she was going to face the next meeting of the Save Yourself for Marriage group, Betsy thought about changing the name to Screw Your Fucking Mother. Reaching up to rub her throbbing forehead, Betsy was horrified to discover the ridges were so deep they felt like corduroy.

In the back seat, Grace pretended to sleep while she tried to listen in on her mother's phone call. Over the constant stream of chatter from AM talk radio, she was only able to make out something about Plan B. At this point, she could almost believe they might hit over the head with a shovel and give her an abortion on the kitchen table. When she was a teenager, Betsy had received the Gold Award as a Girl Scout, the female equivalent of an Eagle Scout. Maybe she had a D & C merit badge. After what had happened that morning, anything was possible.

In their driveway, barely able to wait until Betsy turned off the engine, Grace flew out of the car and ran past her father into the house, nearly tripping over a bunch of black plastic garbage bags that littered the front porch. For the last two hours, she had hardly moved for fear she would wet her pants, and she had been too afraid to ask her mother if they could stop so she could use the ladies' room.

While Grace was in the bathroom, Brad took the opportunity to fill his wife in on his inspired plan. In his mind, the world was black and white—shades of gray were for wimps and losers. "It's the only way, Betsy. Grace needs a shock to the system. Her refusal to do as she was told at the clinic tells me that she is feeling a little too comfortable. I firmly believe we need to reestablish the parental hierarchy, and this is the only way she's going to get the message."

"But Brad, it seems awfully harsh." Betsy had been as furious and hurt as her husband, but throwing their only child out in the street was cruel and unusual punishment. "Are you sure this is a teachable moment, when she's in this condition? Besides, isn't it against the law to refuse to take care of one's own child?" Distracting her husband with a legal issue might take his hysteria down a notch, giving him a chance to regroup and perhaps come up with a less punitive Plan C.

"Look, Bets, you asked me to come up with a Plan B, and this is it. We need to present a united front, and I'm not talking about kicking her out forever. Just a day or two at Jennifer's, and she'll come to her senses. I know my daughter."

Not quite as confident as he professed to be, Brad *hoped* he knew his daughter. But he really believed it wasn't much of a gamble: Jennifer's parents weren't going to house Grace for more than a few days, and after that she had nowhere else to go. They held all the cards. It was just that simple.

Grace reappeared before Betsy could point out that based on what had happened in the back of Nick Salter's car, neither of them knew their daughter as well as they had thought. "What's all this stuff? Why did you put the lawn clippings on the front porch?" Grace asked Brad, who was standing outside the front door.

Brad spoke to her for the first time in nearly a week. "Those are your clothes, Grace. You can't stay here anymore. Since you've chosen to compound your earlier transgression with your latest poorly considered decision, you've really left us with no choice. It would have been so easy to make this thing go away, almost like it never happened. But you're behaving irrationally, threatening our position in this community, squandering your future. This could have remained a private family matter, but now you're choosing to broadcast your disgrace. Your mother and I refuse to be a part of this." His voice boomed as if he were addressing the jury during closing argument.

Even as the lawyer-speak ricocheted around in her brain, Grace couldn't quite believe he was saying what he was saying. "Left with no choice?" she echoed. Admittedly, she had done something stupid, but she couldn't see how this one mistake undid an entire lifetime together. It wasn't like she'd robbed a bank or murdered someone. "You're kicking me out? Where am I going to go?"

"You should've thought of that before you gave it up like some floozy." Not a person who prior to Grace's screened porch confession had made a habit of using such language, Brad continued to find power and comfort in talking like a low-end crime figure in a bad gangster movie. Aware that his chosen words were not exactly Ivy League, Brad wanted Grace to know that if she chose to have this bastard, she had better get accustomed to hearing people say those kinds of things to her, and worse.

Feeling like an actress delivering her lines in some cheesy soap opera, Grace looked up and asked, "But Daddy, what am I supposed to do?" She had known they were beyond furious, but she hadn't in her wildest imagination believed that they would pack all her belongings and kick her out, essentially fire her for poor performance, her failure to meet expectations.

Before Betsy or Brad could answer, an elderly woman, jogging up the driveway like a young girl rather than the octogenarian she was, called out, "Hello. Sorry to bother you. I just want to give you a letter that the postman mistakenly put in my mailbox." As Helen Teitelbaum got closer, she realized she had wandered into the center of a major brawl, and she walked faster, desperate to hand over the misdelivered mail and get out of the way.

Her acquaintance with her neighbors consisted entirely of an occasional wave or "good morning." Just because they lived across the street from each other didn't mean they were the kind of neighbors who popped by to borrow a cup of sugar. The Warrens seemed nice enough, if a little uptight, and not particularly friendly, considering their numerous well-publicized acts of Christian brotherhood and charity. Really, how many lasagnas could one woman throw together while still pursuing a rewarding career as one of Cabot Realty's top closers, while still finding time to run half-marathons to raise money for Children Without Borders or Christian Doctors in Love or some other totally worthwhile cause? Plenty, according to the local paper. Someone at the *Silver Lake Gazette* must owe the Warrens a lot of favors, because their picture found its way onto the front page far too often for people who were neither politicians nor outlaws. Not that the world couldn't use people like that, but to Helen the whole thing smacked of insincerity, like it was all about the recognition part rather than the helping part. Maybe she was wrong—she hoped she was.

"I don't want to interrupt. I'll just leave this here." No one had reached out to take the letter, so Helen put it down on the bottom step of the front porch.

As she turned to go, Helen glanced up at the daughter, who was sitting on the top step surrounded by Hefty bags, her face swollen and tear-stained. This was clearly more than just a minor family disagreement, but Helen had recently been trying, with minimum success, to be less of a *yenta*. Never able to have children of her own, Helen attempted to fill that huge hole in her life by coming to the aid of anyone who needed help. According to her brother-in-law, Jacob, there was sometimes a fine line between benefactor and busybody, and in her efforts to save anybody who looked like they needed a little saving, she was in constant danger of crossing it. Fixing everything was not Helen Teitelbaum's job; not everyone wanted to be fixed, and certain people who looked like they needed fixing were merely exercising an alternate lifestyle choice. That last part had to do with the time Helen found and paid for a six-month lease on an apartment for a homeless couple, who turned out not to be homeless but had merely decided to live off the grid for a year, whatever the hell that meant. Overflowing with good intentions, Helen had further destroyed their social experiment by bringing them a few bags of groceries and buying them winter coats. Who knew that dumpster diving was the latest craze among certain eco-conscious types, and that Helen's charitable works had probably wrecked their chances of getting a reality show on the Green Channel, which Helen didn't even know existed? It was moments like those that made Helen think that perhaps she had lived too long; the world no longer made any sense to her. In spite of that little mix-up, Helen didn't agree with Jacob's assessment of her *yenta*-ing, but she was curious to see if she actually *could* control her urge to stick her nose in other people's business. The earth would not fall off its axis if Helen Teitelbaum missed a day.

One, two, three . . . "Grace, are you okay?" Biting her lip, Helen wondered if maybe Jacob was right, that she was a pathological busybody who needed a support group to teach her how to take twelve steps back instead of trying to solve everyone's problems.

"I'm fine, Mrs. Teitelbaum," Grace sniffed, trying to smile, but only managing to look like she had just returned from having dental surgery.

"Is there anything I can do?"

Helen looked up at the Warrens. She sensed that something very bad was happening, and she was suddenly afraid. On an episode of *The Oprah Winfrey Show*, some psychiatrist had once said it was very important to follow your instincts even if your brain said you were being silly, and Oprah was rarely wrong. Although she doubted that the Warrens were the types who would physically abuse their own child, Helen's gut was telling her not to leave until she figured out what the fight was about. Sometimes these churchy types had weird ideas, and Helen would never forgive herself if a month later she heard on the news that Grace Warren had mysteriously disappeared or fallen down a flight of stairs.

"Not a thing, Mrs. Teitelbaum. You just caught us in the middle of a little family disagreement. Everything's under control," Brad called out from the porch, favoring Helen with a smile that belonged on a politician after a long night of campaigning—his lips turned up, but his eyes were gray ice. Now Helen was certain she wasn't going anywhere.

"Are you sure? Do you want me to send George over with the truck? He could cart away all this garbage for you. It wouldn't be any trouble." Once she explained to George her concern for Grace's safety, and that she was following Oprah's advice, he wouldn't be too annoyed that she'd offered his assistance when he already had more than enough to do mowing *her* lawn and hauling *her* grass clippings.

"We're fine, Mrs. Teitelbaum. Can we help you with something else?" Brad took a step forward and waited, arms crossed menacingly, not above bullying a woman nearly twice his age.

"No, I guess that's all for now." Helen turned to Grace. "If you need anything, I'm right across the street." Slowly walking away, turning to look back every few seconds, hoping that Grace would speak up, Helen reluctantly reached the end of the Warrens's driveway and crossed the street. She looked at her watch. In a few hours she would come up with an excuse to check on things at the Warren household.

"I didn't think we were ever going to get rid of her," Betsy said.

"Bets, in twenty years of practicing law I've lost two cases, and they weren't my fault. I certainly think I can handle a demented old bat with too much time on her hands." Turning to Grace, Brad said, "Think about what we've said. When you've come to your senses, you can come back and we'll take care of this mess properly. Otherwise, you're on your own. You've made your bed, as it were, and now you will lie in it. Betsy, inside."

Although Betsy was not someone who was accustomed to taking orders, she knew that she had failed to hold up her end, and now Brad was in charge. Refusing to meet Grace's pleading eyes, Betsy stepped over a garbage bag and followed her husband into the house.

The front door slammed, and Grace was alone. She started to call Jennifer but remembered that she had gone away for the long weekend with her family. They wouldn't be back until Monday night. Leaving the bags on the porch, Grace walked around the side of the house, hoping that her parents were watching her through the windows and that any minute they would run outside and throw their arms around her, apologizing for their temporary insanity brought on by the shock of Grace's news, and vowing to work through this together. But after a few minutes considering this scenario, Grace nearly laughed out loud. The odds were better that Nick would show up in the next five minutes with a bouquet of roses and a diamond ring. Not knowing what else to do, Grace dragged a chaise longue across the backyard and behind the garden shed. No matter how shaken up she was, she could always take a nap.

A couple of hours later, Grace opened her eyes to find Mrs. Teitelbaum perched at the end of the chaise, quietly filing her nails. "Did you have a good sleep?" she asked.

"What are you doing here?"

"I was just checking on you. When I didn't see you on the front porch, I knocked on the door, but there was no answer, so I walked around the back and there you were, sawing logs."

"How long have I been asleep?" Grace sat up, her brain struggling to arrange the puzzle pieces of the morning. For a second or two, she wasn't sure whether Dr. Ryder had been real or was just a figment of her hysterical imagination.

"It's been a couple of hours since I dropped off that letter." Helen cleared her throat. "I don't want to pry, but might I ask what's going on between you and your parents?" Remembering Jacob's words, Helen added, "Of course, if you don't want to talk about it . . . ."

"I did something very bad, and my parents are angry with me." Telling this prim, angelic looking woman that she was having a baby would be like telling the pope that she was pregnant.

Helen's eyes widened at the vague but ominous explanation. "So what's in the bags?"

"All my clothes."

"I'm getting on in years, so I may be a little slow, but why are your belongings in garbage bags on your front porch?" Slowly, patiently, Helen tried to ask the questions that would get her to the heart of the Warren family feud.

"I'm going to have a baby," Grace whispered and started to cry, her shoulders shaking, all the tears saved up from the morning now flowing freely.

"Sweetheart," Helen said reaching over and wrapping her bird-like arms around Grace's quivering body, "it's not the end of the world.

"Y-y-yes, it is," Grace stammered. "They don't love me anymore."

"I'm sure that's not true. It's not like you just told them that you were a serial killer," Helen said, knowing that this was no time for humor, but hoping she could stop, or at least slow, the torrent of tears.

"I'm not allowed to come home unless I have an abortion." Unconsciously, Grace placed her hand protectively over her stomach.

Sure she must have misheard, or that Grace was so distraught she had confused the facts, Helen said, "But there was a picture on the front page of the paper of your parents at a pro-life rally last month."

"Apparently there's an exception to the rule when it's your own daughter."

Helen stifled a chuckle. Her sixth sense had been right. The Warrens were too good to be true.

"So, at least for the moment, you have nowhere to go?" Helen asked, still not letting go of Grace.

"No. My best friend, Jennifer, is away for the weekend." Grace sniffled, and Helen handed her a tissue that had been tucked in her sleeve. "But I'm sure they'll let me back in before it gets dark. They're just trying to make a point."

Not so sure that Grace's eviction was just a gesture, Helen stood up and said, "Well, until your parents come to their senses, you're coming home with me."

Taking Grace's hand, Helen led her around to the front of the house. "I'll send George over to get your clothes."

The front door flew open, and Brad stepped out onto the porch. He and Betsy had been watching through the windows, speculating on how long it would take Grace to fold, but now the elf in pink cashmere was back, seemingly determined to screw things up.

"Grace, where do you think you're going?" At the sound of Brad's harsh voice, Grace's shoulders tensed and her heart started to pound.

"Mr. Warren, I'm taking Grace back to my house until you come to your senses."

"You're not taking my daughter anywhere," Brad shouted. Betsy stood next to her husband, hands on her hips, saying nothing.

"It seems to me, Mr. Warren, that if you've thrown your daughter out of your home, out of your life, then it is really none of *your* business *where* I take her." Helen mirrored Betsy's hands-on-hips posture and glared back. At five feet tall and barely a hundred pounds, Helen Teitelbaum was surprisingly fierce.

"Well, it *is* our business as you are trespassing on our property, and I'm one minute away from calling the police," Brad said in his best lawyer voice.

Threatening people was one of his favorite activities. A former fatty who had never recovered from the merciless teasing he suffered at the hands of the kids who didn't have to wear Huskies and never chose him for their team in kickball, he spent most of his adult life tormenting others, not so unconsciously trying to compensate for a childhood spent crouched against the chain link fence in the corner of the playground with a transistor radio and his best friend, Mr. Goodbar.

"You can't intimidate me, Brad Warren. I survived the Nazis. My parents and my sister died in the camps. Family is precious, and there are many worse tragedies in this world than an unplanned pregnancy." Not wanting to look at Betsy or Brad in case her bravado was more superficial than she hoped, Helen looked at Grace and nodded. When her mother had woken her at four o'clock that morning, Grace had imagined many scenarios, but this was not one of them. "Grace, come with me. "

"This is really none of your business, Mrs. Teitelbaum. You need to go home. Our family issues are not your concern." Betsy was furious and exhausted, once again being forced to defend her privacy, not quite able to believe what a day she was having. *Since when did raising one's children become a group effort?* she wondered, silently cursing Hillary Clinton and her "it takes a village" crap. If Mrs. Teitelbaum had stayed out of it, Betsy was sure Grace would have backed down before dinnertime and come crawling back into the house, begging for forgiveness. She would have had the abortion, and all would be right with the world. But now Betsy didn't know what was going to happen. She had never seen any grandchildren with Mrs. Teitelbaum, so the old cow was probably desperate to get her hands on a baby, by whatever means.

"But if Grace is no longer living here, what difference does it make to you where she goes?" Helen asked.

Brad pulled his phone out of his pocket and waved it over his head like a teenager at a rock concert. "Trespassing is a misdemeanor, Mrs. Teitelbaum."

Helen wrinkled her nose and sniffed, as if she smelled something unpleasant, having trouble believing that these people could discard their own child as if she were yesterday's trash. "I rode in a cattle car. I was at Auschwitz. You think you can frighten me by threatening to call the Silver Lake police department?" She turned away from Brad. "Grace, you look pale. Have you eaten anything today?" Without waiting for an answer, she said, "Right now you need a good meal and a place to lie down."

Grace realized that she hadn't had a morsel of food since the night before and was in fact starving. As if the mention of a meal had triggered a ravenous appetite, Grace suddenly felt that if she didn't eat something in the next five minutes, she would faint.

"Thank you, Mrs. Teitelbaum." Without looking at either of her parents, Grace took Mrs. Teitelbaum's outstretched hand, and the unlikely pair walked down the driveway and disappeared behind the black iron gates across the street.

Betsy and Brad stood, speechless, surrounded by a sea of black plastic. That was not how it was supposed to go.

"How did that happen? I've a mind to . . . ." Brad firmly believed that Grace needed to learn a lesson, and there was no way she was going to do that if the meddlesome neighbor, who lived in a multimillion-dollar home with a guest house and swimming pool, swooped in to rescue her before she had experienced a moment of discomfort. As Brad understood it, unless Grace faced the logical consequences of her actions, how would she ever grow up? Drinking iced tea while relaxing by a pool was not conducive to introspection and thoughts of remorse.

"To do what, Brad? We kicked Grace out. We have no control over where she goes." Betsy, her shoulders sagging, was beginning to regret their power play.

They would just have to wait it out. What could they possibly say if they marched over there now? They would only look weak and inconsistent, and the first rule of parenting was to look like you were in charge and knew what you were doing, even when you didn't . . . and always, always stick to your guns.

Brad stepped over a bag and opened the front door. "I just hope that houseman picks up these bags this afternoon." Relieved that the drama was over, at least for now, Brad kicked at a bag, sending it tumbling down the front steps, and returned to the comparative peace of his study. Although he had stayed home from work to support Betsy, he had been too distracted to put together a coherent sentence in the brief he was working on. Now his mind was clear. "Let that do-gooder Teitelbaum deal with Grace's mess if she wants to," he muttered to himself.

With loads of time and money and no one to spend it on, Mrs. Teitelbaum was the perfect person to step into the breach. He definitely wasn't up to the task. Part of him realized that this was not a shining moment in his career as a father, but the thought of Grace doing wicked things with some boy made him hate her. She was his baby, and now she was ruined, and he couldn't imagine ever getting over it. Although he realized on some level that he might be overreacting—Grace was nearly eighteen, and he couldn't expect her to remain a child her whole life, as much as he'd like her to—his need to separate himself from the source of his uncontrollable, irrational fury trumped any sense of parental attachment he might have.

CHAPTER 6

Although Grace had said hello to Mrs. Teitelbaum nearly every day since the latter had moved into the giant stone house across the street, Grace knew practically nothing about her, other than that she looked like an apple doll in an endless array of pastel cashmere cardigans. Beyond diminutive, Mrs. Teitelbaum favored crisp white blouses and pearls; a pair of tortoiseshell reading glasses always hung from a chain around her neck. Based on the way she dressed, Grace had assumed Mrs. T. was a retired spinster librarian, although a slight accent, vaguely European, suggested more exotic origins, and of course her house was not what you would expect a librarian to live in. It was massive, surrounded by an acre of lush gardens, a huge black wrought iron fence, eight-foot hedges, and even a small fruit orchard. Grace figured her neighbor must have an unusual back-story, but nothing about her manner had suggested that Mrs. Teitelbaum had spent part of her childhood in a World War II concentration camp.

"Are you okay, sweetheart?" Even as she said it, Helen realized this was a stupid question. How could the poor child be okay? Opening the oversized mahogany front door, Helen called out, "George, where are you? Could you come here for a minute?"

A tall, slender older man in rumpled chinos and a blue work shirt appeared, carrying a toolbox. "I'm right here, Mrs. T. I was just going to fix the squeak in that door upstairs. Do you need me to do something else first?"

"Yes, George, if you could. This is Grace Warren, from across the street. She and her parents have had a, um, falling out . . . and she's going to be staying with us for a while."

George dipped his head slightly. "It's a pleasure to meet you, Grace."

"You too," Grace said. She wasn't sure whether she should shake hands, so she just nodded in return.

"Anyway, George, could you run across the street and get Grace's things? You'll find them on the front porch in black plastic garbage bags. I think there are six of them; you should probably take the golf cart so you can get everything in one trip."

"Garbage bags?" George asked, and Helen nodded. "Sure thing. I'll be back in a flash. Where should I put them?"

George was curious about this girl's sudden appearance as well as her unusual luggage, but it didn't seem like the right moment to ask questions, and it would all come out in good time. His employer was always bringing home strays, although they usually had four legs.

"Let's see, how about the blue bedroom. It's close to mine, in case you need something in the night, and it has a lovely view of the back garden." Helen's eyes sparkled. She got such a natural high when she rescued someone from a bad situation, and she did feel so sorry for this poor little thing. She decided to wait a while before she told Jacob about her latest project. "Come upstairs, sweetheart. I'm going to run you a hot bath and bring you something to eat. There's nothing quite so relaxing as soaking in a warm tub, drinking tea, and eating tiny sandwiches and scones. How does that sound?" One arm around Grace's waist, Helen escorted her new charge up the wide, winding staircase.

"It sounds perfect. Thank you. You really don't have to go to so much trouble for me." A few minutes ago she was a homeless, pregnant teenager, and now she was headed up to a warm bath and a cup of hot tea in a house that could hold three of her own.

"It's no trouble at all," Helen insisted, worried that she was enjoying herself too much when this child had just been abandoned by her parents and was facing the most difficult time of her very short life.

"My mom and dad are just really angry. I'm sorry they were so rude to you. They're not usually like that." Apologizing for her mother for the second time that day, Grace was embarrassed at her parents' outburst in front of a virtual stranger, and as hurt as she was, she didn't want this woman to think terrible things about them. No matter what they said or what they did, they were still her parents and she loved them.

Helen was stunned. This precious girl was trying to protect her vicious parents' reputation? Butter wouldn't melt in their mouths. As vile as Helen thought they were, she didn't want Grace to worry. "I'm sure that's true, Grace. When people are frustrated, they can behave in unfortunate ways. You shouldn't give it a second thought."

Clean and fed and rested, Grace curled up in an easy chair in the corner of her new bedroom. The blue room was wallpapered and upholstered entirely in blue toile. It was like a room in one of the museum houses at Colonial Williamsburg Grace had visited two summers ago, right down to the mahogany four-poster bed. After lunch in the enormous clawfoot bathtub, Grace had taken a long nap, and now she was waiting for Vera, Mrs. T.'s cook as well as George's wife, to ring the bell signaling that dinner was ready. While she was sleeping someone had unpacked for her, and all her clothes were now neatly stowed away in a massive dresser or hung neatly in the cavernous walk-in closet. The bathroom was stocked with every imaginable shampoo, soap, and cream, along with a brand new toothbrush and piles of fluffy white towels. Everything smelled like lavender. It was as if Grace had checked into an incredibly fancy bed and breakfast. She dialed her cell phone. "Hey, it's me."

"Where the hell *are* you?" Jennifer had been convinced that something horrible had happened when Grace failed to respond to texts, phone calls, Facebook messages. "I thought you'd gone and done something stupid." Even though Jennifer couldn't believe that Grace would actually kill herself, desperation could make people crazy enough to do the unthinkable. When Grace had said she wished she would drown in the lake, maybe she hadn't been kidding.

"I'm sorry. I should've called, but it's been a weird day." Grace didn't know where to begin, and she wasn't looking forward to hearing Jennifer's inevitable "I told you so."

"What's up with your parents? When I couldn't get you, I called your house. Your dad just said you'd left, and he didn't know when you would be coming home. What the fuck does that mean?" Jennifer's voice was shrill with concern.

"My mother took me to some clinic in Massachusetts today for an abortion." Had that been just this morning? It seemed like a year since Grace had her feet in the stirrups, felt the cold steel of the speculum. Involuntarily she crossed her legs.

"What?! That's impossible. Your parents? Baby killers?" This was a staggering development—not at all what Jennifer had expected from a couple who always sat in the first pew, right on the center aisle, probably so they could be closer to God. Recovering from the initial shock, Jennifer said, "Well, anyway, that's probably good news overall. How was it? Did it hurt?"

"I couldn't do it. I've decided to have the baby. When I thought about what I would feel for the rest of my life, wondering if I'd done the right thing, I couldn't live with it. That's when it really went to hell. My mother said that my being pregnant would ruin their reputation, and she and my dad couldn't have me in their house anymore." It was embarrassing to say that out loud, basically declaring that her mother and father didn't love her enough, cared about their status more than they cared about her.

"So your parents dread being humiliated in front of their friends at the club more than they fear the wrath of God. Good to know." Jennifer chuckled. "But they're acting like assholes, stupid ones at that. Everyone in Silver Lake is going to know you're preggers soon enough, whether or not you're living under their roof. Wherever you keep your toothbrush, you're still their daughter . . . where *are* you, anyway? Do you want me to come get you? We're only an hour away, and spending the weekend with my parents and my sister—eight-year-olds are so annoying—isn't exactly a vacation."

"No, I'm fine. Mrs. Teitelbaum, the lady who lives across the street in that huge house, wandered into the middle of my eviction and rescued me. My father had packed all my stuff in garbage bags and put them on the front porch. Maybe he thought I'd take my stuff and leave town." Grace had to smile at the mental image of herself standing next to a freeway on-ramp, surrounded by lawn and leaf bags, thumb out, puking her guts all over the place as she waited for a ride.

"Black garbage bags? He's a classy guy, your dad." Jennifer had never particularly liked Grace's parents, had never trusted them—too self-important, too self-righteous. "I can't believe they thought you'd just leave. More likely they thought you'd fold and do what they wanted, but they didn't take into account your crazy neighbor."

"Mrs. Teitelbaum's not crazy. She's the nicest person I've ever met in my life." As Mrs. T. had championed her, Grace would defend her until the end of time.

"And the richest. It's brilliant. Not only did you get rescued in your darkest hour, but you got rescued by a fucking heiress." Jennifer clicked her tongue.

"Heiress?" It was obvious from Mrs. T.'s house that she was loaded, but an heiress?

"You've never heard of HAT Industries?" Jennifer was incredulous.

"Sure, but so what? I've also heard of Apple and GE and Wellington Industries." Although Grace didn't watch MSNBC, she wasn't totally clueless.

"That's your savior's company, dummy. It's like a billion-dollar corporation. They're into precious metals and stuff, I think. Here, I'll look it up on Google."

"Billion? I had no idea," Grace whispered into the phone. So much for the librarian theory.

"How could you miss that? When she moved in, there was a big article in the paper about the old lady and her move from Park Avenue up to the sticks." Jennifer's dad made her read the paper every day, so she wouldn't be just another ignorant, self-absorbed teenager. Sometimes, not often, it came in handy.

"I didn't see it. She's just a really nice person." The fact that Mrs. T. was exceptionally wealthy didn't really matter to Grace, although she had to admit the house was incredible, and she felt like less of a burden knowing that she wasn't imposing on a little old lady on a fixed income.

Quickly scanning the article, Jennifer reported the highlights. "Here it is. HAT stands for Helen and Abraham Teitelbaum. Abraham was her husband. It says here he died three years ago and left his entire fortune to his wife, Helen. They have no children."

"Stop snooping. It's none of our business." To Grace it felt like they were rifling through Mrs. T.'s desk drawer.

"I'm not snooping. This is all public information, available to everyone on the world wide web." Jennifer laughed. "Maybe she'll adopt you, and you and your love child—well, lust child—can live happily ever after on Easy Street."

"You are *so* out of line, Jennifer. Just shut up." Sometimes Jennifer could be so inappropriate. She thought she was being funny, no matter how many times Grace pointed out to her that she wasn't.

"You're right. I'm sorry, but you have to admit it's bizarre. Right?"

It had been a surreal day, and it wasn't over yet. "I guess so," Grace answered.

"You guess so?" Jennifer squealed. "The God Squad pushing for an abortion. The rich old widow rescuing you out of the garbage. Tell me when the spaceship lands. I'll rush right over—I could go for a probing."

Grace was startled by a knock at the door. She whispered, "I've got to go. I'll call you later." In a normal voice, she called, "Come in."

The door opened, revealing not Mrs. Teitelbaum, or George, or Vera, or the housekeeper, Ada, but a boy, a really cute boy, who looked about her age. *Was this the cabana boy?* she wondered. Or did Mrs. T. make it a habit of taking in troubled teens? Although nothing about this guy looked troubled. Straight out of a Brooks Brothers catalog, he had it all under control, right down to his cornflower blue polo shirt that perfectly matched his eyes. In spite of her vow never to look at a guy again, her heart skipped a beat.

"Hi, Grace? I'm Charlie Glass, Helen's great-nephew."

"Hi, it's nice to meet you," Grace said as she slowly stood up, trying not to look as clumsy as she felt, and approached Charlie, who still waited in the doorway. "I didn't know Mrs. T. had a nephew." Jennifer's Internet research had not mentioned the rest of the family.

"Yeah, my grandfather is Uncle Abe's brother." This girl was way too cute, and young, to be in the kind of trouble Helen had described. If he had to guess, he would have pegged her for thirteen at most. She looked like she should be standing outside the ShopRite selling Samoas and Thin Mints for her Girl Scout troop, not deciding whether to have an abortion or give up her child for adoption.

“Who?” Grace asked, feigning ignorance. She didn’t want to look like a busybody.

“Uncle Abe was Aunt Helen’s husband. He died three years ago, right before Aunt Helen moved here. She used to live in New York City, but after Uncle Abe passed away she said it was too sad to walk around Manhattan without him, so she moved up here.” His smile was at least as beautiful as Nick’s. Grace definitely had a thing for teeth. “Come on, why are we standing here? Let’s go outside, if you’re not too tired. It’s a beautiful evening, and after the day Aunt Helen said you had, I think you could use a little fresh air.”

Charlie led the way down the back staircase and into the kitchen. The aroma of roasting chicken and fresh rosemary flooded Grace’s nostrils, and her stomach growled. “Hi, Vera,” said Charlie. “Grace and I are going to go out back for a little while. Dinner smells incredible.”

“Hello, Grace, I’m Vera. I hope chicken’s okay. Let me know if there’s anything special you like to eat, or anything you can’t or won’t eat.” As friendly as her husband, Vera smiled as she whipped egg whites in a shiny copper bowl.

“It’s nice to meet you, and I like everything,” said Grace quietly.

Vera nodded. “Would you like a snack now? Dinner won’t be ready for a little while, and I remember when I was expecting, I was always starving.”

Grace nodded shyly, covering her stomach, as if she could hide the bean. *Expecting.* Cheeks reddening at the word, Grace looked at her feet. For the next seven months, everyone who looked at her would know she was one of those girls who had done the deed and gotten knocked up before she was even out of high school. It was going to be hard to face all those curious, judgmental stares. Vera had been nothing but kind, and Grace was still mortified.

Turning to a cooling rack on one of the white marble counters in a kitchen straight out of a nineteenth-century English novel,

Vera picked up two muffins and handed them to Grace and Charlie. "Fresh out of the oven. Banana nut. You're not allergic to walnuts, are you?"

"No, no allergies. These smell wonderful." Grace gratefully took a bite, savoring the sweetness. If this was a sample of Vera's cooking, Grace feared she would eat everything in sight as long as she was staying in this house. She had no idea how much weight you were allowed to gain during pregnancy.

Outside, Grace and Charlie wandered across the grass and sat down on a glider swing under an arbor covered with grape vines. Suddenly Grace didn't know what to say to this handsome boy, with whom, under any other circumstances, she would have flirted madly.

"So, when are you due?" Charlie asked.

From her hairline down to her toes, Grace felt a surge of heat. "The beginning of April."

"I'm sorry. We don't have to talk about it if you don't want to. But you shouldn't be embarrassed. Not in front of me. I mean, shit happens. I don't judge." Charlie's face turned pink as well. The last thing he wanted to do was make this girl uncomfortable. Her parents were already acting like she'd serviced the entire football team on the fifty-yard line during halftime.

"No, it's fine. I'd better get over it. It's only going to get worse." Grace placed her hand on her stomach, which still gave no clue as to what was going on inside. "I got myself into trouble messing around in some guy's car, and now I have to live with the consequences. I'm stupid and slutty, and everybody's going to know it."

As trite and old-fashioned as that sounded, that was the truth, even in a supposedly liberal, modern society. What made it even worse was that Nick wouldn't suffer for a moment because of this—if anyone did find out he was the father, it would probably only enhance his reputation as a stud. Grace covered her face with her hands. Because of this perennial double standard, it felt odd talking to a guy about stuff like this. But perhaps because Charlie was a stranger, it was slightly less humiliating. Like talking to a therapist.

"Don't talk like that. You think you're the only girl in high school who ever did it in the back of a car with your boyfriend? I don't think so." Charlie shuddered internally.

Not that he was an expert. When he was living in Paris, he had been with exactly one girl exactly twelve times, and every time they'd done it he'd felt like he was doing something dishonest, because he knew he didn't love her, and as hurting as he knew it was, he had no idea how to separate sex from love, even though he had tried his best, all twelve times. If the girl had gotten pregnant, Charlie couldn't begin to imagine how he would have dealt with it.

"He wasn't my boyfriend. It was only our third date. That's pretty slimy, by anybody's standards," Grace whispered, certain that this admission would forever tarnish her image with Charlie. Not that he probably thought much of her anyway. But this would definitely be the nail in the coffin.

Getting naked on the third date *was* a little soon, although for a guy such a pace would earn high-fives, not scarlet letters. Determined not to pass judgment, Charlie tried not to show his surprise. Even if she'd done it on the first date, there was something about this girl that was so *un*slutty. "You did something you regret doing, and you got really unlucky. Are you going to punish yourself for the rest of your life?"

"I think maybe I am. I deserve it for being a moron, if nothing else."

For the most part, she had liked who she was before, except for the geeky aspects. And in the rearview mirror, she really wasn't that much of a nerd—she only owned one calculator, had only seen *Star Wars* twice, and she'd never even been to a sci-fi convention. In retrospect, she wondered why she had felt so lost during junior year. Jennifer was right—if only she had talked it out with someone.

"You shouldn't do that to yourself. It's not healthy, and it's not true," Charlie said.

"But I deserve to feel bad for losing my virginity to a guy I hardly knew. In my heart I knew he didn't really even like me. That's beyond pitiful, isn't it?"

"You really only did it once?" *What were the odds of that?* Charlie wondered.

Grace nodded miserably.

"He didn't use a . . . ?"

"He did, but it's not a hundred percent effective, which is a statistic that I, the math whiz, should have been aware of." Grace couldn't believe she was having a conversation about condoms and sex with a boy she'd just met, and she wasn't stuttering or sweating.

"By definition, one time means you can't be a slut, but I will say you have the worst luck of anyone I've ever met. First time, using a condom, and you still got pregnant."

Charlie shook his head in disbelief. Having lived abroad where people seemed less uptight than in the United States, there was a lot of sleeping around, but he hadn't known anyone who had gotten pregnant, or gotten someone else pregnant. Or maybe they just took care of the problem, and nobody ever found out about it. More likely the case.

"That's it in a nutshell, a really shitty nutshell."

Squeezing her eyes shut, she successfully held back the waterworks. Having already cried buckets, Grace knew they didn't help—it wasn't like she could weep away the bean. Crying just made her face all ugly and scrunched up, and she didn't need to feel any more unattractive.

"If you feel that way about it, and you're not even in a relationship with this guy, then why don't you just have an abortion? Then no one would ever have to know." Aunt Helen had told him that was what Grace's parents wanted her to do, and her refusal to go through with it was why they had kicked her out.

On one level Grace agreed with Charlie. Sixty or seventy years of self-flagellation were impossible to imagine. "You're right, but if I get an abortion, I feel like the ghost of that baby that never got to be will haunt me for the rest of my life."

"A ghost? You believe in that stuff?"

Did Aunt Helen realize what she was getting herself into when she dragged home this stray? This was one messed-up girl. Charlie could understand why his aunt had scooped her up—her eyes glistened with unshed tears like a little girl who had just realized she was lost in a crowded department store, and as she spoke he was fighting the urge to cradle her in his arms and tell her he would never let anyone hurt her again. But she promised to be a handful. Maybe Aunt Helen should stick to the occasional dog or cat.

"Not chain-rattling, white-sheet haunting. Someday, I *hope* I get married and have a family, you know, do it in the right order with the right person. If I have an abortion, when I eventually have a baby because I want to, I'm afraid I won't be able to stop thinking about this one. There's no way to undo that. If I have it and give it up for adoption, I'll have plenty of issues, especially in the short term, but in the long term I know I'll feel better about it. I may end up regretting a lot of things, but at least I won't be asking *what if* for my whole life. Does that make any sense?"

This was heavy stuff to talk about with a complete stranger, who was her age and really kind of hot in a prep school sort of way. But he'd asked, and each time she explained herself, Grace felt marginally more confident that her decision to go through with the pregnancy was the right one for her, in spite of the domestic conflagration she had created by defying her parents.

"Actually, that makes a lot of sense. It would be so easy to get trapped in this moment, only thinking about how you feel today, but you're right, you've got a lot of years ahead of you. I'm sure you'll meet the right guy and have the family you deserve someday, with no regrets."

"It's hard to imagine that happening to me, falling in love, having someone fall in love with me. But I have to make myself think that way, or else I'll lose my mind." She shook her head. "Let's not talk about my mess anymore. You know pretty much everything about me. I want to know about you. Do you visit your aunt often? I've never seen you here."

Grace would have remembered such a good-looking boy wandering around the neighborhood. Tall, with dark wavy hair and startlingly blue eyes, Charlie reminded Grace of a character from a Jane Austen novel, and like his aunt he spoke with the slightest accent, as if he had lived abroad for most of his life. It was a dazzling combination.

"I've only been here a couple of times since Aunt Helen moved out from the City. My father works for Macro Financial. They have offices all over the world, so we've had to move around a lot. Until June we were living in Paris, but then my dad got sent to Moscow to work on some special project for a year."

"You've been to Russia?" Grace's most exotic destination up to this point had been Toronto.

"I spent the summer there, but I didn't want to spend my last year of high school in Moscow, so Aunt Helen offered to look after me."

"Don't they have an American School there?" It felt good to think about somebody else for a change. For a few minutes Grace could almost forget what had happened, how she came to be sitting on this swing with this guy in the first place.

"They do. I've been to the American Schools in Paris, Florence, and Berlin. They're fine, but I was missing home—we haven't lived in the States since I was twelve. It seemed like a perfect opportunity, with Aunt Helen being on her own. And she isn't getting any younger. It'll be good for both of us."

Charlie looked back at the house and smiled. He thought but didn't say that Grace's presence was proving to be a pleasant diversion. If only she weren't pregnant with some guy's baby—but if she weren't, then she wouldn't be here, so maybe it was meant to be. *Beshert*, as Aunt Helen would say—fate, but with a twist.

"Your life sounds incredible. I, on the other hand, am a total hick." Unsophisticated, provincial, and pregnant—quite the prize package. All that was missing were bare feet, a couple of tattoos, and a trailer park, Grace imagined Charlie must be thinking.

"Well I think you're very nice . . . for a hick."

"That's the sweetest thing I've heard from a boy in a long time. It really is." Grateful that Charlie was making the effort to flirt with her a little bit, to make her feel like a girl rather than a science experiment, Grace started to relax.

The sound of a bell interrupted them. "That means dinner's ready. Shall we?" Charlie held out his arm and Grace tucked her hand into the crook of his elbow. This guy was an old-fashioned gentleman, easy on the eyes and genuinely kind. *Where were you a few months ago?* Grace thought sadly. If he had appeared on the scene a little earlier, maybe her life would be completely different right now. But perhaps this was some weird destiny thing, and she just needed to wait for her future to play out in whatever strange way it needed to. For a second, Grace could imagine a decent life after the bean.

Candles provided the only light in a dining room that could easily seat twenty. Two huge silver candelabra sat on the mahogany table, flanking a large blue and white porcelain bowl overflowing with fresh fruit. Sterling flatware and crystal goblets sparkled in the flickering candlelight. It was an oil painting come to life, thought Grace as she and Charlie sat down opposite each other near the end of the table. Helen was already sitting at the head, sipping a glass of wine.

"First, let me apologize for this whole state dinner setup. Vera wanted to make it special tonight to welcome you to our home," Helen said. "But perhaps it's a bit much."

"It's the most beautiful room I've ever seen. She shouldn't have gone to so much trouble for me." Grace was already worried about becoming a burden. She had no idea how she would ever be able to repay Mrs. Teitelbaum for all her kindness.

"Don't worry—Vera loves to do this. She gets bored doing supper in the kitchen every night. But I probably should have brought you dinner in your room—you've had a long day." Helen squeezed Grace's hand.

"No, this is wonderful. Please don't apologize. I don't know how to thank you for everything. I'm sure my parents will get over this pretty soon, and then I can get out of your hair," said Grace, needing to believe that her parents were just having the forty-something equivalent of a temper tantrum. In a day or two they would come to their senses, would realize they had overreacted, would realize how much they missed her . . . she hoped.

Charlie spoke up. "Until they recover, you should enjoy it here. Staying with Aunt Helen is like taking a vacation at a five-star resort—incredible food, heated swimming pool, there's even a putting green behind the apple orchard."

"Exactly," said Helen. "Think of this as a mini holiday, except for the fact that the two of you have to go back to school on Tuesday."

"Thanks for the buzzkill, Aunt Helen. Are you trying to ruin the weekend?" Charlie laughed, as he poured more wine for Helen and some for himself.

"Sorry, children. You're right. Let's talk about something more festive. Charlie, why don't you tell us about things in Moscow? Did you go to the Hermitage?"

It was so wonderful having young people in the house. Vera, George, and Ada were good company, but there was nothing like listening to children chattering away about their lives. On the cusp of adulthood, they found everything exciting and new; the world was rife with possibility. It made her feel lighthearted and free, although she hadn't felt that way herself when she was seventeen. When Helen had been their age, she was still trying to find her way in America, still trying to master the language and lose her thick accent, which had made her feel gauche and ugly. She had been living with a distant cousin, trying not to look like an immigrant, and starting her freshman year at Barnard. It was in September of 1950 that she had met Abraham for the very first time. Two weeks later he had proposed, and by Thanksgiving they had been married. Life was funny that way. You never knew what was going to happen next. Something wonderful could be just around the corner. The day before she met Abraham, she was wishing she had died with her family in Poland—she had been that miserable. She must remember to tell that story, except for the death wish part, to Grace, who could certainly use a little dose of optimism, considering all that had happened to her.

Distracted by all the drama in the last couple of weeks, Grace had nearly forgotten that she still had to get through senior year. During her first three years of high school she couldn't remember any girls with beach balls for bellies waddling through the halls of Silver Lake High School. A dubious honor to be the first. Instead of enjoying the euphoria of senior spring, she would be going into labor in AP Psychology and giving birth in the nurse's office. But Helen's glass-half-full attitude was contagious, and for the first time she thought that maybe everything could work out. Taking a sip of ice water, Grace smiled at her miraculous hostess. As Charlie described the collection of Fabergé eggs at the Hermitage, enamel-covered treasures dotted with diamonds and emeralds, Grace was almost, but not quite, able to enjoy her first evening in her temporary new home.

Lying in bed later that night, unable to fall asleep in spite of the incredibly comfortable bed, Grace wondered if her parents were still awake. Were they thinking about her, or had they banished her from their minds as they had banished her from their house? She stared at her phone, dialing the first three digits of her parents' number over and over, unable to finish. What would happen if she called them? Would they answer, or would they just let the machine pick up?

CHAPTER 7

Dear Baby,
I don't know what you are yet, so I will just call you Baby. Poor sweet Baby. You're almost eleven weeks old, about the size of a lime, and you have tiny fingernails. The baby book says you can swallow and you've started kicking, but you're still too small for me to feel. I'm looking forward to feeling you moving inside me, but I think it will be kind of scary, because then everything will become real. Right now I still find it hard to believe that you are living inside me, like a tiny tenant in a studio apartment who will outgrow your quarters in seven months.
Love,
Grace

It was September ninth, the first day of senior year. Instead of enjoying the relief that should come with gearing up for the last lap of high school, Grace was on the verge of a breakdown, not sure she had the strength to suck it up and slog through the day. Suddenly uncertain if she'd made the right decision about the bean baby, the time for changing her mind was running out. Standing under a tree outside school, waiting for Jennifer, Grace felt certain that everyone knew, that she gave off some fecund pregnancy scent, or that Nick had blabbed, and she might as well have a big red *A* tattooed on her forehead. Rivulets of sweat ran down her back, and her breasts ached inside her painfully tight bra. Certain that pregnancy had caused her to swell up like a pair of cantaloupes, which would be another dead giveaway, Grace wore a sports bra that, while it flattened out her chest, was incredibly uncomfortable. Something had to give, because the way she felt at this moment, she wasn't going to last another week, let alone until April.

Although Charlie had driven her to school in Aunt Helen's gleaming silver Mercedes, he had left her to attend a meeting of some singing group he was thinking of joining. Credit to him, he had said she could tag along so she wouldn't be alone, but she had refused. The time had come for her to stand on her own two feet, at least until Jennifer arrived—or until her ankles became too swollen to hold her up, which she felt was going to happen any second, but according to the pregnancy book was a treat that was still a few months away. Where was her best friend, who had promised her that she would be there through thick and thin, which definitely included being pregnant on the first day of senior year? Checking her watch every fifteen seconds, as if that would hasten Jennifer's arrival, Grace waved and smiled, pretending to be normal.

Already late, Jennifer skidded into one of the last open parking spaces. Checking her face in the rearview mirror, she was startled by someone tapping hard on her window. "What the hell do you want?" she hissed.

She stared up at Nick, hoping he might go away, but he continued knocking. "Let me in. I need to talk to you."

As gorgeous as he was, there was a cool detachment about him that transformed his flawless features into a death mask. Reluctantly, she popped the lock and he slid into the front seat. Trying to sound tough, Jennifer asked, "What do *you* want, asshole?"

"I want you to talk some sense into your crazy friend. You need to make sure she gets this taken care of, *now*." Nick spoke in a monotone and stared out the windshield at a tree. It was like a scene out of a mafia movie. His next line would be something about concrete boots and sleeping with the fishes.

"What exactly do you mean, 'taken care of'?" Although Jennifer knew very well what Nick meant, she wasn't going to make this easy on him. She wanted to make him spell it out and prove what a scumbag he really was.

"Don't play dumb, Jennifer. You know what I'm talking about. She needs to get rid of this thing, this problem. If my parents find out, I'm dead. I don't think she's thought this through."

Realizing that if he came on too strong this girl was going to stonewall him, he tried to soften his voice. If charm didn't work, there was always time to get nasty later. Besides, she was kind of hot in a bitchy way, and it didn't hurt to keep his options open. The type of chick who always had to have the last word, she probably liked it a little rough, and definitely on top. She had possibilities, if she ever stopped talking. But now wasn't the time to think about a potential Number Twenty. Number Seventeen had to be dealt with first.

"Well, it doesn't look like you're going to get your way. Grace is having the baby, and probably giving it up for adoption, you douchebag." Blond hair falling just so over his forehead and miles of white teeth notwithstanding, it was easy to see that this guy was a total bastard. Jennifer wondered how brilliant Grace hadn't been able to see it.

"That's not good enough. This needs to go away, *now*." Playing nice wasn't working. Desperation rising like a wave inside him, Nick could feel his very loose grip on his limited self-control slipping. He didn't know Jennifer all that well, but she didn't look like someone who would give up when her back was against the wall. Taking a deep breath, he willed himself to hold it together, just a little while longer.

"Or else? Are you threatening me, you selfish prick?"

If they hadn't been sitting in the crowded school parking lot, Jennifer wouldn't have been so ballsy. In spite of his reputation as a ladies' man, from what she could see, he was more of a bully. Nick didn't look above hitting a girl if he didn't get what he wanted from her. But the steady stream of kids and teachers made her brave. That and the can of pepper spray she kept under the seat.

"No, I just think that Grace should think a little more about what she's doing. Having a baby isn't like buying a fucking dog. I don't love her, I don't want to be a father, I'm not going to marry her, and I think I should have some say in how this thing plays out, assuming it's even mine." That last bit was unnecessary and incendiary, and, even he knew, ridiculous, but it didn't hurt to keep that seed of doubt alive. "Can't you see what I'm going through?" In spite of the fact that Grace was the one who had to carry the baby, Nick felt like he was entitled to a little sympathy too.

Jennifer shook her head. "You're even more of a shit than I thought. You probably should've considered all those things *before* you took your dick out of your pants. But you don't have to worry your pretty little head. You're not going to be on the hook financially, and Grace doesn't plan on telling anyone who the father is, so why don't you go fuck yourself. And get the hell out of my car." Jennifer sounded way more sure of herself than she felt. As little as she thought of him, he was still intimidating with his perfect profile and testosterone-fueled confidence.

"Just tell Grace what I said. And tell her if she wants anything from me she's going to have to get a DNA test." Nick got out of the car, slammed the door, and stormed off. "That was a waste of time," he mumbled to himself.

Jennifer sat in her car, taking deep breaths and trying to figure out what to say to Grace about her babydaddy. When the first bell rang, she still hadn't decided how to broach the subject, other than to postpone it as long as possible. As her mother always said, bad news keeps. Reluctantly Jennifer got out of her car, pasted a smile on her face, and hurried to find Grace, who had to be furious that she was so late.

"There you are," Grace called out, relieved that Jennifer had finally arrived. There was no way she would get through this first day without a wingman.

"Sorry I'm late. Minor wardrobe crisis." It was not the moment to tell Grace that she had run into Nick in the school parking lot, and that he had urged her—more like threatened her—to talk some sense into Grace about her *problem*, as he called it. Jennifer knew she would have to tell Grace about her little encounter with the devil, but there was no rush.

"You look beautiful, so I guess it worked out," Grace said.

In a short navy blue sundress and red flats, Jennifer did look gorgeous. Grace wondered again why the boys couldn't seem to get past Jennifer's personality issues—her body was amazing, and her hair looked like spun gold. Grace's build was much the same, but she was already mourning the loss of perfect proportion and the advent of miles of elastic that would be needed to encase her rapidly swelling anatomy. This had been the first summer her mother had allowed her to wear a bikini, and now she would probably never look decent in one again. It was a minor problem in the grand scheme of things, but upsetting nonetheless.

"And you look just like you. No one can tell. I swear." Jennifer didn't have to lie. There was no suggestion of a bulge anywhere on Grace's slim frame. But according to the baby books Jennifer had consulted—she owed it to her best friend to be well informed—the change would happen overnight. One day soon, Grace was going to wake up looking pregnant; it was inevitable.

"Thanks for caring enough to bullshit me," Grace replied as the second morning bell rang and they joined the herd of students lumbering into the first day of school.

Miss Tappan, the AP English teacher, tottered into the classroom, a hippopotamus in clam diggers and kitten heels. "Welcome back, children." Her eyebrows rose. "Yes, you're still children. Enjoy it—it's almost over." She perched on the edge of her desk, staring at her class over bright red glasses sitting on the end of her bright red nose. "I know you're all chomping at the bit, desperate to become adults, believing that therein lies some magical key to happiness. But let me be the first to burst your bubble. Adulthood means responsibility, making difficult decisions, some of them wrong, and with no one to come and clean up after you."

Although Grace knew it was practically impossible, she felt as if Miss Tappan were speaking directly to her. Could she know? Her face nearly as red as the teacher's, T-shirt clinging to the damp skin on her back, Grace fought the urge to run out of the classroom. Fleeing would only raise more eyebrows, and her secret, if it hadn't already gotten out, would be that much closer to the surface.

Someone in the back of the classroom raised his hand and asked, "Does this have anything to do with AP English? Are we going to be tested on this? Should we be taking notes?" Everyone laughed. It was a universal sentiment: unless it was on the test, nobody gave a damn.

"Every word I utter and everything you see in this class could potentially be on an exam. So pay attention. You never know what might be significant," Miss Tappan replied, hopping delicately off the desk and clicking over to the white board where she wrote a list of books and poems. "In case you're wondering, write this down—it's important."

Six hours and five classes later, Grace collapsed in the front seat of Charlie's car. More than anything else in the world she wanted to free herself from her clothes, but that would have to wait. She was having trouble getting enough air, but she couldn't decide whether she was simply being strangled by her sports bra or was suffering a six-hour panic attack.

"You made it through the first day. Only one hundred and seventy-nine left to go," Charlie said as he started the car and turned the air conditioning on full blast. Grace's face was on fire, tiny beads of sweat dotting her forehead, even though it wasn't that warm out. It was obvious that she'd had a rough time of it. Charlie pressed a button on the steering wheel, and classical music floated out of half a dozen speakers. It was like a relaxation tank on wheels, but in Grace's state, cool air and a Bach concerto were of little help.

"Don't remind me." Fiddling mindlessly with the thermostat, Grace said, "I don't think I can do this."

"Look, you got through today. You'll see how it goes tomorrow. Take one day at a time," Charlie said, trying to be supportive and sensitive, but worrying that he sounded like a refugee from one of those alcoholics' support groups that meet in church basements once a week to trade platitudes and sobriety chips. Having spent much of his life in all-boys schools, he was a novice when it came to friendships with girls, and Grace wasn't your average teenage girl. That coupled with the fact that he felt different with her left him on edge. She made him nervous, in a really good way, but it was disconcerting. Searching for just the right words to comfort his new friend, he would do or say anything to make her happy, or at least make her feel better. He wished he could fast-forward to next April.

"I'm not sure that I made it through. Between the sweating and the hyperventilating and the paranoia, I have no idea what actually happened today. Even if I go to class, I'm going to flunk all my courses." Grace flipped the visor down and examined the tomato that was her face in the mirror. "Yikes. I look like a pomegranate." She flipped it back up and stared out the window as the glacial, German-engineered air conditioning dried her damp skin and hair. Perhaps if she could go to class in this car she could survive.

"You look fine."

What Charlie really wanted to say was that she looked beautiful and vulnerable and he would do anything to protect her. He had spotted the evil Nick in his history class. With girls swarming around him like bees buzzing around a particularly luscious flower, Nick was impossible to miss. No wonder Grace had fallen under his spell—he looked deep into each girl's eyes, and the way they all batted their lashes and twirled their hair, it seemed only a matter of time until each one found her way into the back seat of the infamous Jeep Grand Cherokee. That this one guy could have random sex with the entire female population of the senior class, along with a healthy quotient of underclass girls, seemed entirely plausible, and that made Charlie even more furious about what he had done to Grace. As bad as it was to be in her unfortunate condition, it was that much worse, because she was clearly only one of many toys in this jerk's playpen. Charlie fantasized about sucker punching him, whispering, "How does it feel to get fucked?" as Nick fell to the floor.

CHAPTER 8

Dear Baby,

You're twelve weeks old. That's the cutoff date, the end of the first trimester. We're in this thing for the long haul now, you and I. No backing out, no more flip-flopping. No procedures involving scraping and vacuuming. The only way you're coming out is head first, screaming your lungs out, and as scary as that is, I'm a hundred percent sure it's the right thing to do. You are fully formed already (I wonder whether you're a boy or a girl), a perfect miniature of a person. Your teeth are starting to grow in your gums. My teeth are pretty good. They're very white and I only had to wear braces for a year, so maybe you'll get lucky. I'm off to see the doctor. Wish me luck.

Love,

Grace

"Grace Warren?" A nurse who looked almost exactly like the nurse at Dr. Ryder's clinic, but in lavender scrubs, was holding a folder and calling Grace's name. Also different was that Betsy wasn't present, and this time Grace knew why she was here and what was going to happen. Helen looked up from a copy of *Good Housekeeping* and smiled encouragingly. When Grace stood, she held out her hand to her new friend and benefactor.

"Mrs. T., would you come in with me? Please?" Not exactly frightened after doing a spread-eagle for Dr. Ryder, all this doctor stuff was still new, and having an adult nearby—one who would offer kind words instead of lobbing insults and accusations—would be comforting.

"Of course, darling. Let's go meet Dr. Weston."

Helen followed Grace back to the examining room, where Grace put on the crunchy paper gown and sat, feet dangling over the edge of the examining table, waiting for the doctor. A few discreet inquiries to Helen's own physician had yielded the name of Dr. Annabelle Weston. She was young, well educated, and, most importantly, not judgmental. Grace didn't need to hear any more disparaging remarks about her moral character, and since Dr. Weston had spent her internship delivering babies at an inner-city hospital where virtually all her patients were under the age of twenty, examining a seventeen-year-old who was twelve weeks pregnant would be just another day at the office.

"Thank you again for finding me a doctor and taking care of everything."

In addition to finding an obstetrician, Helen had a frank discussion with Betsy and Brad, who in their fit of moral outrage had dropped Grace from their health insurance policy. After a twenty-minute debate on the Warren's driveway, Helen, backed up by her lawyer—since Brad had a law degree, it seemed wise to bring her own mouthpiece—convinced them to reestablish Grace's insurance coverage. Not that it mattered financially. Helen would happily have paid all of Grace's medical bills, but she didn't want Grace's parents to get away with such despicable behavior. Grace was their daughter, not their employee, and even if they had made her leave the family home, they couldn't make her leave the family. No matter what happened, Grace was their child, and Helen was determined to make sure they didn't forget that. As incensed as Helen was on Grace's behalf, she held out hope that someday, when the baby was placed with adoptive parents and Grace no longer looked like a pear, Betsy and Brad would come to their senses.

There was no doubt that, in spite of what Helen saw as the Warrens's unforgivable treatment of their only child, Grace would happily run into those reproachful arms, forgiving and forgetting all their cruelty. Children were nothing if not resilient. Bringing that fractured family back together would be the culmination of Helen's rescuing career; at this point, she wasn't sure it could really happen.

"You're welcome, but there's no need to thank me. I enjoy your company tremendously, as does Charlie. You're a wonderful addition to our little household, and I'm sure it will all work out in the end. Your parents are having a hard time with this. Not everybody is able to look at the big picture and see beyond all the potholes that litter the road of life."

"I hope so. But I've never seen them this mad. I can't imagine they'll ever get over what I've done."

How long could she live with Helen? It didn't sound like she would ask Grace to leave after the baby was born, but Grace couldn't stay there forever. So much to think about, and her brain seemed to be stuck in low gear, unable to plan more than a few days, or sometimes minutes, into the future.

"I don't mean to sound like one of those awful inspirational speakers on Channel Ten, but I truly feel that everything works out eventually, even if it doesn't seem possible when you're in the middle of it. With every fiber of my being, I believe that they love you, very much, even if they can't show you right now." Helen spoke as if she were naturally well-adjusted and highly evolved, but it had taken years on Dr. Evelyn Needleman's black leather couch to get to this point.

"You've been through so much, losing your family in such a horrible way. But you're not angry? How is that possible? Do you think it was supposed to be that way?" Although Grace knew she was prying, she needed to figure it out. Did life just happen? Did fate steer your car where it was supposed to go, even if you tried to turn the wheel in a different direction?

"Not *supposed* to be that way. I would give anything to get my family back, but once they were gone, I decided that I had to live my life as well as I possibly could, make the most of it. Otherwise it would have been as if the Nazis had killed me as well."

Natalie, Helen's older sister, had turned seventeen the day before the last day they saw each other, standing in the cold mud in that endless long line of people who had no idea that it was the last line most of them would ever stand in. More than once it had occurred to her that maybe she was trying to channel Natalie through Grace, retrieve a little bit of what she had lost so long ago. Helen wondered what Dr. Needleman would have to say about that.

Helen closed her eyes and she was standing next to her mother and sister, waving goodbye to her father, not understanding that she would never see him again after that day. "Bye, Papa. I love you," she had called to him.

"Be good, my precious girls. I'll see you very soon, and I will tell you the story about your Great-Uncle Max." In spite of the wind and the mud and the snow that was beginning to fall, her father never stopped smiling.

Wondering why her mother wasn't saying anything to Papa, Helen had looked up. At the exact same time, her mother looked down and their eyes locked. Helen was only ten years old, but she could see from her mother's petrified gaze that this was the line that led to the end of the world, and there was nothing left to say. Shaking with terror, Helen flung her arms around her mother's waist and grabbed Natalie's hand in a vain effort to keep her family from being torn away from her.

A soldier raised his gun and yelled something Helen couldn't understand, and her father's line started to move away. He turned back, just before the line went around the corner of a low wooden building, blowing a last kiss to his girls; he was still smiling. Helen smiled and blew a kiss back to him. What else was there to do? And then he was gone.

"Mrs. T., are you all right?" Grace asked.

Waving her hand in front of her face, Helen said, "I'm fine. When you're old, sometimes the memories pop up out of nowhere. I was just thinking about my family for a second. You would have loved my dear parents. They were very special . . . and my sister, too." Helen smiled and patted Grace's hand.

"You're amazing." How could Helen be so good, so understanding, after all that had happened to her? She had every right to be bitter and angry, but she was the warmest, most loving person Grace had ever met.

"Not amazing. Just practical. Ultimately, what's the alternative? Unless you fling yourself off a bridge, you're alive, and as long as you're breathing, you might as well do a decent job of it," said Helen.

The door opened. "Hi, I'm Dr. Weston. You must be Grace. A pleasure to meet you. And this is your . . . ?" Although she was fairly certain this had to be the grandmother, Dr. Weston had once grievously insulted the mother of a pregnant teen by assuming she was one generation more removed than she actually was. How was she to know that the pregnant girl had been a change-of-life baby and the mother had given birth at the age of fifty-two, making her sixty-nine when she walked into Dr. Weston's office with her daughter? Lesson learned: never assume anything, especially with the rampant use of fertility drugs.

"I'm Helen Teitelbaum, a close friend of Grace's." Helen scribbled on her notepad to remind herself to send Dr. Weston an e-mail explaining the specifics of Grace's situation, and suggesting that this young lady could use some extra attention and understanding during this difficult time.

Dr. Weston's eyebrows rose slightly but she said nothing. When a friend accompanied the patient, that usually meant there had been a brouhaha in the family over the unplanned pregnancy. The chart said seventeen, but this girl looked about twelve.

Cutting to the chase, Dr. Weston said, "Dr. Ryder sent me your ultrasound. The notes in your chart indicate that you hadn't yet made a decision about this pregnancy. You're about twelve weeks, so if you're going to terminate, you need to do so immediately. It's not so easy to find someone to perform one, except for medical reasons, when you get much further along."

Grace took a deep breath. "I'm definitely having the baby," she said, hoping that each time she said it out loud she would be more certain that she had made the right decision. Perhaps a few more times, and she would almost be there.

"Very good. So let's talk prenatal care. Are you taking vitamins?"

Grace nodded.

"That's good. And of course, you must eat well, because your baby eats what you eat. You don't look like a Pop-Tarts and Cheetos kind of girl, but keep in mind that you want to eat simply—lots of fruits, vegetables, whole grains, and lean protein. Try to keep the salt down. That will keep the swelling at bay. Avoid caffeine, and of course no booze, no drugs, no smoking." Dr. Weston ticked off on her fingers as she ran down the list of dos and don'ts she automatically recited to every expectant mother.

"I would never . . . ." Grace was more than a little dismayed that this doctor thought she might drink or smoke, or worse.

"Please don't be insulted. It's just boilerplate. I have to give that speech to everyone who comes through this office. I know you would never do anything to harm this child. You're very brave. Having a child at your age is a very difficult thing."

While Dr. Weston was tempted to throw in a few words about thinking more than five minutes into the future when some boy has his hand down your pants, she decided against it—once the horse was already out of the barn, what good would it do, especially with this girl? She didn't look like Dr. Weston's typical pregnant teen patient. Something about the way she perched on the edge of the table, ankles primly crossed, her hair pulled back in a tidy French braid anchored by a pink ribbon, simple pearl earrings—this girl screamed prude. She must have gotten pregnant her very first time. For a second, Dr. Weston wondered if she'd been raped, because she didn't have the look of a girl who would get swept away by a little sweet talk and a couple of Coors Lights. But there was nothing in the chart about that, and Dr. Ryder would certainly have noted such a situation. Some frat guy must have gotten her really drunk on wine coolers, which was ultimately irrelevant—knocked up was knocked up—but fascinating nonetheless. Dr. Weston had yet to meet a teenager who had gotten the message that sex was a dangerous business, and five minutes of messing around really could change one's life forever.

"I'm not brave at all. I'm scared to death," Grace said to the doctor.

"You wouldn't be normal if you weren't afraid. I won't lie to you—it's not a walk in the park. But if it were that bad, no one would ever have more than one child, and the human race would have died out long ago." Dr. Weston smiled and patted Grace's shoulder.

"I guess that makes sense, but it's still scary."

"It's the great unknown. Not having any idea what to expect is daunting. You can read one of those month-by-month baby books, so you know what's happening to your body, but don't read too much, and stay off the Internet. And don't listen to all the horror stories people are bound to tell you about three-headed, twenty-pound babies covered with fur."

It was a mystery to Dr. Weston why otherwise well-intentioned people felt the need to share their *Guinness World Records* carnival sideshow stories. Most of them probably weren't true anyway, and it was hard to imagine why anyone would want to make someone worry about a potential complication that they had probably never contemplated in the first place.

"Thank you, Doctor," said Grace, grateful that Dr. Weston made jokes instead of bawling her out. When the doctor was warning her about drinking and smoking, Grace had feared a morality lecture would follow, which was unnecessary since Grace delivered one to herself twice a day anyway.

"Look, you're young, you're in good health. The odds are with you that you'll have a healthy baby, and I'm sure you'll be a wonderful mother," Dr. Weston said with as much conviction as she could muster, as no seventeen-year-old she had ever taken care of turned out to be a wonderful mother—a teenager couldn't care for a child when she was still a child herself. But maybe this girl would be the exception. Determined not to become a cynic, Dr. Weston sincerely hoped for the best every time she had to tell a girl who was barely old enough to drive that she was going to be a mother.

Helen had remained silent throughout the visit, but now she spoke up. "Grace, didn't you want to talk to the doctor about that?"

"Yeah, um, I'm planning on giving the baby up for adoption. I can't raise a child. I wouldn't even have a place to live if not for my neighbor, Mrs. Teitelbaum. My parents kicked me out when I wouldn't get an abortion a few weeks ago at Dr. Ryder's office." Grace was able to say this without crying now, just barely.

Dr. Weston winced at hearing that this desperate girl's parents could be so cruel. Now all the pieces fell into place. "I'm sorry about that. You're lucky to have such a neighborly neighbor. What about the father? Is he in the picture? Does he support your decision?"

In Dr. Weston's experience, adoption was a smart choice for most girls, but sometimes, rarely, the dad wanted to keep the baby when the young mother didn't, usually because the boyfriend's parents immediately felt like grandparents and couldn't imagine giving that up. Some people found it impossible to imagine their flesh and blood being raised by other people, no matter what the circumstances of that flesh's creation. Such conflicts were painful and could be legally complicated. Dr. Weston hoped that wasn't the case here, as it sounded like Grace already had enough to worry about fighting with her parents—a court battle with the ex-boyfriend's parents would send her over the edge.

"The father wants me to have an abortion. I haven't spoken to him since I told him he got me pregnant, so I don't think he really cares what happens, to the baby, or to me."

Every time she thought about Nick, even so many months later, she kicked herself for not seeing through his gleaming paint job. Now it was obvious to her that he was all surface, but she had been bewitched, plain and simple. Wondering if she would ever stop punishing herself for her foolishness, Grace tried to keep the tears out of her voice. Daily floggings with her imaginary whip were such a waste of energy, and she knew they wouldn't fix anything, but she couldn't help it.

The girl's pain was palpable, but not knowing what she could possibly say that would make Grace feel any better, Dr. Weston simply said, "I'll put you in touch with an adoption agency. Many of my patients have used a place called Children First, and I've only heard good things."

CHAPTER 9

"Hello, may I help you?" Ada asked the young girl standing outside the front door.

"I'm Jennifer, a friend of Grace's. Is she home?" Jennifer knew that Mrs. Teitelbaum was loaded, but she hadn't expected a maid in a uniform carrying a feather duster.

"Yes, please come in. Grace is in the library doing her homework," Ada said, pointing across an acre of black and white marble floor tiles to a pair of elaborately carved doors.

"Um, thank you." Jennifer's footsteps echoed through the two-story foyer, and she marveled at Grace's good luck to be rescued by a millionaire. It might not be such a bad thing if Grace never made up with her parents.

As Jennifer opened one of the heavy wooden doors, she let out a whistle. Grace and Charlie were doing their homework, sitting on either side of an enormous partners desk made of curly maple with an inlaid leather top. Shelves filled with leather-bound books lined all four walls, right up to the ceiling, and two oversized leather chairs flanked a fireplace. An entire herd of cattle must have died just to decorate this room.

"You're living on the set of *Masterpiece Fucking Theatre*," Jennifer said.

Startled, Grace looked up and said, "I didn't even hear the bell. Sorry."

"Doesn't matter. Apparently you have people who do that door-opening thing for you." Glancing over at Charlie, who was listening to music on his iPhone and hadn't even noticed her arrival, Jennifer said, "He's even cuter up close. I can't believe he came with the house."

"Why are you being so weird?" For some reason, whenever she was in this room, Grace felt compelled to whisper.

"Because it's been more than three weeks, and you haven't introduced me to your hottie housemate." At first Jennifer had been insulted that Grace hadn't introduced her to the new family right away, but she had to give Grace a pass—being pregnant and disowned by her family and abandoned by the babydaddy would be enough to make even someone like Grace forget her manners.

"I'm sorry. I'm just so out of it."

"No worries. It's not like I didn't recognize him."

"What do you mean?" Grace asked. Head bobbing in time to the music, Charlie remained oblivious to their guest.

"That whole European vibe, the expensive clothes, the Rolex, the silver Mercedes—he's a celebrity."

"Really?" So distracted by her own shit parade, Grace hadn't been paying attention.

"Yeah, he's like his own MTV reality show. And the fact that he's kind of quiet only adds to the mystery. You haven't heard? Melissa Schwartz is tracking him. She thinks she has the advantage, because of the Jewish thing." Jennifer stage-whispered the last part.

Grace was astounded. She and Charlie hardly ever talked about what went on at school, but now that she thought about it, of course he would attract attention. Next to the typical Silver Lake High School student, who favored torn T-shirts and four-letter swear words, Charlie was definitely out of the ordinary. Well-mannered, incredibly well dressed, with a ridiculously expensive car, he was pretty choice. Grace wondered if he liked Melissa

Schwartz, who was cute but kind of squat with a voice that could crack brass, and she worried that the tightness in her chest might be jealousy, not just heartburn. "Hmm." Saying anything more might betray her real feelings, which she wasn't even ready to acknowledge to herself just yet.

Jennifer's eyebrows went up. "Do *you* . . . . Never mind, sorry to barge, but you weren't answering your phone, and I wanted to know if you'd like to go the mall and help me find a dress for my cousin's wedding. That and the fact that I'm incredibly nosy, and you weren't inviting me over, and I really wanted to see your new crib." Jennifer looked at her phone. "But we have to go right now, because I have to get back to babysit my rotten little sister."

"I'm sorry about not having you over. It just felt funny, inviting you to someone else's house. You know?" As generous and welcoming as Mrs. T. had been, Grace didn't want to make herself too much at home. "And of course I'm a mess generally, so there's that . . . ."

"I know, you and your manners, so I took matters into my own hands. No big deal." Jennifer tapped on the leather desktop in front of Charlie.

"Oh, hi." Charlie pulled the white buds out of his ears, and, ever the gentleman, jumped up and introduced himself. "It's so nice to finally meet you. Grace talks about you all the time. I'm glad she invited you over."

"She didn't. I invited myself," Jennifer said, glaring at Grace.

"Well, however you got here, you're here now. Would you like some tea?"

"Tea?" Jennifer stifled a giggle. He was cute, she thought, but with a little corduroy and a couple of elbow patches, he could be a graduate student at Yale. "Do you have crumpets?"

"I'm sure Vera could find some. Or coffee? Espresso? Scotch?"

Aware that he sometimes came off like a character out of an Agatha Christie novel, Charlie ignored Jennifer's snarky remarks.

When he was living abroad, as soon as a guest arrived, you put the kettle on. Apparently that was not the custom in America. Feeling like a stranger in a strange land, he knew he needed to start acting like one of the natives, which included talking like a teenager instead of a British private school headmaster. He sounded old even to himself.

"Thanks, but I actually just stopped by to see if Grace wanted to go shopping with me." Turning back to Grace, she said, "So, do you?"

"Actually, I have a ton of homework that I have to finish. I don't work as fast as I used to. If you wait until the weekend, I'll go with you."

"If I don't find anything today, that sounds good. Charlie, it was a pleasure to meet you. Perhaps we can have tea on another occasion," Jennifer said, enunciating each word and putting on a slight English accent. She extended her hand, which Charlie took and kissed.

"The pleasure was all mine," said Charlie mimicking her *My Fair Lady* post–Henry Higgins voice.

"Come on, Jennifer, I'll show you out," Grace said, eager to get her more-embarrassing-than-usual friend out of Charlie's house. "What was that all about?"

"I was just playing," Jennifer said. "He was fine with it. I like him, even though he's such a grownup. Do *you* like him?" Grace looked away. "I think you do."

"He's been so nice to me, and right now I can use all the friends I can get. That's all." That was far from all, but Grace didn't feel up to the inevitable ragging that would follow if she admitted to caring about Charlie. Life was complicated enough right now without more boy trouble, and since the byproduct of her first trip around the block was at that moment making her feel vaguely seasick, Grace was determined to proceed with caution.

"I don't mean like him like you like milkshakes, I mean *like* him, like you thought you liked Nick," Jennifer said, gagging on the last word.

Grace blushed. "I'm not exactly girlfriend material right now."

"Your bright red face says it all. Grace loves Charlie," Jennifer sang.

"Be quiet. I don't even know what love is. I'm just thankful for his patience and understanding." Grace looked behind her, grateful they were having this conversation where there was no way Charlie could hear.

"You keep telling yourself that. Now hurry back to your boyfriend. I've got to go dress hunting. See you later." Blowing a kiss, Jennifer ran to her car and sped away.

Back in the library, Charlie was waiting. "So that's your best friend? I never would have put you two together." Even though they'd been at school together for a few weeks, Grace had worked hard to keep Jennifer and Charlie apart, worried that Jennifer's big mouth and Charlie's old-school manners would clash, and then she would be torn between the two.

"Maybe that's why it works so well."

"Probably. But you need to tell her to check her sources more carefully."

"What do you mean?" Grace asked.

"I have it on very good authority that Melissa Schwartz doesn't like boys," said Charlie.

Grace gasped. "You heard all that?"

"Yup."

"Why didn't you say anything?" Grace asked.

"Listening was way more interesting."

"Jennifer's great, but sometimes she doesn't filter."

"Don't apologize for her. I liked her. She's honest; you always know exactly where you stand with someone like that. It's kind of refreshing." If Charlie was going to win Grace over, he knew he had to make nice with Jennifer, and he did appreciate her candor. Most people he had met so far were incredibly phony.

"She's always there for me, sarcastic for sure, but she's got my back." Maybe her two best friends could be friends with each other, and they could face the savages of Silver Lake together—strength in numbers.

"Well, add me to the list. I'm there for you, too." Looking directly into her eyes, Charlie was trying to convey the depth of his feelings in those superficially neutral words. Gazing back at him, Grace hoped he could see how much she liked him. But neither said anything more.

CHAPTER 10

Dear Baby,

You're sweet sixteen weeks and four and a half inches long. Your nervous system works and you can yawn, but you're far from being done. My stomach isn't flat anymore, but nobody knows yet. No offense, but I'm not looking forward to the day when everybody at school finds out you're hiding in there. Someday when you're my age, you'll know how I feel. This afternoon Mrs. T. and I are going to see the lady at the adoption agency so we can find you a good home with two parents who can give you the wonderful life you deserve. I promise to choose carefully. Whoever gets you will have to be very special.

Love,

Grace

When she was seventeen years old, Janet Olson got pregnant at a frat party during the first week of her freshman year at college. Feeling brave and beautiful after one too many plastic cups of garbage can punch, she had fallen into bed with a senior who, through her grain alcohol–glazed eyes, looked and sounded like Harrison Ford when he played Han Solo in *Star Wars*. What this guy had done to her was probably rape, but admitting to that would mean telling her parents what had happened—the underage drinking, the flirting, the messing around. Besides, in

1980, rape was a crime committed by a stranger who dragged his victim behind an abandoned building and assaulted her while she shrieked for help. Janet had floated up the stairs with someone she'd just met and was fantasizing would become her first college boyfriend—no kicking or screaming. When her sluggish brain realized what was happening, that pushing his hand away and shaking her head did nothing to discourage him, she was too out of it to do anything to protect herself. She vaguely remembered him undressing her, her limbs not responding to her unfocused efforts to control them. Even as his hands roamed, flipping her over like some life-sized rag doll, she felt as if it were happening to someone else. Aware but far removed from what was being done to her, she just lay there while some guy who didn't even know her last name made a baby inside of her. Through a fog, she had felt the sharp pain as he entered her, the full weight of his six-foot frame crushing her, the bed springs squeaking rhythmically with every excruciating thrust. The stench of beer filled her nose as he grunted and moaned in her face. To this day, she couldn't stand that yeasty smell. Losing her virginity and getting pregnant all in one go had been an incredibly efficient disaster. It would have made a compelling cautionary tale, an unfunny version of *Animal House,* if only it had happened to someone else.

Afraid to go to the infirmary, too terrified to tell her family, too mortified to tell the boy, whose last name she realized she didn't even know, she ended up having one of those cheap, efficient abortions widely available in the decade following *Roe v. Wade*. At the time it had seemed the only option, but in the thirty years since she had made what at the time had seemed like the only decision, she wondered every single day about that baby that never was, despite the fact that it had existed for only a few weeks, probably never getting much larger than a peanut before it disappeared in a rush of blood.

Ten years after what had turned out to be a defining moment in her life, Janet Olson founded Children First to honor that little he or she who never had a chance, and to give young girls a soft place to land when they didn't know where to go or what to do. While Janet had nothing against abortion—she couldn't stand those self-aggrandizing, illogical lunatics who believed it was okay to kill doctors to drive home the point that it wasn't okay to kill fetuses—she understood that it wasn't the right option for everyone. Her goal was to create a special place where want-to-be parents could build a family out of what had started out as a tragedy for someone else and could, with a little help, end up being the ultimate gift. One person's lemons could be someone else's lemonade. Not that there weren't hundreds of adoption agencies across the country, but Janet felt she could do a better job with these lost girls because she had already walked in their shoes and come out the other side, not necessarily better, but certainly wiser.

Every photograph of every newborn that crossed her desk made her wonder what her own baby would have looked like, and sometimes it was hard to get through a client interview without bursting into tears, but she knew she was doing valuable work. She loved every single one of these infants as if each were her own. Not that they could make up for what she had lost, but helping other people realize their dreams of a family did allow her to sleep at night without dreaming about her what-if, and that was enough. It had to be.

It was tough for Janet to spend her days talking about babies, especially when she had met and married the perfect man and, in the ultimate irony, when she was ready to be a mother, she was unable to get pregnant. But she couldn't bring herself to adopt a child, no matter how desperately she wanted a baby. Her psychiatrist talked about some unresolved Freudian mumbo jumbo stemming from the rape and guilt over the abortion, and although that may have been the right diagnosis, the shrink was unable to deliver a cure. Janet's husband was disappointed, but because he loved her more than he could ever love anyone else, even a precious child, he never pushed her, despite the fact that he thought it was completely illogical that Janet ran a bloody adoption agency but still refused to go through the process herself. So, subscribing to his wife's lemonade theory, they became dog people, proud parents of three miniature dachshunds. Pet ownership could never replace fatherhood, but since nothing could replace an otherwise perfect marriage, her husband made do, and Janet was grateful every single day that he accommodated her craziness, putting their dogs in matching sweaters for their Christmas card photo and not complaining that he was the only Little League coach who didn't actually have a kid on the team, which put him in constant danger of being labeled a dirty old man or worse.

"Welcome Grace, Mrs. Teitelbaum. Please come in. I know this is hard, and you're in a dark place, but let me assure you that you will never regret what you're doing," Janet said, wishing, as she did every day, that her job wasn't necessary, that children like Grace didn't have to make adult decisions that would likely plague them for the rest of their lives.

"I don't think I could feel much worse, so thank you."

Grace wondered if this woman had given up her baby as well. Something about the way she spoke, the look in her eyes that went way beyond professional sympathy . . . this person had definitely been there. If Mrs. Olson had been a pregnant teenager, then Grace knew it could all work out, because this woman was beautiful and normal and there was nothing about her appearance that gave away her mistake.

"I think the best place to start is to talk about the two different types of adoption: open and closed," said Janet.

Having given this speech thousands of time, Janet could practically deliver it in her sleep. But each girl was unique. Some arrived with parents, who could be supportive and understanding or furious and distant, either because they couldn't get past the pregnancy, or because they wanted to keep their grandchild and their daughter didn't. A few girls came with their boyfriends, the rare relationships that survived the shock of an unplanned pregnancy. Janet admired those children, mature beyond their years, and she wondered if those couples would make it through to have another baby at the right time that they would be able to keep. Many girls showed up with their best friend, sometimes the only friend left, to prop them up. And then the saddest ones of all, the girls who wandered in all alone, facing the most difficult decision of their young lives without any support whatsoever.

"I don't know. Doesn't it depend on what the adoptive parents want?" Grace asked. Letting someone else make the big decisions would be such a relief. All she wanted to do right now was go to sleep and wake up sometime in late April, her stomach flat and her breasts small again.

"That depends. If an open adoption is very important to you, then you should only look at potential parents who would agree to that. Some couples won't even consider it. If you want to choose a couple based on other factors, then you can leave it up to them. You have to figure out what your priorities are, Grace."

"What do most people do?"

"It varies. In an open adoption, while you give up all legal rights to your baby, you'll maintain a long-term relationship with your biological child and his or her family. A written agreement between you and the adoptive parents will lay out the extent and frequency of your contact. Typically, the contract might say that the adoptive parents send you pictures every six months, and you get to visit once a year."

"That's weird. Don't you think that's weird, Mrs. T.?" Turning to Helen, Grace needed some input.

"It does sound a little strange. It would be hard to do, at least for me—revisiting a very difficult moment in one's life over and over. But don't a lot of girls choose that?" asked Helen, sitting up and trying to pay attention to the matter at hand.

Instead of listening to the adoption counselor, she had been thinking how stupid she and Abe had been, going through life childless, believing it was God's will that they not be parents. Becoming a parent was not about sharing blood. It was about sharing their boundless love with a sweet-smelling infant with velvet skin, whatever the provenance of that skin. Instead, all of their love that couldn't be lavished on their own precious babies had been piled onto other people's children through myriad charities. Worthwhile for sure, and Helen didn't regret all of the good things they had accomplished, but it had felt so impersonal, and she had no idea what any of those children were doing now. It was a shame that eighty was too old to adopt a baby.

"Many girls find it comforting to maintain a connection with the baby. It's a way for them to show the child that she was given up out of love, not indifference," said Janet.

"I suppose so," said Grace.

It would be awful to worry that her baby wouldn't know how much love had gone into the decision, that it was truly the only thing that mattered. Grace feared the baby would resent her for giving her up, no matter how good the reason. Thinking about what the bean would be thinking about when it was ten years old made her head ache.

"You hear about adoptees who grow up wondering why they were given up and feeling like something's missing. An open adoption is a way to make sure your biological child knows that you've always loved her and you always will."

"I get it, but I don't want to disrupt the baby's life with its adoptive parents. No matter what people say, I think having lunch once a year with your birth mother could be really confusing. Is there a way that I can let it know how much I cared, that I gave it up because I loved it so much?" Grace asked.

She was worried that by showing up once a year with a bag full of toys and a desperate 'please like me' smile, she would screw up the normal childhood she was trying to give her baby by putting it up for adoption. No matter how articulately she explained her decision, it would be almost impossible for a child not to believe that she was given away because her mommy didn't want her. There were no words to explain to a five-year-old the desperation she'd felt when she found out she was pregnant and the boy she thought she was falling in love with barely acknowledged that he, the only guy she'd ever been with, was the father. Grace didn't know how she was ever going to be able to tell this baby that she loved her so much that she didn't want to raise her, after conceiving her in the back of an SUV with a guy she hardly knew, who wanted her to have an abortion. It wasn't going to replace *Goodnight Moon* as a bedtime story anytime soon. Besides, attempting to balance that fine line between loving this child like the mother she was and maintaining the emotional distance that was required because she had signed away her legal rights as a parent seemed an impossible feat. Grace was fairly certain that she lacked the strength of character to step in and out of her child's life according to a schedule drawn up by a bunch of lawyers, a sort-of-but-not-really fake aunt who just happened to bear a startling resemblance to this child.

"Absolutely, I understand what you're saying. It's devastating even when you know it's right. There's a middle ground called a semi-open adoption that might appeal to you. You can meet the adoptive parents, but after the baby is born, you won't have any contact with the child," Janet offered.

"That sounds better. I would like to meet the people who are going to raise my baby, know who's going to take care of her, but I don't think I can manage the rest of it," Grace said.

"Some girls don't even want to see the baby after giving birth. But others need to say hello and goodbye, make peace, you know. That's something else to consider," said Janet.

"It's too much to think about. Do I have to decide today?" Grace asked. Maybe Jennifer in her cut-and-dried, crystal-clear world would have some suggestions about how to handle all these transitions.

"What about keeping track of the baby as she grows up? Do you want to see pictures of her?" Helen asked, still fantasizing about signing up with Children First to find a baby of her own.

"I don't know. That would be okay, I guess. It's so hard to imagine what I'm going to feel like afterwards." Grace sighed.

There were so many decisions she had to make, all stemming from one stupid choice made when she was high on fake love and a flood of hormones. It was truly laughable. Maybe it had been better in the old days when girls like her were hidden away in church-run homes as their stomachs expanded. When the infants were born, they were whisked away to anonymous new families, and the girls returned home, where no one ever spoke of the matter again, except to perpetuate the fiction by talking about the eight-month visit with the relatives on the other side of the country. Most of those children grew up believing they had only one set of parents, and the young girls who gave up their babies without ever laying eyes on them managed to stuff all that pain into the deepest crevices of their souls, growing into women who married and had more children with husbands who believed in their midcentury innocence that their wedding night was the first time their wives had been in bed with a man.

"When the baby's older, old enough to understand, if he wants to find me, then I would love to meet him. But I don't want to confuse him when he's little. That wouldn't be fair." Not knowing what the bean was, Grace kept switching genders when she talked about it.

At the moment, Grace felt most comfortable with a semi-open adoption. Meeting potential parents, getting a feel for them, was important. However, once she made that decision, Grace didn't want to spend the next eighteen years hovering on the fringes of her baby's life. That would make it impossible for her to move on and make a life for herself, which she so desperately wanted to start doing.

Janet slid a large black loose-leaf notebook across the desk. A snapshot and a two-paragraph summary seemed more suited to finding a date than selecting a mother and father for her baby, but what was the alternative? These girls had to start somewhere.

"Look through this book and see if any of the couples jump out at you. Check in with me at the end of the week and we can set up another meeting."

"Thank you, Mrs. Olson." Grace picked up the book and held it close to her. Inside this notebook might be the people who would become her baby's family. While she hadn't ever seriously thought about keeping the bean, it was still strange to be taking this giant step closer to giving it up.

"There *is* one more thing. Although you've said the father has made it clear that he wants nothing to do with this child, we're going to need that in writing. If he doesn't sign away his parental rights, as you will be doing, there is always the danger that he could change his mind and sue to gain custody."

That disastrous scenario had occurred not long after Janet had started Children First, when a seventeen-year-old girl showed up, desperate to find someone to adopt her twins. She claimed not to know who the father was—a drunken one-night stand at a Pink Floyd concert—and Janet had let it go at that. Well acquainted with the hazards of a night of partying, she had no desire to torture the girl by interrogating her about the whereabouts of the dirtbag who had impregnated her. Three days before the twins' first birthday a young man, reeking of pot and an apparent aversion to basic hygiene, stormed into her office, demanding to know where his children were. It had been an ugly court battle, some sleazy ACLU-type ranting about fathers' rights while his client sat like a statue, eyes bloodshot, clearly stoned out of his mind. And while the adoptive parents had ultimately prevailed, it was only after much heartache and the delivery of a big, fat envelope of cash to the on-again, off-again father. From that day forward, Janet tracked down every sperm donor, and if her private detective couldn't find the bum or he refused to sign the paper, Janet refused to take on the client. It killed her to turn away a desperate girl, all the more tragic because the asshole who had gotten her into this mess wasn't stepping up, but she had a business to run, and she couldn't risk some lunatic coming out of the woodwork in search of his baby or, more likely, a quick payoff.

"I think I can get that, as long as no one finds out about it. Nick, the father, he never told his parents, and not that I care about him, but I don't see the point in ruining his life too." Why she felt the need to lighten Nick's burden, Grace didn't know, after the way he'd used her, but wrecking his life wouldn't do anything to repair hers, even if it made her feel better.

"It's just an insurance policy. That piece of paper will never see the light of day," Janet promised.

"Okay." That meant Grace would actually have to talk to Nick. She hadn't spoken a word to him since that day on the lake when she first told him about the bean. At the thought of seeing him again, her heart pounded. Maybe she would take Jennifer with her for backup.

"And if he gives you any trouble, just remind him that if he doesn't sign it, no one will adopt the child, and he'll be on the hook for the next eighteen years. That little secret won't be so easy to hide from his parents." Janet had plenty of experience dealing with reluctant fathers who were wavering when it came time to step up to the plate. Teenage boys were all strut and testosterone, right up until the moment they actually had to behave like grown men, and then most of them turned into stuttering little boys.

"That should do it," Grace said, not sure she had the strength to face him again, but knowing she had no choice, and well aware that she needed to stand up to him if she was ever going to come out of this nightmare in one piece.

"If you like, you can set up a meeting here, and I can explain everything to him myself. I know how hard this must be for you." It was easy to see Grace's anxiety as she chewed ferociously on her lower lip. She was a ball of nerves, and that couldn't be good for the baby.

"Let me think about it," said Grace.

"Just remember what's important. Now is the time for you to think about what's best for you and the baby. Try not to stress about the details. That's why *I'm* here." Janet stood. "I'll get the paperwork together, and I look forward to hearing from you."

"Thank you, Mrs. Olson," Grace said.

"It's been a pleasure, Grace, Mrs. Teitelbaum. You're going through a difficult time, but in that book is the light at the end of your tunnel. I know it." Shaking both their hands, she showed them out through a door at the back of her office that led directly into the hallway. "We like to give our clients as much privacy as possible," she explained.

"We'll be in touch after Grace has had a chance to look through your notebook. You've been a great help. Those worry wrinkles in Grace's forehead are starting to go away already."

Helen had been concerned that having had no mothering experience herself, she couldn't do much for Grace other than providing nutritious meals and a warm bed. But helping Grace find a safe, loving home for this baby was no small thing, and Helen was sure Grace had made the right decision. The process promised to be a little thorny, but it would all be over in April.

"Why don't you take that upstairs and have a look on your own. When you're ready, if you want to talk, come find me." Unable to imagine being pregnant, let alone being pregnant and knowing that you weren't going to make a life with the child growing inside you, Helen was treading lightly. Giving Grace plenty of space and no unsolicited advice seemed the best course. Clearly this girl had a good head on her shoulders, and if she wanted to discuss anything, she knew Helen was waiting.

Flipping through a few pages, Grace felt like she was looking at an L. L. Bean catalog, except they weren't selling flannel shirts and corduroy pants with ducks on them—they were selling the couples wearing them. She didn't know how she was going to figure out who would love her baby more than anything in the world, who could give it the best life. Maybe an artsy couple living in Seattle who owned a coffee roasting company and painted murals on the sides of old buildings in their free time, or a nuclear physicist and his novelist wife who lived outside Boston. The only thing Grace knew for sure was that she didn't want the doctor and the lawyer living in Chicago. Grace's mother had worked throughout her childhood, even though they didn't need the money. As Betsy had explained to Grace when she was three, an unfulfilled woman made for an unhappy mother, and Grace didn't want an unhappy mother, did she? Fulfillment, for Betsy at least, could not be found in endless visits to the playground, afternoons baking cookies, and reading *The Cat in the Hat* for the hundredth time. Not that Grace had any clue what Betsy was talking about at the time, other than the fact that her mother apparently didn't want to spend time with her. Grace decided only to consider couples with wives who stayed at home. If these women wanted her baby, they had better be willing to change diapers and push a stroller, all day long. Superwomen who wanted to have it all need not apply.

In order to do this search properly, Grace knew she needed to be systematic, so she turned back to the very beginning. Couple Number One: Rebecca and Michael Miller lived in suburban Philadelphia. Photographed standing in front of what must be their house, a large brick colonial, the Millers could have been models posing for a magazine shoot. Tiny, with huge green eyes and long black hair, Rebecca looked like a doll next to her husband, who, according to the bio, was six foot four. What a waste of DNA that these two specimens couldn't reproduce. They had met at Princeton as undergraduates and went on to get matching MBAs at Wharton. Working mothers were off limits, but no, Rebecca had worked for five years, then given up the fast lane to pursue baby-making full time, and even when that venture failed to yield any results, she had decided not to return to the workplace. Michael was a successful investment banker, and Rebecca volunteered as a reading and math tutor in the neighborhood public school. These two were so perfect, there had to be some fatal flaw lurking beneath the surface—a drinking problem, a family history of insanity. But Grace didn't know how she would ever be able to find out. Running her fingers over the photograph, Grace stared into the picture, trying to imagine what it would be like to turn the bean over to these two overachievers.

Couple Number Two:. Two plastic surgeons who were active volunteers with Doctors Without Borders. What were they going to do with a baby? Stick it in a carry-on and drag it along on their life-saving missions all over the world? Admirable, Grace thought, but unacceptable.

Couple Number Three: John Pell was a history professor, and his wife taught French literature at a small college in a little town in Vermont. The picture of the Pell's house covered with snow and Christmas lights was a picture postcard of an idyllic life. There was a nursery school on campus for faculty children, and the Pells were active in an organic food cooperative. Without a doubt, the baby would be well cared for and well fed. But while the setting sounded like paradise, and Sara Pell only taught one class, she was working on a book and was a regular contributor to a literary magazine. It sounded time-consuming, despite the fact that she was able to work out of her house most of the time. While Grace didn't begrudge a woman's need to follow her own dreams, and she knew it was perhaps too much to expect a mother to be satisfied solely with her mothering duties, she wanted an adoptive mother who was at least a little less busy than Sara Pell seemed to be. On top of that, Thomas Pell's mother lived with them, and while Grace had nothing against senior citizens or extended family, there was something about the elder Mrs. Pell, who appeared in the photo sitting between her son and daughter-in-law, hand protectively resting on her son's knee, that made Grace uncomfortable.

Couple Number Four lived in Miami. Carlos Perez had been born in Cuba but escaped to Florida with his family as a child. He had met Margaret, his wife of ten years, when she was a senior at the University of Florida and he was a dental student. They had married immediately after she graduated from college, and although Margaret worked as a copywriter at an advertising agency, she planned on quitting as soon as she had a child. Margaret had majored in child psychology and minored in English, so she would know how to deal with temper tantrums and separation anxiety, and someday she would be able to help the bean with his college essays. They lived in a sprawling Mediterranean house surrounded by orange trees, and there was already a playset with swings and a slide set up in the backyard. This pair had possibilities, and the bean would have perfect teeth.

A dozen couples later, Grace's head swirled with images of devoted spouses with perfect lives, except for their inability to make a baby. How sad that all these women in their thirties with doting husbands, large bank accounts, and too many extra bedrooms were unable to carry a child, but teenagers having random sex in back seats and on beaches seemed to be so ridiculously fertile. Life was definitely not fair, at either end of the spectrum.

In spite of the glowing resumes and magazine-perfect photographs of each and every couple, Grace couldn't stop thinking about Couple Number One. There was something about the

Millers that was both familiar and comforting. Was it because Rebecca's dark hair and green eyes unconsciously reminded Grace of herself, or that Michael looked so solid and grownup, yet gentle and kind the way he stood in the photo, his arm protectively around his wife's shoulders? Would they ever tell their daughter that she was stupid or that they regretted having her? Would they kick the bean out of the house if she broke the rules or threatened the family's honor? There was no way to know, but Grace had a feeling these two people wouldn't be capable of such malice. At least she hoped they wouldn't be.

CHAPTER 11

Dear Baby,

Today was one of the worst days of my life, and I probably shouldn't even be telling you that, because it's not your fault, it's mine, and I should be way stronger already, considering everything that's happened and all that's yet to come. The thing is, sweet Baby, they know about you. My baggy sweatshirt isn't baggy enough to hide you anymore, and you're no longer my little secret. I've never been so humiliated in my life, and I'm not sure which part is worse, that everybody knows I had sex with someone (I should probably blab that Nick is the father—at least that would distract those mean girls while they try to figure out why the handsome prince decided to throw a bone to the slimy frog) or that I was dumb enough to get pregnant. It's probably the second part, because all those girls who were talking about me have probably done it, way more than once. They were just smarter about it than I was. I don't know how I'm going to go back tomorrow.

I love you so much,

Grace

After eighteen weeks and no whispers, Grace had almost forgotten to worry about the shit hitting the fan when her baby bump bumped. Wearing sweatpants and oversized sweatshirts Charlie had given her, collected from exotic universities all over the world,

Grace was playing the role of hardcore senior who was too busy writing college essays and studying for her AP classes to waste time on grooming. So far she'd done a good job camouflaging her slowly ballooning figure, because no one had uttered a word—not a single comment from anyone about one too many Hershey bars, or too much reading and not enough running—and thankfully seniors didn't have to take gym class. Either her disguise was working, or Jennifer and the entire student body were being incredibly diplomatic. Not a likely scenario.

But in the third day of her nineteenth week, Grace was in the bathroom before school, where she was spending an inordinate amount of time these days, when her big fat ship hit the iceberg. A break-off herd of girls from Nick's popular planet ambled in. The school day hadn't yet begun, but it was time to reapply their eyeliner and lip gloss before first period. Crowding each other in front of the mirror, each certain that she was by far the hottest girl in school, they pretended that they actually liked each other.

Awesome Girl A: "So did you hear the news?"

Awesome Girl B: "What news?"

Awesome Girl A: "Grace Warren is up the duff."

In a panic, Grace lifted her feet off the tile floor and held her breath. If they discovered she was in the bathroom, they might strip her down to see if it was just gossip or she was in fact packing a little person. The single blessing of obscurity in this whole unblessed event had just blown up in her face.

Awesome Girl C: "What? That's impossible. Straight-A, so-perfect-her-shit-doesn't-stink Grace Warren?"

Awesome Girl A: "That's the one."

Awesome Girl C: "No way. Her mother practically runs our church. She's the parent adviser for this class the pastor runs teaching kids how to keep it in their pants. Grace won't be spreading her legs until her wedding night, if then."

Awesome Girl D: "So who's the babydaddy?"

Awesome Girl A: "I heard it was some guy she met at church camp. He popped her cherry during Bible study."

Awesome Girl B: "Someone's definitely yanking your chain."

Awesome Girl A: "Maybe. Either way, we'll know soon enough. It's not like she'll be able to suck it in for nine months."

Awesome Girl D: "She *has* been dressing like a chunky rug muncher lately. I thought maybe she was practicing for one of those women's colleges."

Awesome Girl A: "Why don't you just ask her?"

Awesome Girl D: "Why don't *you*?"

Awesome Girl A: "Because I don't give a shit if she fucked every member of the chess club and is hauling around triplets."

Awesome Girl B: "If she's got a kid in there, it had to be an immaculate conception. No one but God could be porking Warren."

Awesome Girl C: "Whatever."

Awesome Girl C didn't give a rat's ass what a charter member of the geek squad was up to when she wasn't changing the batteries in her calculator. In her thousand-friend Facebook universe, high school was for looking good, getting hammered, and hooking up, not gossiping about losers who sat at the front of the class with their lips permanently attached to some teacher's fat ass.

When Grace didn't think she could hold it in a second longer, the bell rang and the demons posing as high school girls left. Burying her face in Charlie's sweatshirt, she didn't move. The graffiti-decorated stall—it was only a matter of days until her life story figured prominently in the scribbles on the metal walls surrounding her—felt like the only safe place in the building. Sitting on the toilet, Grace wept bitter tears for the loss of her dignity, the loss of her family, the loss of her flat stomach, and most of all, for the loss of the person she used to be and knew she could never be again.

The late bell rang, and Grace sat up, blowing her nose on a piece of toilet paper. Who had ratted her out? Jennifer had a big mouth, but Grace knew she would sooner cut out her own tongue than sell out her best friend. Nick? No way. His name hadn't come up once in the bathroom conversation, and except for Mrs. T., the doctors, and her parents (who would deny she was pregnant if she gave birth on the altar during Sunday services), nobody else was in the loop. It had to be the sweats. Stupidly believing that miles of cotton fleece would be the perfect smokescreen, Grace had unwittingly outed herself. Coming out of the stall, she examined herself in the lipstick-streaked mirror hanging on the tile wall. That was definitely it. She started to laugh at her reflection, this person she hardly recognized anymore, wondering why Jennifer or Charlie or Mrs. T. hadn't said anything. Unlike her parents, who had no qualms about telling her exactly what they thought of her, those three people loved her so much that either they didn't see the Jabba the Hutt she had become, or if they did, they had the good sense to know that pointing out a blemish that couldn't be covered with Maybelline Cover Stick would be at best a worthless exercise, and at worst, cruel. But she couldn't figure out where the Bible camp fuck buddy had come from.

Not sure what to do next, Grace stared at the floor, as if the answer could be found in the grimy gray tiles. Spending the day in the girls' bathroom wouldn't solve any of her problems, and she couldn't hide out in a stall until the baby was born. Retrieving her backpack from the hook behind the door, Grace took one last look in the mirror and went off to class, or war, or whatever the day would bring.

"Come in, Grace. You're late. Where's your pass?" Miss Hawkins stood in front of the whiteboard, marker poised.

She had been late to class before, and no one had ever asked her for a pass. If a student like Grace was tardy, there had to be a good reason, so a note from the office would be a waste of paperwork. "I'm sorry, Miss Hawkins, I don't have one. I was in the restroom." Twenty-three snickers combined into a single deafening guffaw.

"Whatever. Take your seat, and next time try to take care of your business at home."

Resuming her lecture, Miss Hawkins droned on about Skinner boxes and operant conditioning. Collapsing into her seat accompanied by a second round of sniggering, Grace dug out her notebook and pen and pretended to listen to her teacher. If her not-so-delicate condition was obvious to her classmates, didn't that mean that the teachers, who were certainly smarter and less self-absorbed than their students, must also have solved the whodunit . . . or whodidher? That would explain the unprecedented request for a late pass and the snide comment.

The bell finally rang, ending Miss Hawkins's attack on video games as modern examples of Skinner boxes, destroying America's youth and threatening to become the one-way ticket to last place for the United States. "For your sake, for the sake of this country, you people need to rethink your priorities. Our futures depend on it. Check the syllabus for your homework. Class dismissed."

Miss Hawkins turned to erase her whiteboard in preparation for the next round of fertile young minds. It was only 8:30 A.M., and she didn't know how she was going to make it through the morning, let alone the five years she had to endure until she could retire with a pension.

"Boooo!"

"You just haven't found the right joystick, Miss Hawkins."

"Don't be such a noob!"

"If you'd ever fragged someone, you wouldn't be saying that."

"This class is a total wankfest!"

Slamming her hand down hard on her desk, Miss Hawkins turned to face the class and spoke through gritted teeth. "That's exactly what I'm talking about. Such disrespect didn't exist twenty-five years ago. You're a bunch of animals. Not worth my time. Get out of my classroom."

Too curious to leave it alone, and also wanting to apologize to Miss Hawkins for being late—she was still the good girl, no matter what her uterus said—Grace stopped in front of Miss Hawkins's desk. "I'm sorry I was late this morning. I had the start of a migraine or something. It won't happen again."

"I hope not. You and your associates need to get your collective acts together. You're seniors, not a bunch of wide-eyed freshmen who don't know up from down. It's so disappointing for us as teachers to see young people throwing their lives away like empty soda cans. Squandering one's gifts is an unforgivable sin. Do you understand that, Grace?" Miss Hawkins stared not at Grace's face, but at her stomach. Maybe she was reading Moscow Institute of Physics and Technology, or maybe she was trying to decide if Grace looked any fatter than she'd looked a few weeks earlier.

Close to melting down, Grace just nodded. Second period students began trickling in, and Grace blinked back her tears. Another bell rang, but instead of going to her next class, Grace lumbered towards the office. Having inadvertently mutated into one of those disappointing young people the teachers were wasting their precious time on, Grace knew she would need a late pass to get into AP English.

CHAPTER 12

School had become a walking, talking bad dream. Based on how Grace felt every day since she'd come out of the closet, or the bathroom stall, she would gladly stick pins in her eyes if it meant she could stay home. But what was the alternative? Dropping out like those girls on TV, taking classes online so she could get her GED. After all that had happened, Grace still wasn't ready to give up on the dream of going to a first-rate college, and dropping out of high school in the middle of her senior year because she couldn't take the whispers and smirks was beyond chickenshit. At some point they had to get bored with her, had to get tired of smiling hypocritically, asking where the father was, suggesting names for the baby—"Loser" worked for a boy or a girl.

Within a week, everyone from the night janitor to the Chinese transfer student who only spoke three words of English knew about the Girl Scout who'd gotten storked at church camp. Rumors spread faster than the flu at Silver Lake High School, and the moral demise of a member of the National Honor Society and an AP Scholar was far more interesting than someone in the vocational training program getting knocked up. That would be business as usual; this was news. Grace used to feel like she was the only one who hadn't done it, but now she felt like she was the only one who had. Her slowly expanding stomach advertised her moral depravity and was reflected in the condescending stares and snickers of those either smarter or luckier than she had been. Even girls she thought were her friends were blowing her off.

"Hi, Kim," Grace said to the girl standing at the locker next to hers. They had been lab partners in biology, teammates on the mathletes, and had known each other since elementary school.

Kim didn't answer, just put her books away and zipped up her backpack.

"Kim, what's the matter?" Grace pleaded. Without a word, Kim, who wasn't even part of the cool crowd, who Grace had always thought was a sweet, compassionate person, turned and walked away. Even her fellow geeks were abandoning ship.

Every night Jennifer spent an hour on the phone with Grace, trying to convince her to give up Nick. "Why are you protecting him? He's a first-class douchebag. He'd stab you in the back without a second thought. You get that, don't you?"

"I do, but . . . ."

"But what? You're not still into him, are you? Dick can't be that powerful. Besides, you said it wasn't even any good." Sex was still a mystery to Jennifer, but she couldn't imagine anything on earth could command that kind of authority over a brain with an IQ of 145.

Grace cringed. Tact, subtlety, and sensitivity were not part of Jennifer's makeup. "It has nothing to do with that. I hate him. I hate every part of him, including *that* part of him." As Jennifer had so succinctly pointed out, if she could allow his junk inside her, she should be able to say the word for it out loud, but it still stuck in her throat.

"Well, that's good news. So what's the problem? If you tag him as your sperm donor, I guarantee you there will be significant heat transfer to his sorry ass. Can you imagine? No one has any idea that the biggest man on campus is the one who stole your v-card and planted his seed. People will be talking about it for years, like where you were when you found out Michael Jackson died."

"But that's exactly my point. If I tell the world that Nick is the father, that'll just add fuel to the fire. Instead of jokes about Bible study and virgin births, they'll be laughing about how Nick had to fuck me for community service or how he was trying to win a bet about whether or not my encyclopedia was stapled shut. The possibilities are endless, and horrible."

"It would be so worth it, though, to see Nick get dragged through the mud. He deserves to suffer." Jennifer rubbed her hands together gleefully at the thought of Nick being burned in effigy at the homecoming game.

"You just don't get it. No matter what, I'm going to be the villain in this story, and Nick's always going to be the hero—it's simple genetics. The only thing that'll bring an end to this nightmare is getting away from here, but I've got no place to go. So I'll just have to suffer through it." At the thought of at least twenty more weeks of taunts and whispers, Grace's stomach dropped. It was going to feel like twenty years.

"You're giving up too easily. You can't be sure that's how it would play out."

"This from the person who didn't think that we, co-captains of the math team with matching 4.9 averages, were geeks. Shows you how in touch with reality you are."

Shouting into the phone, Jennifer was determined to straighten Grace out. "I love you, Grace, like a sister, but you need to pull your head out of your ass and realize that high school isn't the fucking Academy Awards, and those small-minded assholes you're so afraid of aren't the Oscar winners you think they are. They're not even extras in the movie that is our life. They're losers who just haven't gotten the memo yet. But they will, and when they do, you and I will be collecting our diplomas from Princeton and deciding which six-figure job we should take. So, Grace, you're the one who needs to get in touch with reality."

"I want you to be right," Grace whispered. "I need you to be right."

"Don't worry, I am," Jennifer said with her unshakable confidence. "Now that we've got that misconception cleared up, let's talk about what you need to do *today*."

"I'm still not outing Nick, no matter what you say. I don't want to have anything to do with him ever again. It's too upsetting."

"Fine, whatever. But you still need to deal with him at least one more time. If he doesn't sign off on that document, you're going to have to find a new adoption agency or practice your diapering skills."

"I know. I will."

While Jennifer had generously, and a little too enthusiastically, offered to track down Nick and explain to him about giving up his parental rights, Grace decided it was a task that she needed to do herself. Every time she saw him at school, her heart jumped into her throat, even as Nick quickly turned away, not even acknowledging her presence, as difficult as she was to miss as the bean grew into a melon. After several attempts to catch him in the hallway at school, in which he fled like a pickpocket through a crowd in Times Square, Grace decided to catch him when he wasn't expecting it. One morning she stationed herself behind a tree, a hunter tracking her prey, and waited until he pulled into the parking lot, still driving the scene of the crime. After he shut off the engine—less danger of him driving away or running her over—she dashed, more like plodded, over to the car. His deer-in-the-headlights look told her that she'd succeeded in surprising him.

Looking around to make sure no one was watching, he rolled down the window and said, "What do you want now?"

There was no point in pretending anymore: she was way past the point of no return. This baby was already a baby. But then his brain caught up with his emotions, and he realized that now, more than ever, he needed to keep his cool. As promised, Grace hadn't revealed his role in her problem, and except for Jennifer, who even though she had a big mouth had proved she knew how to keep a secret, nobody knew he was the father. He had no idea why Grace had chosen to take the high road. Even *he* could see that he was being a total dick, from start to finish, if you were looking at it solely from her point of view.

"I need to talk to you about something," Grace replied, trying to slow her pulse, which was banging so loudly in her ears that she could hardly hear her own voice.

"Then get in the car, in the back," he hissed, worried that if anyone saw them talking, they would easily put the pieces together, and the entire school would be calling him Daddy before first lunch block.

When Grace slid into the back seat, the smell brought everything back, crashing down on her like a tsunami, and she stifled a scream. Turning around, Nick asked, "What the fuck's the matter with you?"

"The smell of your car, it's making me sick." Gagging, hardly able to talk through her panic attack, Grace breathed through her mouth so she wouldn't have to smell it.

"Nice." If she threw up on the leather, he'd kill her.

Not that she owed him an explanation, but she wanted so much for him to understand how she felt, to exhibit even the slightest bit of interest in her. "Your car smells the same as it did the night we . . . ."

"You still need money?" he interrupted, eager to get this conversation over with. "You didn't listen to me before, so what do you want now?" Nick wished she would just handle this on her own and leave him out of it.

"No, I don't need your money." Although she didn't care about him as a person anymore, he still had the power to disappoint her. Grace was still hoping to hear some compassion, regret even, for what had happened between them. Not expecting actual empathy, or even an apology, she just wanted him to prove that he was at least human, if not for her sake, then for the sake of the baby, who would be inheriting not only his cheekbones, but possibly his cold, dead heart. She trembled involuntarily.

"So what do you want from me? Jennifer says you're giving it away. You should have just gotten rid of it, but I guess this is better than keeping it." Sometimes Nick had nightmares that Grace decided to keep the baby and he was working at a gas station to make money to buy diapers, because his parents had kicked him out and he'd had to turn down the college scholarships so he could support his accidental family. He would wake up in a sweat to the sound of a baby screaming, but it was his own cries that had woken him.

"That's kind of what this is about. In order to give the baby up for adoption, we both have to sign away our parental rights," Grace said, trying to maintain a neutral tone.

She couldn't shame him into being a good person, and she needed to stay calm if she was going to get through this conversation without losing it. Trying to assure herself that his stony indifference to the baby, to her, was a product of some failure on his part, not her own inadequacy, she waited for the next selfish, childish rant to spill from his perfect lips.

"Why do I need to do that if no one even knows I'm the father? I'm not signing my name anywhere. If I admit to being the father, then I could be on the hook. I could lose everything." I, I, I . . . even Nick heard what a self-absorbed asshole he sounded like, but that didn't change how he felt. There was no way he was going to throw himself under the bus now, when Michigan had pretty much promised a full scholarship, preferential athlete housing, the whole works.

"The woman at the adoption agency said no one would ever see the document you sign. It's just legal stuff. Otherwise she won't help me, won't help *us* with our problem, and then we might have to keep the baby." Nick needed to be reminded that though he had remained anonymous so far, she could throw him to the wolves at any time. It was only because Grace had mercifully spared him that his future wasn't in ruins. A single telephone call to his parents could change everything. "Besides, even if you never sign anything, never admit to anything, a simple DNA test will accomplish the same thing."

That did it. The blood drained from Nick's face as he realized Grace wasn't quite the simp he'd taken her for. She knew how to play hardball, and she wasn't afraid of him anymore. He decided he'd better watch his tongue. "Why can't you just go to another agency? You can just say you don't know who the father was, that it was a one-night stand and you never knew his name."

"All the agencies I spoke to require both parents to sign off. Maybe some less reputable ones don't care, but I want our baby placed with the best family, and this is the agency I want to use."

Grace hadn't looked at any other adoption agencies, so she didn't actually know if what she said about the rules was true, but there was no way she was going to tell anyone that she'd had anonymous sex with some stranger just to protect Nick. Up until this moment, Grace had let him have his way, given him the gift of anonymity, but now she was drawing the line. This wasn't about him and it wasn't about her—this was about the poor, innocent life they had so stupidly and cavalierly created together, and they both owed it to this child to redirect its life from its inauspicious beginning.

"Fine." Smart enough to know when he was beaten, Nick turned around and stared out the windshield. "So where's this piece of paper?"

"You have to come to the agency, because your signature has to be witnessed by a notary public." Grace handed him one of Mrs. Olson's business cards. "Here's the address. You need to be there tomorrow afternoon at four."

"Okay. That's all I have to do?" In the back of his mind, he wondered if this was a setup, whether Grace's dad would jump out from behind the door, flanked by her mom and the pastor of their church, ready to make Grace an honest woman and wreck his life.

As if she had read his mind, Grace said, "Don't worry, it's not a trap. After you sign, we're done. I never want to speak to you again."

If only she'd had a crystal ball back in July, had been able to see that Nick's beauty was barely skin deep and that sex didn't necessarily have anything to do with real love. As she got out of the car, Grace turned once more to look into those eyes that had wielded such power over her a few months earlier. Now they were just eyes.

At 4:15 the next day, Janet turned to Grace and said, "Do you think he lied to you, that he won't show up?"

"He'll be here. He knows I mean business. I kind of told him that if he didn't sign it, no adoption agency would help us and we would have to keep the baby," Grace answered.

"Brilliant. Veiled threats. Actual threats. Whatever it takes to get the job done." When they first met, Janet had worried that Grace was so fragile she might fall apart under the stress of pregnancy and the adoption process, but she could see that under the delicate, uncertain façade, Grace was tough as nails.

As if on cue, the door to Janet's office suite opened and Nick strolled in, his posture belying his discomfiture at being so deep in enemy territory. Glancing around quickly, even checking behind the door, he was relieved to see that Mr. Warren and Reverend Halvert were not present, wedding rings and Bible in hand. Maybe Grace wasn't trying to ambush him after all. Janet stood and walked towards him slowly, hand out, as if approaching a wild animal. *No wonder Grace's common sense went out the window*, she thought. Embarrassed that she could be so physically attracted to someone who could easily be her son, Janet hoped that the heat she was feeling wasn't evident in her cheeks. Even though she knew what a lowlife he was, she couldn't control the visceral response to his broad shoulders and sculpted features. Janet's heart broke for poor Grace—she'd never stood a chance. But one thing was certain: it was going to be a beautiful baby.

"You must be Nick. I'm Janet Olson." She couldn't say it was a pleasure to meet him or that she'd heard a lot about him. Either one would be inappropriate, and she didn't want to rile this kid up. From what Grace had told her, he was a loose cannon, and now that he was here, she didn't want to risk him bolting.

"Hi."

For the first time in his life, Nick was standing in front of an attractive woman and had nothing to say. He had a little thing for cougars, though he hadn't yet nailed one. According to a couple of guys on the lacrosse team, it was a good time: they tried really hard, were incredibly grateful, and even paid for dinner. But this particular cougar was all business. Usually women of all ages gave him an appreciative once-over, but Mrs. Olson never looked away from his face. He realized Grace must have told her everything, and his natural urge to charm would be a total waste of time. He just needed to sign the paper and get the hell out of there.

"Let's get this taken care of, shall we?"

As much as she wanted to launch into a tirade about sexual responsibility and respect, Janet held her tongue. She understood that as much as this boy deserved a dressing down, he would merely be a stand-in for the now-middle-aged man who had violated both her body and her trust in the back bedroom of a frat house. Years of therapy had taught her that nothing she could do could erase the past, and blaming others for one's own situation only delayed one's recovery. This kid would get his. The next girl he knocked up might not be as civilized as Grace, or maybe he would catch a nasty STD that would permanently take the lead out of his pencil. One could only hope.

"Yeah," he said softly. Grace was sitting in one of the two chairs in front of Janet's desk. Nick nodded at her but said nothing.

"Okay, have a seat. Nick, when you sign these documents you are giving up your parental rights to this child. That's forever. Under no circumstances can you reassert your rights. This piece of paper effectively trumps your biological connection. Do you understand?"

"Yes," Nick said with a little smile.

"Fine," Janet said, handing him a piece of paper. "Read this over. Take your time. If you have any questions at all, now is the time to ask."

After a couple of minutes, Janet spoke. "I'll assume your silence means you fully comprehend what you've read. Please sign and date the document." It was such an emotional moment, but it was important to remain businesslike, at least until the paper was signed and she had put her notary stamp at the bottom.

Nick scribbled his name casually and sat back. His nightmare was over. One stroke of a pen and he'd gotten his life back. He paused, certain that anything so easy had to have a catch. "Is that it?"

"You're all done," Janet said, wanting to add, *until you knock up the next one, you self-centered putz.* "Grace will sign after the baby is born, and that's it." Although she had hoped this scare would change Nick's attitude toward sex and girls, make him understand that sex was more than just a carnival ride, the vacant look in his eyes and the way he slouched in his chair told Janet that this kid was still thinking with his penis, and nothing she could say was going to change that.

"Okay, see you later," Nick said to the room, barely able to keep the smile off his face. "By the way, do you know what time is it?"

"It's five to five," Grace offered, realizing as she said it that those were probably the last words she and Nick would ever exchange.

They had made love—well, they had had sex—made a child, and now their last conversation was about the time. It had truly ended with a whimper.

"Thanks," he said as he opened the door to leave.

He was late to meet Amy, but she wasn't going anywhere. Their late summer thing had continued into the fall. She was the best fuck he'd ever had, and she had this little stick implanted in her arm that meant there was no way she could get pregnant. Sometimes he didn't even wear a condom, even though he knew she was probably screwing other guys, which he knew was stupid on his part, but doing it bareback was amazing. Willing to try any freaky thing he suggested, Amy was like a female version of himself, and he was under her spell. Instead of waiting for the elevator, he ran down the stairs.

CHAPTER 13

Dear Baby,

Happy Thanksgiving! You're twenty weeks old. The doctor says you're six inches long, and you can hear things. So now you know what my voice sounds like and that I listen to the Beatles in the middle of the night when I can't sleep, which happens a lot. I can feel you wiggling around inside of me. It's not time for you to come out, so just relax. The doctor told me that you're a girl, and I cried. Not because I was sad, but because now I know I'm having a daughter.

I know I'm not keeping you, but I need to call you something other than Baby. Can I call you Molly for now? I know that your adoptive parents will give you a name, but for now it's just you and me. Remember how much I love you and how sorry I am that I did this backwards, but I'm going to make it right. You're going to have the best mommy and daddy I can find. I promise.

Love,

Grace

When Grace walked into the kitchen on Thanksgiving morning, Vera was rolling out a piece of pastry for a piecrust and Helen was sitting on a stool at the counter polishing the silverware. An assortment of copper pots bubbled away on the oversized range, and the air smelled like cinnamon and coffee and vanilla. As much as she tried to block the thoughts, Grace couldn't help wondering what her parents were doing. It was nine o'clock, so they were probably already at the soup kitchen, up to their elbows in vats of mashed potatoes and gravy, full of empathy for those less fortunate than themselves. Their ability to sympathize with strangers and not their own daughter made Grace both sad and angry. Maybe if she were living on the street, strung out on heroin instead of pregnancy hormones, they could find it in their hearts to forgive her. *No, don't go there*, she warned herself. Determined not to ruin the day, Grace stomped on all her bad thoughts and vowed to live in the moment, to appreciate all the good things she had. It was Thanksgiving, after all.

"Good morning, Vera. It smells amazing in here. Mrs. T., thank you for inviting Jennifer over. She's going to join us for dessert."

"I'm so glad. I know this must be a difficult day for you, and having your best friend with you seemed like a good idea."

Earlier in the week, Helen had ventured across the street to invite Grace's parents to Thanksgiving dinner. This silent treatment was going on way too long, and it was time for the Warrens to start acting like adults. Thanksgiving seemed like the perfect opportunity to put the past behind and make a fresh start. But although Helen could hear footsteps on the other side of the door, no one answered, and after ten minutes of knocking and doorbell-ringing, she gave up and went home. Grace's parents had to be crazy—there was no other explanation.

Grace shrugged. "I'm okay. Every day it gets easier being away from them."

That was a lie, but Grace was committed to making it true because she didn't have a choice in the matter, and it was a waste of time and energy ruminating over a situation that was out of her control. She had begged, literally on her knees, for their forgiveness, and they had slammed the door in her face. Since that awful day, she had left three notes in their mailbox saying that she loved them and was sorry for what she had done, basically repeating what she had told them that very first night, hoping that the passage of time might have softened their seemingly impenetrable outer shells. But there had been no response, and it looked like the cold war was going to continue through the winter.

"I'm sure that's not true, darling, but you've done your best to mend the rift, and now we simply must wait for your parents to find their way out of the woods. As Dr. Needleman used to tell me every week, the only behavior you can control is your own."

"I know, but I just wish I could make them understand why I'm doing this. Why don't they get it? They raised me to think this way, and then they went and changed all the rules." Grace's voice cracked and she turned away, swiping at her tears with her sleeve.

Putting down her polishing cloth, Helen came around the kitchen island and put her arms around Grace. "Shhh. They'll figure it out eventually. Come, sit down and have a little breakfast. Vera and I were about to take a coffee break."

"Thank you, Mrs. T., for everything," Grace whispered into Helen's soft sweater, feeling the stamina of every one of Helen's eighty years in those narrow but sturdy shoulders.

"It is my privilege, *mamala*, and my pleasure," Helen whispered back.

"Good morning. Happy Turkey Day, ladies. Did I miss the group hug?" Charlie put his arms around Helen and Grace and kissed each of them. The feel of his hand on Grace's back and the smell of his soap made her pulse speed up just a little bit. It frightened her.

"Good morning, darling. Grace and I were just having a moment. Holidays are kind of emotional. Speaking of which, we should call your parents sometime today. What's the time difference in Moscow? I always forget."

"It's eight hours later there. I already Skyped them. They're doing Thanksgiving at the embassy."

"That sounds exciting," Helen said. "I'm afraid I can't compete with that."

"Last year, we had Thanksgiving at the embassy in Paris. You've seen one, you've seen them all. I'm much happier here with you, Aunt Helen. You're way better than any ambassador." Charlie was talking to Helen, but he was looking directly at Grace. "I wouldn't trade my time here for anything."

Grace blushed, picked up the silver cloth, and started rubbing vigorously at the tines of a serving fork, trying not to look flustered, and failing. Charlie poured himself a cup of coffee and sat down across from Grace.

"Have you had breakfast yet?" he asked, sounding more parental than he intended.

"Not yet." Grace blushed again, not sure why such a neutral question would provoke such a response. "I'm going to have some cereal. I'm fine. I just woke up."

"Sit," Helen ordered. "Vera and I made a quiche this morning, and we're all going to have some."

After breakfast, Helen excused herself. "I think I should give your folks a call myself. Just say hello. We e-mail, but I haven't spoken to them in a bit, and as long as I'm looking after you, I should probably let them know that you're thriving under my tutelage."

"I'm sure they would love that. Do you want me to set you up on Skype?" Charlie asked.

"No, dear, the telephone is much better for someone my age. I'm sure your parents don't want to be staring at my prune face right before they have dinner."

"Aunt Helen, don't say that. You're beautiful, and timeless."

"Just like the Sphinx, my love. Now, while I do that, why don't you and Grace set the table. The cloth is already on. The dishes are on the sideboard. You just need to rinse the silver first. Otherwise everything will taste like Tarn-X. There will be five us—the three of us, and George and Vera—make that six, since Jennifer is coming for pumpkin pie."

"What about Ada?" Charlie asked.

"Ada has taken a couple of days and gone to visit her family, so it's just us."

In the dining room, Grace and Charlie walked around the table, arranging cutlery, plates, and glasses. "Your aunt has such lovely things." Grace held a cut crystal wineglass up to the light.

"She does. It's nice that Jennifer is coming over," Charlie said, not particularly interested in Helen's dishes or her guest list, but feeling awkward in Grace's presence. Small talk set his teeth on edge, but he couldn't think of anything else to say.

"Mrs. T. thought having my best friend here would make the holiday a little easier . . . since my parents aren't around."

"That's a good idea."

"It is, but she didn't need to. I feel so close to you . . . and to your aunt. It's weird, but you've become my family these last few months."

The pause wasn't lost on Charlie, and he smiled, although when she said family, he prayed she didn't think of him as a brother. "I'm glad. When we finish here, do you want to go for a walk?" Maybe his tongue would untie itself if he exposed it to a blast of cold air.

"Before . . . my dad and I always used to go for a long walk on Thanksgiving Day."

"We don't have to, then. I don't want to stir up bad memories."

"No, it's all good. I'd love to go for a walk with you, Charlie Glass."

The sky was a silvery gray, and only a few brave leaves still clung to the branches as Grace and Charlie walked up the trail by the old reservoir. It was the same hike Grace used to take with her father.

Grace looked up at the sky. "It feels like it might snow if it were just a little bit colder."

"Are you warm enough? Here, take my coat." Charlie started to take off his jacket.

"No, Charlie, I'm perfectly warm. But thank you. Where do you come from? No boy has ever tried to give me his coat before."

"I don't think lending you my jacket is exactly going out on a limb. It's not like I'm offering you a kidney or something." If it ever came up, Charlie was fairly sure he would, but Grace didn't need to know that right now.

"But you're so good to me. You're always thinking about what I might need or want." Grace was on a fishing expedition out at the reservoir, hoping Charlie might give her a hint as to his real feelings. Was he simply the most thoughtful person on the planet, or was it something more? Not daring to hope that it could be something more than just good breeding, Grace tried to find the right words to force the issue without sounding like she was making a play for him.

"I'm good to you because we're friends," Charlie said simply, afraid to say anything more explicit.

In the weeks and months since they had become unlikely housemates, Charlie had tried to find things wrong with Grace in a useless effort to contain his rapidly growing feelings for her. But the more closely he examined her, the more smitten he became. Her uncertainty and her vulnerability highlighted her strength of character. Her slowly blossoming body was incredibly feminine and sexy. Her quiet sorrow over her undeserving parents showed how honorable and loyal she was.

"I think you're my *best* friend these days. I love Jennifer to death, but sometimes I think she's kind of annoyed with me for not going through with the abortion. In her mind, I made my life ridiculously complicated for no good reason. I wish I could make her understand."

They had reached a steep part of the path, and Charlie took Grace's hand to guide her. If she fell, he would never forgive himself. When the trail flattened out again, he didn't let go, and she didn't either.

"It's a very personal decision, and what's right for one person may not be right for everyone," Charlie said.

"You should be hanging out at the embassy with the other diplomats. What would *you* do if you were seventeen and pregnant? Or your girlfriend was?"

Charlie stopped walking and took Grace's other hand so they stood facing each other.

"I would love her and stand by her, whatever she decided to do, because we're in this together." He had purposely switched tenses, hoping Grace might pick up on his subliminal suggestion that *he* wanted to be the one standing by her.

"Oh." A single tear rolled down Grace's cheek as she stared up at Charlie, hating herself for not waiting for someone who looked at her the way Charlie was looking at her at that moment. A lifetime of thoughtful decisions abandoned on a balmy evening on a country road, and now she was looking at the face of what should have been her future, but now could never be. Even if Charlie and Mrs. T. could accept her many imperfections, his perfect parents never could.

Charlie leaned over and kissed Grace's cheek. It would have been so easy to kiss her sweet mouth, to telegraph his longing to be something more than her other best friend. But something stopped him. So disoriented, Grace would probably kiss him back, but what would it mean? Better to be patient and be sure.

When Charlie drew back, Grace exhaled slowly and looked at the ground. She had been so sure he would kiss her on the lips. When Charlie gazed into her eyes, she felt as if they were the only two people on earth, but she had obviously misunderstood. It had happened before. Nick's adoring looks had been vacant promises. Best friend would have to do. It was better than nothing.

At the top of the trail they peered over the rocky edge into the pewter-colored water. Stepping back quickly, grabbing onto a tree trunk to anchor herself, Grace made a face. "I don't like that."

"Don't like what? Do you feel sick?"

"I'm afraid of heights . . . along with all the other things I'm scared of."

"I'm sorry. I didn't know. I shouldn't have brought you up here." What was supposed to be a romantic walk in the woods was turning into a therapy hike. Charlie felt like jumping into the icy water. Nothing he tried was working.

"No, I need to start facing my fears, so I'm glad we came here." Grace smiled up at Charlie, wishing she had the nerve to tell him how wonderful he was, how she never wanted to let go of his hand.

"I'd say you spend plenty of time facing your fears these days."

"Trust me. I've barely scratched the surface."

"Well, I think that's enough for today. Let's go home."

Charlie held out his hand and Grace took it, knowing that she should be grateful for this special friendship, instead of wasting time wishing it could be something more. No boy on earth, not even one as sensitive and mature as Charlie, would hitch his wagon to a girl who had someone else's bun in her oven. She knew she had no right to expect a miracle.

Thanksgiving dinner at the Teitelbaum home was nothing like the Thanksgivings Grace was used to. As formal and gracious as Mrs. T.'s setup was, that's how casual the meal was. Because it was a holiday, everyone was pitching in. Vera was the only one not allowed to get up from the table, because she had done all the cooking. Everyone had to say what he or she was grateful for, which ran from Grace thanking everyone assembled for treating her like a member of the family to George thanking Mrs. T. for buying a space-age snow blower for the coming winter. Conversation was light, and they spent as much time laughing as they did eating.

At Grace's house, although the setting was far more casual, the meal was anything but. There was lots of talk about politics and the economy and the state of the Supreme Court. Sometimes Grace felt like she should be taking notes, because there might be a test before dessert. Having never spent a holiday with anyone but her own family, Grace had assumed that was normal. But after a relaxing meal that did not include a single reference to the president or the Middle East, Grace began to see that her parents were just serious people. Maybe they were simply unable to lighten up, which would partially explain, although not excuse, the fact that they couldn't see past Grace's pregnant belly.

Jennifer knocked on the back door as Grace was stacking dishes next to the sink. "Hey, Princess Grace. Here." Jennifer thrust a pie covered with Saran Wrap into Grace's hands. "My mother said I couldn't come empty-handed, but once you taste her pecan pie, you'll wish I had." Jennifer stuck out her tongue.

"I'm sure it's delicious. I hope you didn't act like that in front of your mother."

"Not to her face."

Charlie walked in carrying the turkey carcass on a huge silver platter. "Ah, the man of the house. Grace, how did you train him so quickly?"

"Shock collar, and lots of positive reinforcement," Grace said.

"I'm into discipline," Charlie said, baring his teeth and growling.

"Enough," Jennifer said, clapping her hands over her ears. "You two need to get a room already."

Charlie cleared his throat and flipped the switch on the coffeemaker. "I'm just going to finish clearing and bring in dessert. Grace, why don't you and Jennifer go sit down and relax in the dining room."

When Charlie was out of the room, Jennifer whispered, "Either he's trying to impress you, or he's channeling Martha Stewart. Which is it?"

Grace shook her head. "He's not gay. He says things, and the way he looks at me sometimes . . . . There's no way. And he had a girlfriend when he was living in Paris."

"Elton John used to be married . . . to a woman. I'm just saying."

"He's not gay. I'd bet you anything," Grace whispered just as Charlie came through the door, juggling plates and bowls.

"The dining room is that way," he said, putting down the dishes, picking up two pies and disappearing through the swinging door.

Jennifer said, "Let's go meet the in-laws. And by the way, it's a bet. I want proof, straight proof. Bring me his boxer shorts."

After another hour of laughing and more eating, Thanksgiving was over at the Teitelbaums'. Charlie jumped up. "Aunt Helen, you and Vera and George are dismissed. Jennifer, Grace, and I will clean up."

"But sweetheart," said Vera, "there's so much to do, and I'm an old pro. It won't take me long."

"Absolutely not," said Grace. "You made such a wonderful meal. The least we can do is wash a few dishes."

"Don't argue with them," said George.

"Goodnight, children. Thank you for letting the old people go to bed. I must admit I am a bit tired." Helen blew a kiss and went upstairs.

Charlie clapped his hands together once. "Okay, Jennifer, you wash, I'll dry, and Grace can count the silver to make sure we didn't accidentally throw anything away."

"Why do you get to be in charge?" Jennifer demanded.

"It's his house," Grace pointed out. No wonder Jennifer couldn't attract a guy.

"Sorry, sir." Charlie saluted. "I await your orders."

Not expecting Charlie to give in so quickly to her brattiness, Jennifer said, "What you said was fine, but why can't we stick everything in the dishwasher? You have two of them."

"The detergent will ruin the sterling, and the gold trim on the plates will wash away in the dishwasher," Charlie explained.

"That's stupid."

Grace laughed. "That's all you've got?"

Jennifer scowled and turned the hot water on full blast, squirting way too much dish soap into the sink. After she'd washed exactly two dishes, her cell phone buzzed with an incoming text. "That's my mom. She says I have to come home and wash *her* dishes. Sorry."

"Why are you smiling?" Grace asked. "Dishes are dishes."

"Not true. Our crappy dishes aren't made of gold and our stainless steel silverware can go in the dishwasher. See you later. Grace, remember what we talked about. And Chuckles, you wash and let Grace dry."

With one last evil cackle Jennifer was out the door, and Grace and Charlie were alone in the quiet kitchen. "You heard the boss. Here's the towel, unless you're tired, and then you should go to sleep. I can finish this myself."

"Charlie, I'm pregnant, not sick. And there's no way you're doing all of this cleanup yourself." Grace snatched the towel from Charlie's hand and stationed herself next to the sink. "Let's get to it."

"It's so bright in here. Can I turn off some of the lights?" Charlie flicked off the big fixture over the marble island. With just the lights on over the kitchen table and the sink, it was almost romantic, in spite of the piles of dirty dishes and leftovers. "So what were you and the mean girl talking about before?"

"Nothing," said Grace quickly.

"You expect me to buy that?" Charlie rolled his eyes.

"It was nothing. Just Jennifer being Jennifer."

"She doesn't like me, does she? She thinks I'm kind of a freak, which I guess I am. It's just so different here than it is in Europe."

"No, she likes you." Grace tried to figure out a way to put Jennifer's bet to rest without humiliating herself *and* Charlie. "She just thinks it's impossible for anyone to be as nice as you are—there must be something else going on underneath the surface."

"Like what?" Charlie asked, blowing a handful of soapsuds at Grace.

"I don't know," Grace said, knowing how dumb she sounded when she tried to play dumb.

"Maybe I'm nice to you because I like you," Charlie said, wondering if his sudden attack of bravery was a consequence of being alone together in the dimly lit kitchen, or more likely, the four glasses of wine he'd drunk with dinner.

"I like you, too," Grace said.

"I kind of think I might like you more," Charlie said, drying his hands on the towel Grace was holding, pulling her towards him.

The kitchen light flipped on, and Helen was standing in the doorway. Grace and Charlie stepped away from each other, and the wet towel fell to the floor.

CHAPTER 14

"Tell me again why we're in the children's section of the bookstore," Jennifer said as a toddler ran up to her, threw his arms around her knees, and then backed away crying and hiccuping, having realized that he was not hugging his mother. "It's so noisy . . . and sticky, and the chairs are really, really tiny."

"Don't you listen to anything I say? I've decided that I don't want to have contact with Molly while she's growing up, but I do want to give her a birthday present every year, so I want to buy all of them now, and then her parents can give them to her."

Books were such an important part of Grace's life, and she wanted to share her favorites, which she had read over and over, with Molly. They had been milestones in her own childhood, and she knew that even if she couldn't sit at the end of her daughter's bed and read these books out loud, Molly would be able to feel her love flowing through the words of E. B. White and Beverly Cleary. Even if Grace couldn't be there, knew she shouldn't be there, she realized she had a lot of things she wanted to share with the bean.

"Are they going to tell her they're from her real mother?" Jennifer asked.

"Biological mother," Grace corrected. "I hope so. Whatever happens, I just want Molly to know what she means to me."

The whole parent-child thing was never far out of Grace's thoughts, not just because of Molly, but also because of the mess with her own mother and father. It had never occurred to her before the bottom dropped out of her world back in August that the relationship that had defined her life could be shattered as easily as her father's coffee cup on the slate floor of the sunroom.

"You could have ordered them on Amazon. It would be way easier than crawling around in munchkin land."

As much as Jennifer adored Grace, she was having trouble relating to her friend's overflowing love for what Jennifer still considered to be nothing more than a bean, albeit a girl bean. Of course, she knew the baby was more real to Grace, who could feel the little bugger swimming around in there, but she couldn't understand how Grace could feel so strongly about this baby when Nick was the father. She knew it wasn't the baby's fault that she had a fuckface for a dad, but how could Grace fall in love with the thing that had pretty much trashed her life? If Jennifer were in Grace's shoes (not that that would ever happen, considering she was nearly eighteen and had never gotten past first base), she would have run to the abortion clinic without a backwards glance. In Jennifer's eyes, two wrongs definitely didn't make a right, and bringing an unwanted child into an already overpopulated world, even if some yuppie couple was waiting to carry it off into the sunset in their BMW SUV, was definitely a second wrong. Under no circumstances would she ever share these secret thoughts with Grace. What good would it do to second-guess Grace's decision, which, as tortured as it was and as complicated as it had made her life, was for her clearly the right way to deal?

"But this is fun for me. I wanted to do this because I want to remember the buying part of it, since I won't be around for the reading part."

In five or six years someone else was going to be reading *Stuart Little* to her daughter. Grace wouldn't be there to hear Molly giggle when Stuart's father lowers him down the drain to retrieve the ring or ask the question she had asked her own mother—how can human beings give birth to a mouse? When she thought about those moments, Grace was plagued with second thoughts about her decision, but then Jennifer's sometimes grating but always practical voice would cut in, telling her that giving up her own life to raise a child she wasn't ready to have was the opposite of good parenting. And then Grace would be jolted back to reality—giving her baby to perfect strangers wasn't how it was supposed to be, but when you fuck things up you're not allowed to fuck things up more by being selfish on top of it.

"I get it," Jennifer said, even though she didn't. "Why don't you record your voice reading a book out loud? Those two kids who gave up their baby for adoption on *Teen Mom* did that when they went to see their baby for her first birthday. It was kind of cool."

"Maybe. I'll have to talk to the adoptive parents about that. They might think that's too pushy."

A pleaser from birth, Grace was always worried that she might say or do the wrong thing and offend someone. Maybe if she'd been less worried about pleasing Nick . . . no point in wandering down that road again. It always led to the same place: the inn of self-loathing and depression, which always had a deluxe room for her.

"But it's not their baby until you say so, so don't you get to make the rules? They want your baby, so won't they do whatever you want, as long as they get to take the baby home in the end?" Looking around at the little kids crawling all over the floor, way more interested in stacking the books like building blocks or wiping their boogers on the carpet than in actually reading, Jennifer wondered what all the fuss was about.

"I don't care about having control. I care about doing the right thing for Molly. Nothing else matters."

Grace's certainty about protecting her baby sustained her. If she did everything right from here on out, maybe she could make up for all the things she'd done wrong before. It was an overly simplistic karmic equation: spreading your legs for a stupid boy you hardly knew canceled out by behaving irreproachably for the rest of your life.

"All right. Give me a job so we can get this done and get the hell out of here." The bookstore, teeming with tiny bodies, looked like an ant farm, and Jennifer was starting to get itchy.

"Here's your half of the list." Grace tore the sheet of paper she was holding in two and gave one piece to Jennifer. "You get the baby books."

Jennifer looked at the piece of paper in her hand. *Goodnight Moon, Welcome to Busytown, D. W. the Picky Eater, Horton Hears a Who, Yertle the Turtle, Caps for Sale, Harvey's Hideout,* and *I Love Me.*

Leaving Jennifer to her assignment, Grace headed for the middle grade and young adult sections. *Charlotte's Web, Stuart Little,* the entire Ramona series, the Little House on the Prairie series, *The Twenty-One Balloons.* Then on to books for teenage Molly. *To Kill a Mockingbird*; anthologies of short stories by F. Scott Fitzgerald, J. D. Salinger, and O. Henry; Daphne Du Maurier's *Rebecca*; *The Time Traveler's Wife*; and *The Namesake.* That should get Molly through her eighteenth birthday.

Grace handed the clerk an American Express Platinum Card. "Do you think you could gift wrap them?"

"Of course. All together?" the saleswoman asked.

"No, each one separately, if it's not too much trouble."

"Since when do you have a platinum credit card?" Jennifer asked. Her own parents kept her on a tight budget. Cash and carry all the way.

"Mrs. T. gave it to me." Living with Aunt Helen apparently had perqs beyond gourmet meals and fancy cars.

"Getting disowned by your parents doesn't look so bad from over here. I'm always broke," Jennifer said.

"Yeah, but your parents love you, talk to you, let you sleep in your own bed." Grace would trade any amount of money to have her parents love her without reservation, without preconditions.

"I'm willing to bet your father never called you a whore." Almost more than anything else, Grace couldn't get over her parents' contempt for her. It almost felt like they'd been waiting for her to screw up so they could say what they'd really felt all along.

"I think I'd be okay with that if I could have a credit card without a spending limit," Jennifer replied, covetously eyeing the gray plastic rectangle.

"As much as I appreciate everything Mrs. T. has done, and Charlie's pretty amazing, I miss my parents."

"You miss being screamed at and told you're nothing but a no-good slut? I didn't know you were a masochist."

"Shhh. Keep your voice down. Remember where we are," whispered Grace. At the word *slut* a woman with a toddler glowered in their direction.

"Sorry. Well?" Jennifer whispered loudly.

"I don't miss the mean stuff, but I do miss how it used to be, before."

"That ship sailed. You'll never be able to go back there." As she said it, Jennifer bit her tongue. She didn't know for certain that Grace's relationship with her parents was irreparable. Miracles happened every day.

"Here you are miss—um, ma'am," said the sales clerk as she placed two large shopping bags filled with Molly's books on the counter. Was a pregnant girl who looked fourteen but was using a platinum card a 'miss' or a 'ma'am'?

CHAPTER 15

Snow floated silently past the windows, like feathers from some extraterrestrial pillow fight. Helen's attic was a cozy refuge from the real world, and Grace and Charlie treated it like a secret clubhouse, sprawling at either end of an enormous and ancient leather sofa. They talked, read, and listened to music, their feet meeting under an antique, moth-eaten striped wool Pendleton blanket. It was heaven, and Grace wished they could stay up there forever. No one could hurt her in this cluttered fortress, and for an hour or so every evening, she could block out the daily torture being meted out by the suddenly high-minded, moralistic students at Silver Lake High School.

"You're more than halfway there." With each passing day, Grace seemed a little bit sadder, and Charlie was trying to think of ways to lift her spirits. Pointing out the light at the end of the tunnel couldn't hurt, although nearly four months seemed like a long time, even to him.

"So what? I'm used. I'm damaged goods. Who's going to want to get involved with a girl my age who's already had a baby? I only did it once, but I'm screwed for life." Grace was too depressed to recognize her own bad pun.

"It's going to take some time, but you'll get past this. I know it's a huge trauma, but once you graduate, no one has to know about it unless you tell them. I'll never tell anyone. You can go off to college and make a fresh start."

Charlie was finding himself more attracted to Grace every day. He kept reminding himself that this girl was a walking nuclear disaster. She had a bowling ball under her sweater. And her parents had kicked her out. And she wasn't Jewish. But he couldn't help himself. The kiss that they had almost shared on Thanksgiving haunted him. All he could think about was how soft her lips must be, how sweet she must taste. It was sick and perverted to have those kinds of fantasies about someone who was pregnant, not even by him, and yet every time he looked at her, he imagined what she must look like naked—all perfect curves and glowing skin. He should gouge his eyes out for having such wicked thoughts. It had gotten so bad he could no longer wear his shirt tucked in when she was around. Like in middle school, when his body had a mind of its own, and the woman in the hairnet with the wart on her nose behind the counter in the cafeteria would say, "You wanna breast or a thigh?" and he would get a raging boner, even though she looked like a witch and was talking about fried chicken.

What was driving him? Was it Grace's sweetness in the face of the shit blizzard that was her life that he found so incredibly appealing? Or was he just horny and desperate? Maybe—and he hoped this wasn't the case—he was falling for a girl who had way more checks in the *cons* column than in the *pros* column. Whatever the reason, he wished he had better control over the part of his brain that controlled his sexual fantasies.

"I don't just mean mentally. I've got stretch marks everywhere. It's gross, take my word." Grace held up her hands. "And my fingers look like those sausages that come in the little cans."

Even her stretch marks and swelling sounded hot to him. Without thinking, Charlie grabbed her hand and lightly kissed each fingertip. "You don't look disgusting. You're incredibly beautiful, even with that tiny ball under your shirt. And in a few months, your body will be back to normal, and who cares if it's not exactly like it was before? Did you plan on joining a nudist colony or making a living as a stripper?"

Grace blushed, wondering if Charlie could actually think about her as something other than the guest of honor at a nine-month pity party. The Thanksgiving almost-kiss might have been an aberration—he *had* drunk nearly an entire bottle of wine. Realistically, what decent boy would want anything to do with her after what she'd done—she was an untouchable, and no purifying bath or magic word could change that. Doing it with Nick had ruined what should have been the most special part of her life. Sex would never be the intimate, transcendent experience she had read about in novels and seen in movies.

And after what had happened with Nick, Grace had been certain she would never feel *that* way again about a boy. Not only did she no longer trust boys in general, she didn't trust her own feelings about them. Every kiss, every touch would take her back to Nick's Grand Cherokee. Whatever her future held, it was hard to imagine falling in love with someone, ever actually making love to someone.

But Charlie was different. He didn't avoid her eyes when she looked at him, and he didn't seem horrified by what she had done, or that she looked like a monster truck in stretch denim. In fact, when they were together, she felt pretty much like her old pre-Nick self. At first Grace had assumed he was nice to her to please his aunt, and it was obvious he felt sorry for her. Over the last few months, they had spent so much time together, doing homework, taking long walks, and talking about everything under the sun. Sharing a house, sharing Helen, they had become extremely close. He really was like a second Jennifer, but without the sharp tongue, and it was impossible to forget how cute he was.

Now he had said she was beautiful, and such a compliment wasn't something a guy said if he was just being polite. Or maybe well-mannered, private school boys *did* toss flattering remarks around, and she was reading too much into it. Maybe she was just desperate for a little validation after so many months of self-loathing, and he *was* just the kind of person who would see how needy she was and try to help her feel better. Teenage girls, even pregnant ones, spent a tremendous amount of time worrying about whether or not they were pretty. There were so many reasons for him to be nice to her that were more likely explanations than that he was actually attracted to her.

"You don't have to say that. I know I'm a whale. But thank you for taking the trouble to lie. It means a lot."

Since Thanksgiving, they hadn't talked about their feelings. But the unresolved question still hung in the air, at least for Grace. Tired of spending every waking moment wondering if he truly had feelings for her, Grace needed to know, and she realized she cared about him enough to let him off the hook if he was just trying to be a good friend, trying to build her flagging self-esteem. If he said nothing now, there would be an awkward moment—perhaps a pregnant pause, she laughed to herself—but at least she would know where she stood, and then she could move on, as difficult as that might be.

"I'm not lying," he murmured.

Placing his hand gently on the mound of her belly, Charlie leaned over and kissed her, his lips barely touching hers. He waited a few seconds. When she didn't pull away, he pressed harder, caressing her lips with his tongue, coaxing them apart. She tasted even better than he had imagined. Feeling like the world's biggest degenerate but unable to stop, he moved his hand upward, cupping her breast. He was definitely going straight to hell, but it was worth it. Grace moaned, and he pulled away in a panic. "Did I hurt you? Is the baby okay? I shouldn't have done that. I'm sorry. I crossed the line, didn't I?"

Grace didn't know whether to laugh or cry. "Don't apologize. You didn't hurt me. Just the opposite. I haven't felt anything like that, ever—not even with, um, you know. You just surprised me. That's all."

In his chinos and crisp button-down shirts, Charlie looked like someone who spent all his free time reading the *Wall Street Journal* and polishing his penny loafers. Apparently not. Gentle but assertive, respectful but passionate, he was everything that Nick was not.

Trying to slow his breathing and erase the sensation of her lips on his, Charlie said, "I really wasn't planning on doing that. It just kind of happened."

"Don't apologize. It just wasn't what I expected."

"Was it that bad?" Having grown up overseas and made out with girls of many nationalities, he considered himself an above-average kisser. Apparently all those girls had only been exceptionally polite, or American girls had an entirely different set of standards.

"No, it was amazing. But boys like you aren't supposed to kiss like that." Grace's heart was still thundering. *Could this be bad for the baby?* she worried.

"Boys like me?" *What did she mean? Was this a Jewish thing?* He hoped not.

"Yeah, polite, preppy, smart. You look so clean, but you kiss so, um, so dirty. You know what I mean?" Totally tongue-tied after what had just happened, Grace knew her attempts to explain herself were beyond clumsy, and she blushed mightily.

"I'm not sure, but if dirty is good, then I'll take it." This girl was insane, but she was also funny and sexy as hell.

"Dirty is definitely good. But I'm afraid. Kissing leads to touching and that leads to . . ." she said, pointing at Exhibit A, which seemed to have grown even bigger in the last hour.

"There's no law that says you have to get naked with every boy you kiss. Nick was your first, but he wasn't your first kiss, was he?" Charlie asked. Grace shook her head. "You obviously have self-control, even if it briefly went AWOL. You'll never forget again."

Charlie was in a tough spot. Though he knew she had every reason to be gun-shy, he hoped that she wasn't going to run away from him, from any possibility of a relationship, because she had been so badly burned her first time out. And starting a relationship with her in the middle of her second trimester smacked of poor judgment—not to mention what his parents would say if they ever got wind of this. Hopefully Aunt Helen was either unaware of his feelings or good at keeping secrets.

"I know. It's just that I can't stop thinking about everything. And I feel like a, well, like a slut. Pregnant with one guy's baby and kissing someone else." Grace desperately wanted Charlie to understand that she didn't want to push him away. It was just that she didn't know what to do, didn't want him to think she was *that* kind of girl, didn't want to have a baby on board when she fell in love with Charlie, which she could easily see happening.

"Are you in love with him?"

It hadn't occurred to him before, but if Grace was in love with that slimeball, Nick, then Charlie had seriously misjudged her. Anyone who could care about someone who had used and discarded her was majorly fucked up, and as attracted as he was to Grace, Charlie was no masochist. That he was sure of.

"No, of course I don't love him. I hate him. I hate him for tricking me, for luring me in with his voice and his looks, for not considering anyone's feelings but his own."

"Guys are assholes. I won't deny it."

Nick was a bastard, but that overwhelming urge to see a girl without her clothes and touch her all over was a feeling every guy could relate to. The difference was that *nice* guys had self-control and empathy, and they actually thought of girls as more than just tits on a stick. As much as part of him wanted to push her back onto the ancient Chesterfield sofa and run his hands over her tantalizing curves, make her moan again, he liked her too much to do that. Both of them had to be ready; otherwise they would be over before they got started.

"Not all of them," Grace said softly, tapping Charlie's shoulder. "And it's not just that I hate Nick. I hate myself for being shallow and shortsighted, because I didn't think that's who I was. I'm afraid of what I've become, and whether I'll ever be able to go back." Something about Charlie's face made her want to tell him her deepest, most frightening thoughts, knowing that he would understand exactly what she meant.

"You're going to be fine. Underneath, you're still you. The last thing I want to do is make things more difficult for you." Charlie was sad but sincere. This clearly was a mistake, at least for now. "But you're going to have a life after you give birth. You can't torture yourself forever." *Or me.* Unconsciously, he licked his lips. For him, there was no going back, but he kept that to himself for fear of spooking her. She was even more brittle than he had thought. If he handled her the wrong way, she would surely break in two.

"Stop apologizing. That kiss was the most amazing thing you could have done. You made me feel almost normal again, and I can't tell you how much that means to me. But . . . ."

Charlie grimaced. The big but. "But you're not ready. I get it. I promise to control my less than honorable thoughts. You tell me if . . . and when. I'm not going anywhere." It felt good to be candid with her, and to hear her being honest with him.

"Thank you for understanding. Promise me you won't forget those thoughts. I like you, so much, and I don't want to ruin it by starting a new chapter before I finish this one. Does that make sense?" She held her breath, hoping Charlie had a lot of time and patience. Talking openly and honestly to a boy after such an earth-moving kiss was incredibly weird, but also really exciting. This was how it was supposed to be.

"Very good sense. Until you give birth, I promise to keep it completely platonic, as far as you know." Smiling, he reached over and kissed Grace lightly on the forehead. "In my mind, that was lower." The baby was due on April third, and not that he wished for it to be born prematurely, but he didn't know how he was going to wait that long.

CHAPTER 16

Now that he had declared himself to Grace, instead of feeling relieved that she seemed to reciprocate at least some of what he was feeling, he was obsessing about her more than ever. No matter where he was, no matter what he was doing, she invaded his every thought. Even standing at a urinal in the boys' bathroom, reading the nonsense scrawled on the tile wall—*ken q. is a motherfucker*, and below it, *ur mother says hi, ken q.*—and other equally eloquent observations about life, Charlie couldn't stop thinking about Grace. He wondered if she would ever be ready for a real relationship with a normal guy. While he knew *he* could get past the Nick thing, he wasn't sure she ever would. At the sound of another guy peeing, Charlie woke from his daydream. Glancing to the left, he saw Nick Salter.

"What are you looking at, homo?" Nick said, glaring at Charlie.

"Studies show that the more homophobic a man is the more likely he is to possess latent homosexual tendencies." *Did I just say that out loud? How gay did that sound?* Charlie thought, wishing he could retrieve his words.

"What?" Nick looked genuinely puzzled. "Are you calling me a fag, faggot?"

"Your command of the English language is impressive." Biting his tongue, Charlie knew he sounded like a creepy college professor, which wasn't helpful when talking to someone like Nick.

Recovering, he said, "I'm not calling you anything, man. Just leave it."

As much as Charlie wanted to get into it with this scum, defend Grace's honor in some small way, he couldn't bring himself to pick a fight with this loser. Ultimately it would accomplish nothing, except possibly getting him suspended, which could really screw up his college applications. Wishing he didn't think so much, he longed to be more emotional, less cerebral, so he could just go whale on this jerk.

"What the fuck's the matter with you? You sound like my grandfather."

"You want me to talk like a regular guy? Okay, here goes. Just because you'll stick your dick in anything that moves, you think that makes you special? Just because every other word you say is 'fuck' doesn't make you special." Charlie zipped his pants and walked over to the sink, turned on the water, and stared at his reflection in the filthy mirror.

"And what does, you prissy prick?"

"Definitely not screwing as many girls as you can just to prove how macho you are . . . and then abandoning them when they get pregnant," Charlie said quietly.

"So that's it. You've got a hard-on for that chick Grace. Pretty fucked up to be chasing after someone in her, um, condition. But I don't know why you're talking to me about it. *I* never fucked her." Lying had become like breathing for Nick. "Not that it's any of your business." Nick glared at Charlie's starched shirt and V-neck sweater, wondering how such a poof had the guts to talk to him and whether it was Grace or Jennifer who had ratted him out.

"That's not what I hear, you pathetic excuse for a human being. You got her pregnant and walked, no, ran, away." At that moment, Charlie wanted to kill this douchebag who had stolen something precious from Grace and left her with permanent scars.

Suddenly Nick was standing behind him, looking over his shoulder, smiling dangerously at Charlie's reflection. "Don't you say that out loud ever again, you fucking queer. You understand me?"

"Which part? The part about how you knocked up Grace or the part about you being pathetic?" Before he could turn around, Nick punched him in the kidney and Charlie grunted, doubling over in pain. "Shit," he groaned. This was not how his fantasy attack on this asshole was supposed to go. *He* was supposed to be the one doing the sucker punching.

"You think you're funny? I'll beat the living crap out of you." Nick couldn't believe that he'd come in for a simple piss, and now he was trading punches with some shithead who had the hots for Grace.

"You think?" Charlie spun around, fist up, his punch landing squarely on Nick's exquisite nose. Blood gushed, staining Nick's pristine white T-shirt and dripping onto the tile floor.

"You stupid fuck. Now you've done it." Nick's flawless profile that had escaped injury in spite of years of contact sports was ruined.

Three minutes and two black eyes later, the newly elected president of the freshman class wandered into the bathroom and discovered two bloody, bruised seniors flailing around on the blood-smeared floor. Doing a quick about-face, in spite of the fact that he really needed to use the bathroom, he ran to the principal's office to report the crime in progress.

"So what were you two geniuses fighting about?" Principal Stanley stared impassively across his desk. Based on their appearances, there was no clear winner. Pushing a box of Kleenex towards Nick, he said, "You're dripping on my new carpet."

Nick grabbed a handful of tissue and held it up to his nose, which was running like a faucet.

"It was just a misunderstanding, Mr. Stanley," Charlie offered. "We worked it out."

"Yeah," Nick echoed in a nasal voice, grateful that Charlie didn't seem eager to share his secret about Grace.

"I have your files in front of me, and I see that you, Mr. Salter, are being recruited by a few powerhouse schools who would like to exploit your athletic abilities. And Mr. Glass, you're Ivy League all the way. Fighting in the bathroom like a couple of thugs is not the smartest way to achieve either of your goals. Would you boys agree with that assessment?"

"Yes sir," the boys said, staring straight ahead.

Mr. Stanley was in a tough position. Helen Teitelbaum had written a large check with no strings attached to the PTA when she enrolled her nephew at Silver Lake, and hoping that her generosity was not an isolated incident, the principal was reluctant to inflict a punishment that might cause her to slam her checkbook shut. Besides, from what he knew about Charlie Glass, he was a good kid—a straight-A student with English boarding school manners. Nick Salter was what the kids called a "playah," who was constantly being oohed and aahed over by a gaggle of adolescent girls in tight jeans. He wondered how the kid could make his way down the hall through the throngs of admiring females; it was an enviable predicament. Neither one was a troublemaker, so there was likely a good reason the two had come to blows, but after thirty years of listening to children either spill their guts or lie like thieves, he was losing interest in getting to the bottom of things. At the moment, all he cared about was surviving until June, when he could retire with a full pension and spend his days building ship models in the glorious solitude of his basement.

"Today's your lucky day, gentlemen. It's my wife's birthday, and I'm feeling festive. So in the spirit of giving, I'm going to let you off the hook with a very stern warning," the principal said, peering over his reading glasses at two kids who in a few months would be old enough to vote and defend the United States in a war, but now, as they slumped in their chairs in their torn and bloodied clothes, looked like a couple of little boys fresh from a schoolyard skirmish.

"I'm really sorry, Mr. Stanley. I don't know what I was thinking, and I promise it won't happen again."

Charlie had never been called into the office of the principal or headmaster of any of the many schools he had attended all over the world. Never before had he allowed his emotions to trump his good sense. That could mean only one thing: he was definitely in love with Grace.

"I'm sure you are, Mr. Glass. Mr. Salter, do you echo your compatriot's sentiments?" Mr. Stanley looked expectantly at Nick, tapping his pen as he waited for a response.

"Yes, sir," Nick mumbled.

Barely able to see out of his right eye, Nick was fuming less over getting into a fight with the pansy-assed prepster who was mooning over the one girl he regretted fucking than he was over the fact that his perfect face was going to be considerably less perfect for the foreseeable future. Although, if he really thought about it in a glass-half-full kind of way, girls were nurturers, so he was fairly certain he would be able to find a few biddies willing to take off their clothes and nurse him back to health.

"You two are so close to the finish line, I'm fairly confident that you'll find the wherewithal to control your caveman urges in the future. But if you don't, be warned, I'm going to throw the book at you. And you know what that means—no Division One, no ivy-covered halls."

"Yes, Mr. Stanley."

"Why don't you two take the rest of the day off? And next time, use your words instead of your fists."

"Yes, Mr. Stanley." Both boys shuffled out, heads down, and walked quickly in opposite directions down the hallway outside the principal's office.

When Charlie walked into the kitchen, Helen and Vera were sitting at the table, heads together, doing the crossword puzzle. Vera looked up and screamed, causing Helen to spill coffee all over the newspaper. Both women jumped to their feet and started babbling at once.

"I don't look that bad, do I? Vera, could I have a bag of peas to put on my eye?"

"That kind of shiner needs a steak, young man," said Vera as she went to find just the right cut of meat.

"Charlie, what happened?" Helen asked, wondering how she was going to tell Charlie's parents that he had gotten beaten up on her watch.

"I got in a fight. It was nothing. Vera, I'm not putting a piece of raw meat on my face. A bag of ice or frozen peas will be fine."

"You, a fight? Who would start a fight with you? You're the most civilized young man I've ever met," Helen said as she stood in front of Charlie, smoothing his wrinkled, bloodstained shirt and gently patting his swollen cheek.

"It was kind of mutual, actually. I ran into Nick in the bathroom, and we got into it." Now that it was all over, Charlie wasn't sure whether he was proud of or embarrassed about his bathroom scuffle.

"Nick? Grace's Nick? Got into what?" Helen was completely confused. Silver Lake had the reputation of being the kind of town where you didn't need to lock your doors, and at midnight you were as safe on Main Street as you were in your own bed. Apparently that was a falsehood.

"Oh my gosh, Charlie. What happened? Who did this to you?" Grace cried as she walked into the kitchen.

"You should see the other guy." Charlie, who had never traded punches with anyone in his life outside of the week they learned how to box in PE class in the seventh grade, had always wanted to say that. He tried to smile, reopening the gash in his lip, sending a trickle of fresh blood down his chin.

"*That's* hard to believe," said Grace, although she regretted her words as soon as they were out of her mouth. Telling a guy he didn't look like someone who could hold his own in a fight was more than a little insulting.

"Thanks, buddy," Charlie replied, as Vera handed him a bag from the freezer. Unfortunately, Grace didn't see him as the knight in shining armor, riding to the rescue of the fair maiden.

"We're out of peas. Are blueberries okay?" Vera was still convinced that a New York strip would be more effective, but she wasn't in charge.

"Perfect. Thank you, Vera." Charlie sighed with relief as the icy balls of fruit numbed his throbbing eye.

"So what happened to you?" Grace had a sneaking suspicion that Charlie's run-in with someone's fist somehow related to her.

"I saw Nick in the bathroom and we started talking, and the next thing I knew we were rolling around on the floor trying to kill each other."

"But why? You don't even know each other, do you? What could you two possibly have to talk about?"

"I may have said something that set him off," Charlie said.

"Like what?" Feeling like a lawyer trying to tease information out of a reluctant witness, Grace wanted to reach down Charlie's throat and yank the words out.

Helen interrupted. "Are you sure you don't need to go the doctor? How do you know you don't need stitches?"

"I'm fine, Helen. A few minutes with these blueberries and a hot shower and I'll look like myself again," Charlie answered.

"Come, Vera, help me find the first aid kit. I think it's on the top shelf in my bathroom, so you'll have to reach it for me." Helen took Vera's hand and led her out of the kitchen, whispering, "I think they need to talk," loud enough for both Grace and Charlie to hear her.

"So what did you say that made him want to rearrange your face?" Grace asked again once Helen and Vera were out of earshot.

"I told him he was a loser because he'll screw anything that moves and he abandoned you when he got you pregnant. Please don't be angry, Grace. The words just came out. I couldn't stop them." How could he explain to her that seeing Nick Salter standing next to him with his dick in his hand, the same dick that had defiled the girl that Charlie was head over heels in love with, was more than he could take?

"Damn it, this is all my fault. Charlie, you don't have to avenge my lost honor. We're not living in medieval England."

"But it's so unfair. He's still out partying, having the time of his life, and you're . . . ."

"Screwed. True enough, but he'll get his someday. Good looks and good luck can't last forever. At least that's what I keep telling myself." Revenge fantasies in which Nick lost his junk in a freak masturbation accident, or crazier ones where Nick himself got pregnant, had become a regular part of Grace's daydream rotation.

"You're being awfully philosophical about all this. Don't you want to kill him every time you see him? I don't even know him and I want to kill him," Charlie said, fists clenched, wishing he'd landed a second punch in Nick's mouth, forever ruining the smile that had probably hustled a hundred gullible girls.

"I did, but not anymore. What choice do I have? Ultimately, don't I have to take responsibility for my own behavior? I can be angry at Nick for being a total creep after I got pregnant, but I'm as much to blame as he is for everything that happened up to that point."

"But you're so . . . and he's so . . . from what I hear he's done it with half the girls in school. Did he know you'd never done it before?"

Grace reddened. "I told him I was still a virgin on our very first date. I knew he had lots of experience, and I didn't want him to think I knew what I was doing when I didn't."

"Then he had no right to lure you into his web when he knew you were a total babe in the woods," Charlie said, furious at Nick for treating Grace so casually, and annoyed with Grace for not being more worked up about it.

"But I'm not a total moron. I could have just said no, and I didn't."

"The fact that you were so innocent probably made him want you even more." Charlie himself was tremendously attracted to her clear-eyed sweetness, which remained untainted by her growing belly.

"Whatever the reason, I could've stopped him if I'd wanted to." In Grace's limited experience, it had never occurred to her that sometimes boys didn't take no for an answer.

"Are you sure about that?" Charlie asked. The vitriol with which Nick had attacked him made Charlie certain that even if Grace had refused him that night by the lake, Nick would have gotten what he wanted no matter what.

"Does it really matter?" Grace was feeling fat and tired, and talking about all the what ifs didn't change the fact that her feet were killing her and she had to get up three times a night to pee.

"I suppose not." Part of Charlie—a large part, he hated to admit—wanted Grace's encounter with Nick to be less about her own desire, whether for Nick himself or simply to belong, and more about Nick's forcefulness. Even though she would have ended up in the same place, it made her less culpable, innocent in spirit if not body.

"Look, Charlie, I know where you're going with this. I'm not such a good girl as you think I am. This is all of me, the good and the bad," Grace said as she spread her arms and thrust out her stomach. Afraid she would be unable to live up to the squeaky-clean image that Charlie seemed determined to have of her, Grace was desperate to dispel the mythology. If he could ever love her, he would have to love every facet of her, including the broken, not so shiny bits, and there were lots of them. "I did a bad thing, and now I have to live with the consequences every day, and if you want to be my friend, you're going to have to live with that wicked, awful, brain-dead part of me too. Don't you understand that I would do anything to take back that night, take back my virginity that I stupidly threw away so I could feel like I belonged to a group of people I don't give a flying fuck about?" Exhausted, Grace plopped down on a kitchen chair.

"You're *all* good, Grace, and I'm sorry I upset you. I'm just being an idiot. That guy is such an asshole that I can't imagine the two of you, how you would ever . . . with him . . . unless he . . . ." Even though Charlie's sexual experience was limited to one girl he had only kind of liked, he still held onto the romantic belief that sex was supposed to be between two people who were actually in love.

"Raped me? No, I was willing. Did you take a good look at him before you tried to bash his face in?" Grace asked, not wanting to make Charlie feel bad by pointing out Nick's obvious attributes. But he really did need to understand that the choice to do it with Nick had been hers, a stupid, awful, horrendously poor choice made for shallow, ill-considered reasons.

"He's definitely a good looking guy." Discussing Nick's physical gifts was the last thing Charlie wanted to be doing.

"Well, girls aren't any different than guys when it comes to a beautiful face and a hot body," Grace pointed out.

Disappointed that no girl would likely ever lose her self-control in *his* presence, Charlie said, "You just don't seem like that kind of girl."

"What kind of girl is that, Charlie? A whore?"

"That's not what I mean." Not even sure what he meant anymore, Charlie wished he could put a padlock on his mouth, or at least redirect this conversation so he sounded less like a Neanderthal.

"Smart girls get horny too," Grace said, feeling more than a little defensive. "And you can take your 1950s double standard and go fuck yourself."

"No, that's not it. All I was trying to say, not very well, was that you seem like such a thoughtful person, I still can't imagine you making such a big decision with so little thought. That's all. I'll never say another word about it."

Grace started sobbing. "That's exactly what Jennifer said, and I don't have an answer for why I didn't use my brain that night, and I'll never forgive myself. Feel free to hate me, because *I* sure hate me." Swimming in a sea of regret, Grace feared she would drown before she ever reached the shore.

"And now I'm just making it worse," whispered Charlie as he stood behind Grace's chair, stroking her hair, trying to stop the tears he had so stupidly provoked. Talking things out was definitely overrated. "I'm so sorry."

"It's not your fault."

"Just let me love you," Charlie whispered into her hair, but she didn't hear him.

CHAPTER 17

The college essay Grace had originally written back in July, before her world had come crashing down around her—something about getting lost on a camping trip when she was ten and how it had affected her—sounded stale and irrelevant. Reading it over, she felt as if she were reading about the life of a stranger. How could she have changed so much in so short a time? Sitting down at her computer Grace let her emotions loose, the words flowing as easily as her tears.

Who Am I?

In a matter of minutes I had transformed from a good girl into a cautionary tale. A few well-chosen words, a wandering hand, a five-minute lapse of judgment, and I have become a totally different person. Or have I? Am I only the sum of my experiences, or can I choose to be something else, something more?

When I walk down the street, people turn to stare at my swollen belly, making me feel like the bearded lady in a carnival sideshow. But am I a freak? Studies say that about half of all seventeen-year-old girls have engaged in sexual activity, so my current condition, while unfortunate, is not statistically unexpected. Condoms are only about ninety percent effective; somebody has to be in that unlucky—some might say stupid—ten percent.

But is that it for me? Will I be an unwed mother for the rest of my life? Has my identity been cast in stone because of my careless behavior? I prefer to believe that this single thoughtless act will be just that, an isolated moment in a life that I hope will be remembered for other reasons. Ultimately it is my choice. Just as I chose to give it up in the back of a 2005 Jeep Grand Cherokee, I can opt to address my future with the care and consideration that I now understand it deserves. For this reason, I have found a loving couple who are perfect parents except for their inability to make a child of their own. My baby, although conceived unintentionally, is by no means a mistake; she is a gift, a life worth living, no matter how inadvertently she began. In the caring arms of a mother and father who are ready to commit to the ultimate sacrifice that is parenthood, my daughter will live the life she deserves.

I cannot undo my poor judgment, I cannot bridge the abyss that now divides me from my family, and I cannot recapture my lost innocence. But I can make the best of this little detour, learn from it, and move forward into a brighter future. I am more than the sum of my experiences. I am whatever I choose to be.

It wasn't pretty, but it was the truth, and even if every school sent her a thin envelope, Grace knew she had done the right thing by being honest. Not that it would probably matter. College cost a fortune, and the sum total of Grace's assets consisted of her laptop, her iPhone, and a Tiffany heart locket her parents had given her for her thirteenth birthday.

"I'm so proud of you, Grace. Even with all of your distractions," the guidance counselor said, trying not to stare at Grace's midsection, "you've managed to get your applications in on time—early, no less. It's very impressive."

"Thank you, Mrs. Evans." It was December twenty-third, the last day of school before Christmas vacation, and even though she was not even six months pregnant, Grace felt like she had swallowed a volleyball. She had only gained seven pounds so far, but it was all in one place. "I do have a question. My parents are having trouble dealing with my, um, distraction, and we're kind of not talking to each other right now. They made me move out of the house back in September."

"Oh Grace, I'm so sorry. I had no idea. That must be very difficult. Are you staying with relatives?" Grace was not the first pregnant student to wander through her office, but she was the first who had actually been given the boot. It was common knowledge that the Warrens were hardcore conservatives, but Mrs. Evans couldn't imagine how they could reconcile this move with their Christian values. After thirty years helping young people navigate the college process, Letitia Evans had thought she'd seen everything, but there was always something new under the sun.

"I'm staying with my neighbor. She's been great, so that's not a problem right now. My problem is this: if I do get into college, how am I going to pay for it? I don't have any money of my own, and if my mom and dad aren't talking to me, I kind of doubt they're going to shell out fifty thousand dollars to pay for school."

"That *is* a problem. You're not eighteen yet, right?"

"I'll be eighteen in June." Grace felt more like a hundred and eighteen.

"So you're still a minor, which means they're still legally responsible for you. But of course there's no law saying they have to pay for college, although the financial aid office will be looking at your parents' tax returns to determine your eligibility . . . interesting dilemma." As she spoke, Mrs. Evans flipped through a notebook on her desk.

"Are there scholarships for idiotic pregnant girls? Maybe a *pathetic* scholarship instead of an *athletic* scholarship?" Grace asked.

Mrs. Evans chuckled. "It's good to hear you've kept your sense of humor, kiddo. I'm going to do some research, but I think your best course of action may be to go to court and get emancipated from your parents. If you do that, their income will not be considered by colleges that offer need-based grants. While your grades and test scores are fantastic, the colleges you're considering don't offer merit-based scholarships." College counselors weren't supposed to give legal advice, but in Mrs. Evans's mind this was a special situation, and Grace was a special girl.

"Emancipated?"

"It's a drastic move, for sure. You'll have to think long and hard about your relationship with your parents and if there's any possibility of reconciliation. Have you had any contact with them since September?" Mrs. Evans was uncomfortable advising a student to legally divorce her parents, but Grace was bound to get into some top colleges, and it would be a tragedy if she couldn't afford to go. Spending senior year pregnant was punishment enough; the poor girl shouldn't have to suffer the rest of her life.

"I saw them once, and I tried to talk to them, but it didn't go well. I even wrote to them asking for their forgiveness, apologizing and everything. But they didn't answer."

Grace cleared her throat and wiped away a stray tear. Even though months had gone by and she was managing pretty well, all things considered, it was still hard to talk about it. No matter what happened, they were still her mother and father, and she couldn't quite believe that it had turned out this way.

A few weeks earlier Grace had bumped smack into her mother at the market. Vera needed lemons for a pie, and Grace had offered to pick them up for her. If she had been paying attention, Grace would have remembered that her mother always did her big weekly shopping on Wednesday afternoons after work, and Grace could simply have gone to a different store. But she had other things on her mind than her mother's rigid schedule, so she wandered right into her path. Betsy had been as startled as she was.

"Mom," Grace cried, dropping the bag she was carrying, sending lemons rolling in all directions.

Betsy considered ignoring her daughter, not for solely punitive reasons, but mostly because she had no idea what to say to her. Peering at the small bulge visible under Grace's sweatshirt, Betsy stood gripping the shopping cart handle, worried that if she let go, she might collapse on the filthy linoleum floor. Prior to the front porch debacle, Betsy had never gone more than a day without talking to her daughter. Even when Grace went away to summer camp, she called every night on the cell phone Betsy had insisted she sneak into her duffel bag, because phone calls home were officially limited to one a week. Now it was the second week of December, and they hadn't exchanged a single word since the beginning of September. And the subject of their rift, as Betsy chose to view it, was no longer merely a blue cross on a test stick or a notation in a medical chart. It was a full-fledged baby, poking its tiny head against Grace's shirt, announcing its existence to the world. This was really happening, and even though she and Brad had chosen to ignore it, there was going to be a baby, a grandchild, in another few months. It felt strange being totally isolated from this person she had created, who had spent nine months in *her* belly. Through some elaborate scheme of rationalization, Betsy did not even consider that this separation was ultimately a product of the parents' behavior, not the child's. Self-pity now joined the anger, resentment, and humiliation that had continued to simmer in Betsy's brain over the past few months.

"Hello, Grace," Betsy said coolly, determined not to reveal the emotional strain she was under. Letting Grace know how much she had affected her mother would only shift the balance of power away from Betsy, and being a parent was all about retaining the power position. Without that, there would be chaos.

"Mom, how are you? How's Daddy?" Grace didn't know whether she should kiss or hug her mother, but Betsy's stiff posture was like a barbed wire fence with a Keep Out sign on it, so Grace just stood, hands at her sides, trying to think of the magic words that would break the ice.

"We're fine. You?" Pretending she was chatting with someone she had run into from her book group rather than her daughter, Betsy tried to hang onto her equanimity. It wasn't easy.

"I'm fine. Mrs. T. has been really nice to me." There was no need to go into details about how Mrs. T. had basically taken over Betsy's job for the past few months. "I'm just finishing my applications and trying to keep my grades up." Hopefully the mention of college applications might spark a conversation about next year. Maybe Betsy would let Grace know which way the wind was blowing, although Betsy's raised eyebrows when she looked at Grace's belly probably meant that not much had changed.

"Oh." Betsy's mind was reeling, and though she was rarely at a loss for words, nothing was coming to her, even though she had imagined this moment nearly every day since Grace had left. Dozens of speeches of varying tones, from forgiving to vicious, had been rehearsed as she drove down the highway, ran on the treadmill, raked leaves. But now that the moment to speak her piece was at hand, she drew a blank.

"Yeah, I rewrote my common application essay. It was a risky move, but Mrs. Evans said it was really good."

Grace wanted to ask if her parents were going to send her to college, but she didn't, and Betsy just stood there. Unable to believe that her parents were really done with her, that they really thought she was such a terrible person, Grace tried to see what was going on behind her mother's eyes.

Then from behind a pyramid of tuna fish cans stepped Grace's father. Brad rarely went to the grocery store, but he had come home early from the office, just as Betsy was leaving, and on a whim he had decided to go with her. With him always gearing up for the next trial and Betsy always doing her do-gooding or selling houses, they had precious little together time, and he had vowed to make an extra effort to do a couple of things with her. Especially now that Grace was gone, Betsy seemed a little fragile, a little quicker to accept the glass of wine the waiter offered on Sunday nights at the club, a little more likely to borrow one of his Ambien, just because she had an early day tomorrow and needed a good night's sleep. His wife was no longer the woman he married, no longer the unflappable helpmate who knew what he needed before he needed it. Wanting the old Betsy back, he had no idea how to make that happen. Talking about how they had handled their daughter's unfortunate situation, reconsidering the wisdom of the Hefty Bag Solution, never occurred to him. Running errands together, however, seemed like a step in the right direction, and it was way easier than reexamining his values or his parenting skills. Besides, going to the grocery store was a pleasant distraction, like visiting a food museum where every iteration of food known to man was displayed in brightly colored packages, all vying for his attention and his money. It blew him away that there were nearly a dozen different kinds of raisin bran. Running into Grace had spoiled his tour of salad dressings and condiments.

"Daddy, hi." Grace smiled up at her father, hoping that an unplanned meeting might be just the thing to start the mending of their fractured family. At the very least, maybe Brad would be more loquacious than Betsy.

"Oh, Grace, it's you," he said, nonplussed, staring straight at the swelling under Grace's shirt.

Bile rose in his throat as his brain thought about how his little girl had ended up in this condition. Images of sweaty bodies entwined in the back seat of a car, his daughter's bra hanging from the rearview mirror, moans of illicit pleasure, invaded his brain. The saying was definitely true—out of sight, out of mind. Now he would never get this picture of his pregnant daughter out of his head. Secretly he had hoped that Grace wouldn't reappear until after the baby was gone, when she would look like a regular person, not like a slowly inflating Macy's Thanksgiving Day balloon.

"I was just telling Mom that I finished my applications. Senior year isn't terrible so far. I really like my AP Psych class." Always able to connect with her father on the topic of school, Grace hoped that his internal geek wouldn't be able to resist a chat about neurotransmitters and mental illness.

Betsy continued to stand, holding tight to her shopping cart, looking like a department store mannequin except for her periodic blinking. Brad, however, had not been rendered paralyzed by the unexpected appearance of their daughter. "About that, Grace. Where did you end up applying?"

Perhaps the cold shoulder had begun to melt. Grace's hopes soared. Maybe that bullshit about time being the great healer wasn't bullshit after all. "I applied to Princeton, Penn, Dartmouth, Georgetown, University of Chicago, and NYU."

"That's ambitious. Those are some pricey colleges. Have you considered how you plan on paying for one of those schools, assuming you even get in?" Brad said, still staring at Grace's stomach, refusing to look her in the face.

There was nothing remotely warm or encouraging in Brad's voice. So much for a thaw. His chill tone sounded more like the dawn of a nuclear winter.

"I hadn't really thought about it. I've been too busy writing essays and keeping up with my schoolwork."

Her father sighed histrionically and said, "Well that's not too bright, is it? Did you assume your mother and I were going to pay for it?"

Grace shrugged. Feeling her father's eyes burning into her belly, she crossed her arms protectively and looked pleadingly at her mother, who remained catatonic and surgically attached to the cart.

"Robert Louis Stevenson said something about everyone eventually having to sit down to a banquet of consequences. Grace, I think your table is ready. Bon appétit." Brad had read that quote in a book on financial planning the week before, and he smiled to himself at his own cleverness. "Betsy, I'll meet you at the car. I need to stop at the drugstore."

Without a backward glance, he sauntered away, as if he had just run into his accountant, rather than his estranged and very pregnant daughter to whom he had just spoken for the first time in months. To Brad, this ability to move through life without being burdened by sentimentality was a gift. It would be many years before he realized how much he had missed.

Not knowing what else to do after having been so mightily dissed, Grace bent down and retrieved the runaway lemons. At least she knew where she stood now. Based on her father's reaction, Grace understood that this feud could outlast all of them.

"Bye, Mom." Grace briefly placed her hand on her mother's shoulder and then walked quickly away, leaving Betsy in front of a huge bin of walnuts, a single tear rolling down her otherwise expressionless face.

Trembling from head to toe and unsure whether she could safely drive home, Grace had sat for a few minutes, trying to slow her breathing and her hammering heart. Looking down, she realized she had walked out without paying for the lemons, but she was too upset to go back. A second encounter with her stone-faced mother would surely do her in.

Grace sat back in her chair. Repeating the story was enough to get her adrenaline pumping. "So I don't think they're planning on helping me."

"That's such a sad story. You poor little thing. Well, based on that," said Mrs. Evans, "I think your only shot is to go the emancipation route. It's unlikely you're going to find two hundred thousand dollars in change between the couch cushions."

"I'll think about it over Christmas vacation. Thank you for listening, Mrs. Evans."

"No problem, Grace. Try to have a merry Christmas." Giving Grace a hug, Mrs. Evans doubted that was possible.

Talking to her counselor about that day at the market was a relief, because Grace had never told Helen about the lemon encounter. It would only make her hostess and savior more sorry, more worried, more determined to compensate for Betsy and Brad's shortcomings. Although Grace hadn't intended on telling Charlie either, that proved impossible as Charlie took one look at her face when she returned home and forced her to spill the beans, which she did only after she made him swear he wouldn't tell anyone, especially Helen.

After dinner on what would have been Christmas Eve at Grace's house, but was just a regular winter evening in the Teitelbaum home, Helen and Grace sat in the solarium, drinking herbal tea and listening to the rain pounding on the glass ceiling. "Grace, darling, I want to talk to you about something."

"Of course, Mrs. T. Is everything okay?" Grace asked, suddenly worried that she'd done something wrong and ruined this wonderful friendship.

"Everything's fine. I just want to talk to you about next year. You know that Abe and I were never blessed with children, and the closest I have to a grandchild is Charlie. It would be my honor to help you in whatever way I can, which includes sending you to college."

Charlie's promise to Grace not to divulge her run-in with her parents had been a hollow one, and he had told Helen everything, including the bit about divorcing Betsy and Brad. It made Helen sad that Grace hadn't felt comfortable sharing her burden, but she understood Grace's reluctance was not a result of a secretive personality, but rather that she didn't want to look like she was asking for money. The hardest part was going to be getting Grace to agree to let Helen help her.

"How did you know about . . . ."

Grace could hardly believe her ears. She was seriously considering the emancipation option, especially after her father had made it clear where he stood. And if that didn't work out, she could always get a job and go to community college. Lots of people managed to get an education that way. At this point, Grace knew she needed to be flexible. Her old dreams about ivy-covered buildings and classes with Nobel Prize–winning professors might be destined to remain dreams, and that was okay. Life was playing out differently than she had thought, but she was learning to take each day as it came. Having to take a detour didn't mean she wasn't going to get there—it just might take a little longer, and the road might not be as scenic as she had hoped.

"Charlie told me. Don't be mad at him. He's so fond of you, and he rightly felt I should know what was going on with you."

"But just because I'm staying with you doesn't mean that you have to solve all of my problems," Grace said.

"Listen to me. I have lots and lots of money, and I can't take it with me. Using it to help people while I'm still alive makes me happy. Don't you want me to be happy, Grace?" Helen's eyes were bright in the light of the candles scattered about the room.

"But you've already done so much for me. I can't accept any more." Mrs. Teitelbaum's generosity was boundless, and Grace vowed she would try to be as giving as this extraordinary woman, with whatever she had to give. "My guidance counselor said I can go to court and get emancipated from my parents, and then I'll probably get financial aid from whatever college I get into, assuming I get in anywhere." Although Grace definitely had the grades, she was suffering a global crisis of confidence, and it wouldn't surprise her if, like her parents, every college in the country rejected her.

"You don't need to do that. Someday your parents will come to their senses. I promise you they will. It may take a long time, but they will come around. And in the meantime, we can help each other," Helen said.

"How could I ever help you?" At this point, Grace felt her only contribution to the world was to make other people feel better about their own lives, but from what Grace had seen so far, Mrs. T. had a pretty fabulous life, except for World War II and the loss of her family, and what could Grace do about that?

"You've helped me more than you know, my dove. You are a very special person. Trust me—I know about these things. And think of it like this. I was going to give that money away anyway. Better I should write a check to help some strangers? I can't imagine a more worthwhile way to spend my money . . . and even if I end up putting you through medical school, there will still be plenty left. It's not like I'm going to be eating dog food anytime soon." Helen wrinkled her nose. "My dear, Abe left me in a *very* comfortable position. College tuition will not break the bank."

More tears, of joy and relief this time, rushed down Grace's cheeks, mingling with Helen's as the two hugged and kissed. "Thank you, Mrs. T. Thank you for everything."

"You're so welcome. There is one thing you could do for me, though."

"Anything."

"Please stop calling me Mrs. T. I'm Aunt Helen, or just Helen. Okay?"

"Okay . . . Aunt Helen," Grace sniffled.

"I'll call Sidney in the morning, just to make sure. He'll tell us what to do, and then he'll take care of everything." Helen jotted down a few words on the pad of paper she always kept in her pocket. "All we'll have to do is wait for the acceptance letters, so he knows where to send the check."

"Sidney?"

"Sidney Schneidman, of Schneidman, Schwartz, and Smith. He's my lawyer and accountant. I haven't bothered him in a while. Let him earn his retainer." This was exciting. Writing large checks to charities to benefit thousands of anonymous people all over the world felt good, but looking directly into the eyes of someone who needed a helping hand and telling her that everything was going to work out, at least financially—the sensation was beyond satisfying. Granted, Grace wasn't underprivileged in the traditional way, but in Helen's mind she was no less needy than the starving urchin dressed in rags and running barefoot through the streets of Calcutta.

CHAPTER 18

"Today you're going to meet four of the couples you picked out of the book. Remember, you don't have to decide on the spot, and if you don't like any of these people, we can keep looking," Janet explained, hoping to alleviate some of the nerves that were visible in Grace's hunched shoulders and uneven breathing.

"But how will I know if they're the ones? On paper, they're all pretty perfect."

There was no greater responsibility than choosing the two people who would be raising her child. What if she failed to notice that the would-be dad was an alcoholic, or the mom wasn't just organized, but had obsessive-compulsive disorder? What if someday the couple she chose had a biological child? Would they love this baby less because she wasn't their flesh and blood? Desperate to find a way to think of all the potential pitfalls so she could protect the bean forever, Grace was on the verge of a full-fledged panic attack.

"You'll know. Every girl wonders how she'll be able to choose the right parents, but it's just a feeling you'll have. I'm not sure how to explain it, but I've seen it happen over and over."

In all the years Janet had been doing this, only one young woman found it impossible to select adoptive parents for her baby—each couple was almost, but not quite, right. Ultimately she ended up keeping the child, which was no surprise. In her heart, the girl had never made the decision to give the baby up in the first place. As long as the birth mother was certain about the adoption process, it worked out.

"As long as *you're* sure, I guess I'll get there," Grace said, still unconvinced.

"That's my girl. Ah, there they are, the Perez family."

"I feel like I'm on some bizarre game show, and Molly's the grand prize, but I already know I've lost," Grace mumbled, wondering if this was the couple who would be taking her place.

Once pleasantries had been exchanged, the three adults and one-and-a-half children sat at Janet's conference table, awkwardly trying to get to know each other. "So, Grace, please feel free to ask Carlos and Margaret whatever you want," Janet said, trying to get the ball rolling.

Sometimes things just clicked, but more often both sides were struck dumb, afraid of saying the wrong thing. For the potential parents, this meeting was like the ultimate job interview. Teenagers were touchy creatures: a single word taken the wrong way, and they would be out on the street, still desperate, still childless.

"Well, all I really want to know is if you'll love her with all your heart, and if you ever have a child naturally, will you still love her as much?" Grace had decided that was all that really mattered. Whether they were church regulars or agnostics, Democrats or Republicans, meat-eaters or vegans—none of that made any difference. The only question was whether they would love Molly completely and without reservation, no matter what.

"Of course," Margaret and Carlos said simultaneously. "We've been trying to have a baby for a long time, but it looks like it's not going to happen the old-fashioned way, so here we are," Margaret said.

This kid was really pretty, and according to Janet, a brilliant student as well. Wondering about the competition in this race for a baby, Margaret was desperate to say whatever it was this girl needed to hear to seal the deal.

Two hours later, Janet peered at Grace. "Are you sure you're up to one more? I can easily reschedule. The Millers are in town until tomorrow."

"No, I'm fine. Making small talk, trying to analyze every word, figure out who's the right one—it's really hard, and tiring, but I just want to finish."

"So, any vibes? Do you think you've met the parents of your baby?"

"Honestly, I don't know yet."

"My grandmother always said a good night's sleep makes everything clearer. You need time to sift through everything you've heard," said Janet. "Here they are. Ready?"

"As ready as I'll ever be," said Grace, knowing full well she wasn't ready for most of what had happened to her since July second.

Awkwardly making her way to a standing position—Mrs. Olson's chairs were comfortable, but deep and low—Grace looked up into the faces of the two people she suddenly knew were going to be Molly's parents. It was like the first time she'd laid eyes on Charlie—a feeling of recognition. Something about them struck her as familiar and comfortable. Was this the sensation that Mrs. Olson had been describing?

"Grace, thank you so much for meeting with us. We saw your picture, and we felt like we knew you. It was so strange." Rebecca Miller took Grace's hands in hers and gazed warmly at her, knowing that empty chatter wasn't necessary. There was no uneasiness to compensate for.

Not expecting such a powerful connection, such a sudden certainty, and worried that her palms must be sticky and sweaty, Grace answered, "Me, too."

"Shall we all sit down and get to know each other?" Janet hadn't missed the electricity that had passed between Grace and Rebecca. There would be no need to keep searching. Bringing people together for adoption was in a way not that much different from running a dating service. What attracted people to one another went beyond the physical or the intellectual; some intangible bond that defied reason seemed to apply to adoption as well as marriage.

Not really needing to ask any questions, Grace felt she owed it to Mrs. Olson to go through the motions. "Do you think you'll keep trying to have a biological child after you adopt a baby?"

"We found out last year that we can't make a baby," Michael said, taking his wife's hand and smiling sadly.

"I'm really sorry," Grace said, now knowing for sure that the Millers were the ones. Inside her, Molly kicked—the decision was unanimous.

CHAPTER 19

Evidence of her cardinal sin was straining against her sweatshirt. Thirty-four weeks into her pregnancy, Grace felt like a planet with stretch marks and swollen ankles. Dirty looks and snide insults uttered in hushed tones had been replaced with outright rubbernecking and really loud cheap shots: "Nice abs, Warren!" and "Beep! Beep! Beep!" like the sound of a truck backing up. Nobody thought it was bullying because getting pregnant wasn't like having a stutter or a lazy eye—getting knocked up had been Grace's own fault. She had gotten herself into this fix, and now she had to stand there and take it. When she walked down the hall, the crowd parted like the Red Sea, everyone wanting to get a good look but no one wanting to touch her, like they thought that pregnancy was contagious.

Knocking frantically on Mrs. Evans's office door, Grace tried to keep herself from hyperventilating. Her heart was racing after navigating the hallway of condemnation. Not that the taunting had been any different yesterday or the week before, but the straw had broken the camel's back, and she couldn't take it for another minute.

Mrs. Evans flung open her office door. "Grace, what's the matter? Did something happen?" Eyes shiny with tears, face bright red, Grace looked like she was going into labor.

"I can't stay here anymore. It's too hard."

"You're okay? The baby's okay?" Unequipped to handle emergencies beyond the hysteria students experienced when they were rejected by their first-choice college, Mrs. Evans reached for the phone. Her first aid skills were definitely a little rusty. She knew you were supposed to boil water when someone was having a baby, but she couldn't remember why.

"The baby's fine. I'm fine." Grace's voice was hoarse with pain, but not the kind that came from contractions.

Mrs. Evans collapsed into her chair with a sigh of relief. "Thank goodness. Then come in and sit down." She handed Grace a bottle of water and said, "Have a drink, and tell me what happened."

"Everyone stares at me and laughs all day long, and I can't concentrate on school. I feel like I have three heads or something. I don't think I can deal with being a circus freak for the next six weeks." Tears coursed silently down Grace's cheeks. Spending most of her lunch hour every day crying in a bathroom stall, Grace had perfected the art of bawling without making a sound.

"Oh, Grace, I'm so sorry. I wish I could slap each and every one of those brats and tell them to tuck their eyeballs back into their heads, but I'm afraid I can't do anything about it. You'll just have to muscle through, or . . . ."

"Or what? I can't muscle through. I really tried, and I thought I could do it, but I can't." Even though she was in the final act of her nine-month pregnancy play, the days seemed to be getting longer, and Grace was beginning to question her sanity.

"I get it. Kids can be incredibly mean. You could do independent study at home. With your grades, it probably wouldn't be a problem to get approval. Other girls in your situation have gone to a night program in Chester, but they don't offer any AP courses, so that wouldn't work." Most girls in Grace's position were headed to beauty school or a cashier job at the local Walmart. None of the unfortunate girls Mrs. Evans had counseled over the years had been taking five AP classes and applying to Princeton.

"I promise I won't let my grades drop. With the Internet, I'll be able to send in all my papers and keep up with the assignments. Please, Mrs. Evans, don't make me go back out there." Grace sat on the edge of her chair, leaning towards her counselor's desk, beseeching Mrs. Evans with her body as well as her words.

Knowing she couldn't abandon this poor girl who was clearly at the end of her rope, Mrs. Evans said, "Fine. Let's try it. I'll send a memo to your teachers. I doubt they'll mind. I've heard whispers in the faculty room that your, um, condition is a little distracting to the other students, so I'm sure everyone will make a sincere effort to make your homeschooling work."

"Thank you so much. I knew school would be bad, but I didn't think it would be this awful."

"I think that because you are who you are, your pregnancy is more—how do I say this—interesting to your fellow students than if you were just any girl. You do realize you're probably the last person anyone would expect to turn up pregnant," Mrs. Evans said.

"I was the last person *I* would expect to get pregnant, but that doesn't make it any less horrible to deal with," said Grace.

"Teenagers are cruel, there's no doubt about that, and when a girl who is otherwise perfect—smart, beautiful, nice—stumbles, you're going to get a lot of attention and a certain amount of schadenfreude. It's not fair, but it *is* human nature."

"Schadenfreude? You really think me being pregnant is making other people happy because I'm *me*?" Grace was dumbfounded. "I'm getting worse treatment because I was the teachers' pet? I just thought they were being cruel because that's how kids are."

"Unfortunately, on some level I think that your accomplishments, your specialness, have made you a compelling target."

"That's the dumbest thing I've ever heard," Grace said. Kids she didn't even know were teasing her, pointing and laughing as she struggled down the hallway, belly sticking out in front, backpack behind.

"Jealousy is a pretty basic emotion, and although I doubt you were ever aware of it, a lot of people were jealous of you."

"Jealous of *me*? That's impossible. Who would be jealous of a misfit like me?"

"You may see yourself that way, but that's not how your classmates see you. Take my word. As a guidance counselor, I hear everything. For some reason, kids think they can say anything to me. It's like this office is a confessional."

In spite of the fact that Mrs. Evans's primary duty was to ferry students through high school in the context of college applications, most kids treated her like their own personal psychologist, seeking her advice about boy trouble, bullying, and birth control. No matter how many times she referred them to the school psychologist or the nurse's office, they would inevitably wander back in, only sometimes taking the trouble to ask her a question about the SAT before launching into the real reason for their visit.

"I wish I'd known that before," Grace muttered, mostly to herself. If she'd had more self-confidence, she likely wouldn't have gotten herself into this dreadful situation. If only she'd been less concerned with what other people thought about her, especially when she'd been totally wrong about what they'd been thinking.

"One thing I've heard many times over the last few years is how kids look up to you, what you've achieved. Unfortunately, that also means they feel better about themselves when you fall." Trying to explain the mixed-up adolescent mind to a very mixed-up adolescent was like trying to explain the terrible twos to a toddler.

"Great. I tried to get a boyfriend so I would be less of a loser, when nobody actually thought I was a loser, but now, because I was totally clueless and insecure, I really *am* a loser," Grace said.

"Just because you made a mistake—and it was a doozy, don't get me wrong—it doesn't make you a loser. You have to believe that," Mrs. Evans said.

"But I can't see my feet anymore, and people make foghorn sounds when I walk down the hall."

"It's all just temporary. In not so many weeks, your life will start to get back to normal. Just be patient for a little longer."

"Each day feels like a year," Grace sighed.

"Look, you have my permission to hide out until this is over. I agree that your mental health is important, and I'm sure you can handle the workload on your own with no trouble. But I expect to see you back here in April . . . afterwards."

"Okay. I really appreciate you backing me up, Mrs. Evans. I promise I'll work really hard," Grace answered, although at that moment she couldn't imagine ever going back.

"You'd better. Those AP exams in May are for real. If you mess those up, you could jeopardize your college acceptances."

"I know." Grace stood to leave, and Mrs. Evans came around from behind her desk, arms outstretched. Grace was one of the good ones, and she was sorry to see her go.

"Good luck, Grace. You're in the home stretch. Just hang on. Call me if you need anything."

"I will. Bye."

Although Grace had gone to Mrs. Evans so that she could withdraw from school, now that she had done it, she felt sad and kind of scared. Grace hadn't discussed it with Helen beforehand, fearing she would talk her out of it, but now that it was done, Grace wondered if she'd taken the coward's way out. Now she had to go back to the house and break the news to Helen and Charlie.

"Okay, if that's what you want to do," Helen said when Grace told her, clearly surprised, but as usual, not judging or scolding. "They're going to send your work home?"

"Everything is online, so as long as I have my computer, I can do all the work, and Mrs. Evans said the teachers will send me the tests. Since I've always been a good student, I don't think anyone's worried about me cheating."

Charlie was less receptive. "But you look fine, and who cares if a few morons act like a bunch of ten-year-olds? You shouldn't quit school just because of them." In truth, Charlie was going to miss driving back and forth with her every day.

"Thank you, but I look like the Goodyear blimp, and it's more than just a few. Every day feels like a public stoning, and I can't even focus on what the teachers are saying anymore. What's the point of going to school just so I can have a nervous breakdown in the cafeteria?"

"Grace is right, Charlie. No matter how sympathetic you are, you can't possibly imagine what she's going through. Besides, the decision has been made, and it's our job to support Grace in whatever she does. That means you can bring home her work from school and help Grace however you can," Helen instructed. When she put it that way, Charlie realized Grace's hermit period might not be so bad.

It had been a long day. Dropping out of school had been exhausting. "I think I'm going to turn in early. I don't think I've ever been so tired in my entire life."

"You do look like you could use a good night's sleep, dear. Everything will look brighter in the morning. I promise," said Helen, opening her arms for a hug. Dr. Needleman always said that nothing was more therapeutic than the touch of another human being, and Grace needed to feel that she was loved, even if it wasn't the loving embrace of her parents.

"Thank Vera for a delicious dinner. Night, Charlie." As Grace passed his chair, she briefly rested her hand on his cheek and he tipped his head back, smiling sadly, wishing for the thousandth time that he could do something to take away Grace's pain.

"Goodnight, Grace. Sleep well."

He wanted to run upstairs and tuck her in, but he realized that might frighten her. Although he knew he needed to stow his emotions on a high shelf, Charlie was having trouble compartmentalizing. Every time he looked at Grace or heard her voice, he thought of their incredible kiss in the attic. It had been etched in his brain, and no matter how hard he tried to ignore it, the feel of her, the taste of her, flashed through his mind. Knowing he was acting like a girl who couldn't get over her first kiss, Charlie wondered what it had meant to her. He watched Grace trudge up the stairs, desperate to know if she spent half as much time thinking about him as he spent thinking about her.

When she heard Grace's bedroom door shut, Helen said, "You like her, don't you?"

She wasn't at all sure whether or not she should even broach the subject. How many teenage boys would be willing to discuss their love lives with their old widowed aunts? The last thing she wanted to do was make her cherished nephew uncomfortable.

"Is it that obvious?" Charlie had thought he'd been hiding his emotions pretty well.

"All those longing glances? I can practically see the little hearts floating over your head."

Thinking back to the early days of her relationship with Abraham, Helen sighed. That feeling was probably the thing she missed most about being young. If her heart started to pound at her age, she would be more likely to think she was having a heart attack than falling in love. But she would give anything to experience that again, even for just a moment.

"Are you mad at me?" If Helen disapproved, Charlie wasn't sure what he would do. As much as he cared about Grace, it would break his heart to disappoint his aunt.

"Why would I be angry?" Helen asked.

"Well, she's not Jewish, she's pregnant, her parents have disowned her—the girl has a few issues." Although on paper Grace was radioactive, Charlie was transfixed by the real, live girl.

"That she does, but she's a wonderful person, and I firmly believe that a person should not be judged for any single act, and certainly not for the acts of her parents. Grace is much more than a young girl who's gotten herself into trouble. Besides, you can't control what your heart feels, can you?" Helen ruffled Charlie's hair.

She didn't have a problem with her nephew falling in love with a semi-homeless, pregnant *shiksa*, but she wasn't so sure his parents would be so open-minded. Having seen the worst of human nature during the war, Helen wasn't one to get bogged down in the minutiae of religious differences and social convention. Life was short, and such prejudices were nothing more than a waste of precious time. But not many people, thank goodness, had witnessed hell on earth, and therefore few people possessed Helen's clarity. As much as she regretted having gotten caught up in the horrors of the war, her childhood literally up in smoke courtesy of the Nazis, it did have one major benefit: it allowed her to view the world completely without preconception or intolerance.

"I can't. And it's not just like; I think I love her." Charlie hadn't meant to say that out loud, but if anyone would understand, it was Helen.

"Have you told her that?" Helen asked

"Of course not. I kissed her, though, and I think that scared her, so I'm kind of in a holding pattern until the baby comes."

"Probably a good idea to take things slow. She has about as much as she can handle right now."

"Besides, how do I even know I'm really in love with her, or is it just that I think she's beautiful and I'm caught up in all her drama?" Charlie desperately wanted to sort out his feelings, and as bizarre as it was to be talking about his love life with his eighty-year-old great-aunt, she understood him better than anyone else.

"You've never felt like this about a girl before?" Helen was quite enjoying this conversation. That Charlie felt close enough to her to confide his most deeply felt emotions thrilled her beyond measure, and she wanted to offer him the support and guidance he deserved. But as it had been so many years since she'd felt those first pangs of falling in love—all the confusion and insecurities—she wondered if she had the expertise needed for the job.

"Never. I can't stop thinking about her." Images of Grace in yards of white silk and himself in a tuxedo, dancing on his aunt's terrace, tiny lights shimmering in all the trees, floated through his mind on a nearly daily basis. He knew it was beyond abnormal for a guy to daydream about his wedding day, especially with a pregnant girl he'd only known for six months, but he couldn't help himself.

Trying to remember how she had felt more than half a century earlier, Helen said, "Well, at your age that could just be hormones. If you're attracted to her, it could be easy to confuse sex and love."

When Abe had proposed, exactly fourteen days after they'd met, Helen wondered how he could have fallen in love with her that quickly. At that point she didn't even know what that kind of love felt like. Perhaps he just wanted to go to bed with her, and in those days nice girls didn't give it up until their wedding night, which didn't leave horny, well-bred young men with too many options. Although she soon realized that he loved her body and soul, it wasn't so clear at the beginning.

Charlie blushed. Maybe this wasn't such a good idea. But it wasn't like he could talk to his guy friends about having the hots for a girl who was having some other guy's baby. "I've been physically attracted to girls before, but this is totally different. It's not just the way she looks; it's all of me needing to be with her. I'm already missing her, thinking about her going to a different college."

"You've got it bad, kiddo. But I can't fault you for falling in love with her. I love her, too—it's as if she's the granddaughter I was supposed to have. I guess she's just our type." *What an adorable couple they would make, and what beautiful babies they would have someday*, Helen thought.

"What about Mom and Dad? They're not like you, Aunt Helen. They're going to be furious when they hear about her." Charlie paused. "You haven't told my parents, have you?"

"Just the vaguest details. But I didn't spill the beans about you having feelings for Grace. That's your job to tell them, if and when you want to." Charlie was almost eighteen. He could manage his own business. But if it ever came to that, Helen would do everything in her power to convince Charlie's parents that Grace was worthy of Charlie's, and their, love.

"Do you think Grace might love me back?" Charlie asked. Although he knew she liked him, seemed to be as attracted to him as he was to her, he wasn't sure she had the capacity to fall in love, at least for the time being.

"I think so, even if she doesn't know it yet. Just be there for her, in whatever way she needs you. When all the noise in her life goes away, you'll be holding her hand, and she'll see all of you. At that moment, how could she *not* fall in love with you?" Helen pinched Charlie's cheek and smiled mischievously at him.

"Thank you for listening, Aunt Helen. How did you get so good at this? You would have made a great mother."

"That's the highest compliment you could have paid me. I love you, dear boy, and I'm so glad you came to stay with me. I'm having the most wonderful time."

"Goodnight, Aunt Helen."

"Goodnight, sweetie. And don't worry so much. Lord knows, it won't change anything." Helen clicked on the television. "I'm just going to watch a little *Masterpiece Theatre* before I go up. Sleep tight."

Staring at his reflection in the bathroom mirror, Charlie debated with himself. *You owe her an apology. It can wait until morning. But what if she's upset? You just want to see her without a bra on, you pervert.* He knocked gently on Grace's door. Not sure what he was going to say, he knew that he couldn't go to sleep without talking to her.

"Come in."

Grace was already in bed, reading a book. In a pale pink nightgown, with her dark hair lying in swirls on the white pillowcase, Charlie thought she looked like an angel. He had never seen her look more beautiful.

"I just wanted to apologize for earlier. I shouldn't have said anything. Of course I can't begin to imagine what you've been going through at school." Charlie took a step into Grace's room, wanting more than anything to crawl into bed with her and wondering how he could make that happen.

"It's nothing. And you're right, I shouldn't let people I don't even care about make important decisions for me, but I'm just so tired." Grace sighed and put her book on the nightstand.

"I'll let you go to sleep," Charlie said.

"No, please don't go. Do you want to sit with me for a while?" Patting the bed next to her, Grace nodded. "Would you read to me?"

"Of course." Charlie gingerly sat down on the edge of the bed and picked up Grace's book. "*Mansfield Park*?"

"It's the only Jane Austen I haven't read yet. You look like you're about to fall off. Come over here. Get comfortable," Grace said, propping a pillow against the headboard next to her.

Charlie stretched out next to Grace. "Okay, here goes." He hadn't read out loud to anyone since the third grade. When he came to the end of the chapter, he looked over at Grace to see if she was asleep. "Do you want me to stop?"

"If you want," Grace said, and yawned.

"You need your rest. Goodnight, Grace."

Leaning over, Charlie intended to kiss Grace's cheek, but she turned her head at just the right moment, and his mouth met hers. Knowing he should pull away, that they had agreed to wait until after the baby was born to try this again, Charlie was unable to stop. And when Grace made that sweet little meowing sound and opened her mouth to his, he let himself go. Her body was rounder and riper than it had been that first time, and his hands were desperate to explore. With one hand tangled in her hair, Charlie let his other hand slip inside Grace's nightgown. He knew what he was doing was wrong, was probably illegal in some countries, but he kept going, kissing his way down her neck, not stopping until his tongue was teasing her nipples. Grace moaned in his ear. He was nearly ready to come just from the sounds she was making.

"Grace," he breathed. "I . . . ."

Charlie's voice snapped Grace back to reality, and she pushed him away. "Charlie, we can't."

She could hardly catch her breath, and from the neck down, the last thing she wanted to do was stop, but in her heart she knew they would both regret carrying this to its logical conclusion. It was not the right time, no matter how incredible it felt.

Jerking upright and leaping off the bed, as if it had metamorphosed into a red-hot stove, Charlie turned away from Grace so that she wouldn't see his hard-on, which hadn't yet gotten the message that storytime was over. "I'm so sorry. Please, Grace, you have to forgive me. I didn't come in here to do that. I swear."

"I know that, Charlie. You didn't do anything wrong. I was right there with you," Grace said, pulling the sheet up to her neck, the tingle of Charlie's mouth on her breasts lingering like a delicious phantom pain. Still unable to believe that he could look at her, let alone touch her, in her puffed up state, she wanted to laugh out loud. The most perfect boy in the world wanted her, bloated body and all. "It's okay."

"No, it's not. I promised not to bother you, and then I attacked you." His hands splayed ineffectively over his crotch, Charlie couldn't shut off the movie of their too-brief love scene that was already replaying in his head.

"Stop." Grace felt hot all over, and her heart continued to pound. "Go to bed, Charlie."

"But . . . ."

Grace had to giggle at Charlie's obvious distress. "Go take care of yourself. I'll see you in the morning." She blew him a kiss and turned off the light.

CHAPTER 20

When Grace awoke from a dream in which she had peed in her pants in front of the entire student body of Silver Lake High School, she realized that while she was not standing in front of a thousand howling teenagers, she was still soaking wet. On top of all the other humiliations she had suffered in the last nine months, now she could add bedwetting to the list. But as she floated up through layers of sleep, she realized that it was the first of April, and the doctor had told her that her water could break at any time. Thank goodness. But if her water had broken, that meant she was in labor. Molly was on the way. Grace tried to stay calm, reminding herself that this was perfectly natural, exactly what was supposed to happen. Her efforts to soothe herself failing, Grace looked at the bedside clock: 3:45 A.M.

She tiptoed into Helen's room and stood by the bed, staring down at the tiny sleeping form, still wondering whether this could wait until a more civilized hour—she had already inconvenienced Helen in so many ways—when her belly seized up in a single enormous contraction. "Argh!" As hard as she'd tried to control it, the groan slipped out between her gritted teeth.

Helen sat up straight and looked around. "Sweetie, what's wrong? Are you in labor?" Having mentally prepared herself for this precise moment for weeks, she felt like a rookie fireman hearing the alarm bell, about to slide down the pole on the way to her first real fire. It was simultaneously exhilarating and terrifying. But she knew she needed to put on a calm front for Grace, make her feel like everything was under control. Throwing back the blankets, Helen leaped to her feet, ready for duty. In anticipation of just such a middle-of-the-night emergency, she had been sleeping in a sweatsuit for the last two weeks, so she wouldn't have to waste precious time getting dressed and could focus all of her attention on getting Grace to the hospital. Aware that she didn't move as quickly as she used to, Helen didn't want to risk Grace giving birth in the car because an old lady's arthritic fingers took forever to button her shirt.

"I think my water broke. Either I'm in labor, or something's really wrong. Helen, I'm scared," Grace whimpered, tears streaming down her face, more from fear than from pain.

"You're going to be just fine, my darling. Remember what Dr. Weston said. Everybody gets through it. And I'll be with you all the way."

Soothed by Helen's reassuring words, Grace rallied. "Okay, my suitcase is downstairs. I guess we should go."

Helen grabbed her cell phone and dialed the doctor's answering service as she took Grace's hand and led her back to her room. "You're drenched, dear. First let's get you into some dry clothes, and *then* we'll go."

Five minutes later they were in the car on the way to the hospital. "How are you feeling now?" Helen drove with one hand on the wheel and the other one stroking Grace's arm. "Don't forget to breathe."

"It still hurts a lot, but not as bad as before," Grace said, not sure she was going to be able to make it through without drugs.

"Were we supposed to be timing the contractions?" asked Helen. There were so many details to remember, and she had left her little notepad on her nightstand. Now she would have to wing it.

"Probably."

"It doesn't really matter. The book said that if your water breaks you should go to the hospital. We'll let them figure everything out. That's what doctors are for." As they pulled up in front of the emergency room, an orderly magically appeared with a wheelchair. Five-star treatment, for sure, and Helen briefly wondered if everyone got that kind of service, or whether the hospital staff had been put on notice after receiving her donation the previous week. It was a worthy cause, and as Sidney always said, it didn't hurt to grease the wheels.

CHAPTER 21

"You're six centimeters dilated and nearly eighty percent effaced," said the nurse as she withdrew a gloved hand from under the sheet. "You're more than halfway there. Good job."

As intense as the pain was, like a giant fist clenching and unclenching inside of her, Grace had thus far refused an epidural. Partly because she didn't want Molly exposed to any drugs, and she had heard that a spinal block could slow down her labor. But more than that, Grace viewed each searing contraction as part of her punishment for getting herself into this mess. Experiencing every second of this gut-wrenching agony was exactly what she deserved, and if she managed to get through it without folding, she might be able to forgive herself for her dreadful mistake and move forward with her life.

Helen put down the magazine she had been pretending to read and came over to the bed. "Grace, you don't have to be a hero, you know. Everybody gets an epidural."

"I know, but it's not that bad," Grace said, her voice raspy with the effort. It was more than that bad, and as every hour passed there were fewer minutes of relief between the contractions. Her insides felt as if they were twisting themselves into a Gordian knot.

Grace's paler-than-usual skin told Helen that Grace was lying, but she didn't say a word. Whatever Grace's reason for refusing medication, it was none of anyone's business, and before the advent of modern medicine everybody had natural childbirth, so as unpleasant as it appeared to be, it wasn't impossible to endure. Hopefully, if it couldn't be pain-free, at least it would be quick.

"If you change your mind, let me know, and I'll have the anesthesiologist here in one minute, okay?"

"Okay," Grace said, once again grateful for this magical old lady who had rescued her like an abandoned dog found at the side of the road, feeding her and loving her like her own. She wondered if Betsy and Brad knew she was in the hospital.

Once again displaying a flash of clairvoyance, Helen asked, "Do you want me to call your parents and let them know what's happening?"

In fact, Helen had already called the Warrens and left a message on their answering machine informing them that the birth of their granddaughter was imminent. That was three hours earlier, and there hadn't been any response. Apparently time did *not* heal all wounds. If Grace wanted them, however, Helen would call Sidney and he would have one of his guys kidnap them and drag them to the hospital. Whatever Grace wanted.

"No, I doubt they'd want to be here, and this is hard enough without worrying about what they're thinking," Grace said, grimacing as another contraction stabbed her body. If girls knew how excruciating labor pain was, they would never have sex.

Helen's phone rang, but it was Charlie, not the Warrens. "Helen, is everything okay? I just found your note." When Charlie had woken up that morning, he had found Helen's note (drafted two weeks earlier as part of her baby preparation: *Dear Charlie, The big day has arrived. Have taken Grace to the hospital. Love, H*), and now he was in the car on the way to the hospital.

"Everything's fine, darling. Grace is doing beautifully. She is so incredibly brave." Helen paused, listening. "I'll ask her. Charlie would love to come and hold your hand, but he understands if you don't want him here."

Grateful that Charlie had the good sense not to just show up, Grace shook her head. “I don’t want him to see me like this. Thank him for me, but could he wait until it’s over before he comes?”

“Of course, sweetheart. Charlie, I’ll call you, okay? I think this is kind of a girls’ outing today, you know?”

“I understand. Tell her I love her,” Charlie said, disappointed that he wouldn’t be there to help her through it, but hopeful that she would want to see him afterward.

“I’ll let you tell her yourself, later. I love you, sweet boy. Bye.”

When Helen hung up the phone, Grace said, “I don’t want to hurt Charlie’s feelings. It’s just that I don’t want him to see me so out of control. He’ll never be able to forget this moment, and I don’t want a screaming, sweaty, bloody blob to be his default image of me.”

“Don’t be silly, sweetie. He understands perfectly. All Charlie wants is what’s best for you. Trust me. He really cares about you.” Stopping short of telling Grace the whole truth, Helen was fairly certain that Grace reciprocated Charlie’s feelings. They just needed time to work it all out.

“I know, but he thinks I’m this fallen angel or something, like I was this perfect piece of crystal that Nick dropped and now I have a crack, and Charlie feels like it’s his job to glue all my pieces back together.”

“Charlie does come from a family of fixers. And the only reason he’s put you up on a pedestal is because he likes you so much. He just needs to learn that as much as he has enjoyed putting you up there, it’s no place for a girl to live.”

“That’s exactly right. I can’t be half as good as he thinks I am.”

“You are just the right amount of good, Grace Warren, and Charlie knows that. Men aren’t very good with their words, especially in a crisis. But just pay attention to how Charlie behaves, even if he’s saying all the wrong things, because his actions will show who he really is.” Even though Helen was certain Charlie would get there on his own, she couldn't resist helping things along.

"Do you know absolutely everything, Aunt Helen? Owwww, that hurts so much." Grace squirmed in the bed, but she could hardly move, because she was tethered to so many monitors—her heartbeat, the fetal heartbeat, blood pressure, IV.

"By the time you get to my age, darling, you've had plenty of time to make mistakes and figure things out. I wish you just such an education, my pet."

A knock at the door interrupted their heart-to-heart. "Come in," called Grace, hoping it was the doctor to tell her that Molly was ready to be born and the torture would be over in the next few minutes.

"Hi, ladies," said Janet. "How are you doing?"

"Okay, I guess." Determined not to cry, not to appear weak, Grace managed a tight-lipped smile.

"You're almost there. The Millers are in the waiting room, and when the baby leaves the delivery room, your job will be done."

Although she had witnessed literally hundreds of births, Janet was always floored by the guts these children had. Having a baby was stressful for a thirty-year-old woman with a husband and family to hold her hand, but these girls, for the most part, were getting the job done all by themselves. The strength of the human spirit was extraordinary.

Grace nodded. So lost in the pain and worried about how she was going to push something the size of a large chicken out of such a small opening, she had completely forgotten what was going to happen directly afterwards. Still uncertain whether she wanted to see Molly at all, not wanting to forge a bond that would immediately have to be severed, Grace still hadn't decided whether she should hold her daughter before she gave her up forever. Would she just be causing herself more pain if she kissed her hello and goodbye, or would she regret missing that opportunity for the rest of her life? If only there were someone who could tell her what to do.

"I'll see you after," Janet said, and went to sit with Rebecca and Michael in the waiting room.

Another knock on the door, and Jennifer marched in. "Your study buddy just called me, so I ditched school and here I am."

Not wanting to admit that she hadn't thought once about her best friend these last several hours, now Grace was glad she was here. "Hi," Grace moaned as another contraction tore through her body.

"Hello, Mrs. Teitelbaum. Nice to see you," Jennifer said, doing a little curtsy. There was something almost regal about the little old lady who was wearing her signature pearls with her pale blue velour tracksuit.

Helen smiled. "You too, dear. Thank you for coming, and I'm sorry I didn't call you myself. I left my list at home."

"No worries. You look like shit, babes," Jennifer said, turning back to Grace, taking in all the wires and beeping machinery.

"Thanks. You always know just the right thing to say to make me feel better." It hurt too much to laugh, but Grace was grateful for the distraction.

"So when do you have to do the magic trick?"

"Magic trick?" Grace asked, thinking she had misheard through the veil of pain.

"Yeah, when do you have to push the watermelon out of your—"

"What's the matter with you? Is my entire life just an excuse for you to make jokes?"

"Pretty much," Jennifer deadpanned.

"Well, I'm not fully dilated yet, but Dr. Weston said when I feel an uncontrollable urge to push, that means I'm ready."

"Yeah, I read in that baby book it's like taking a giant dump," Jennifer said.

Grace cleared her throat and looked meaningfully at Helen, who was smiling into the pages of the *New Yorker*. "Do you always have to say exactly what you're thinking?"

"Just trying to find the humor. I can see you want to laugh."

"Yes, that's exactly what I feel like doing right now," Grace grunted as her entire body stiffened with another contraction. "Owww, I feel it, I need to push! Helen, I think it's time. Please get Dr. Weston."

Helen jumped up. "Jennifer, press that red button. I'm going to find the doctor," she ordered as she sprinted out of the room.

"She moves pretty fast for an old bag," said Jennifer. Seeing the pain and fear in Grace's eyes, she said, "Hold my hand. We're going to get through this. Whatever you do, *don't* push. Otherwise *I'm* going to be the one catching the bean, and that would not be good."

A minute later, Dr. Weston dashed in, followed by a breathless Helen. "It sounds like someone's ready to have a baby," Dr. Weston said.

"Yes, right now. I need to push, so bad," Grace panted. "It hurts like crazy. I can't hold it in. Please let me push so the pain will go away."

"Okay, let's just have a look," said Dr. Weston as she slipped on latex gloves and lifted the sheet over Grace's legs. "Yes, ma'am, that baby is on her way. Mrs. Teitelbaum, and Grace's friend, do you want to help?"

"That's why we're here," Jennifer said. "What do we do?"

"Grace is going to push hard, and you're going to hold her feet so she has something to push against. Like this," said Dr. Weston, demonstrating.

Helen, tears already gushing, and Jennifer got into position as Dr. Weston stood at the end of the bed. "All right, young lady, it's all you. Take a deep breath, hold it, and push from your bottom, like you're having a bowel movement, for ten seconds at a time. Don't make a lot of noise—it just wastes your energy."

Grace nodded, desperate to get on with it. She had been afraid she wouldn't know what to do when the time came, but the need to push was so primal, so natural, it was as if her body had been programmed.

"Go," ordered Dr. Weston, and as Grace pushed, Jennifer slowly counted to ten. "Okay, rest. You're an excellent pusher. This isn't going to take very long at all. Are you ready? When you feel the next contraction, go with it."

Pleased that Grace had risen to the occasion, Dr. Weston looked up at the clock. This delivery would be over before one-thirty, so she would be able to make it to her own daughter's parent-teacher conference. Sometimes it was possible to juggle everything and have it work out.

"That was excellent. When you feel another contraction, do it all over again," Dr. Weston said. "You're so close, Grace. Just hang in there a little longer."

Eyes wide, Jennifer couldn't believe what she was seeing. The top of a tiny bald head was emerging from between Grace's legs. Every smartass comment she had been considering vanished, and she stood bracing Grace's foot, for once speechless, mesmerized by what was happening in front of her. It really *was* a miracle.

Certain her eyes must be popping out of her head with the effort, Grace held her breath and pushed. As painful as it was, feeling as if her body had split down the middle, it was an incredible relief to push. Suddenly Dr. Weston said, "Stop! Her shoulders are out. Don't move. You're almost done. There. Now one tiny push. Good girl!" Dr. Weston, knowing that Janet Olson and the adoptive parents were waiting outside, wanted to focus more on Grace and less on the beautiful baby she was holding. "You've given birth to a healthy baby girl," said Dr. Weston as she handed the infant off to the nurse. "Terry's going to clean her up. Do you want to hold her for a minute before she goes?"

It was all happening so fast. Nine months of uncertainty and aggravation had crawled by, interminable days that she thought would never end, but now time seemed to accelerate. Grace just wanted to freeze this moment, so she could think clearly, figure out what to do next.

"Yes, I want to hold her," she blurted out.

Helen and Jennifer had backed away and stood against the wall, watching quietly as Grace nuzzled the tiny blanket-wrapped bundle, no bigger than a bag of flour. "Sweet baby, I love you, forever and ever," Grace whispered into the pink seashell of an ear.

For a fleeting second, Grace couldn't imagine letting go of this precious creature who for so many months had been her traveling companion. Molly's deep blue eyes stared into Grace's, as if she understood exactly what was happening and didn't want to miss anything. Was it possible that on some deep, almost cellular level a newborn infant could internalize and remember something that happened when she was only a few minutes old? Although Grace knew that Molly wouldn't consciously recall this moment, she was comforted by the belief that her words were somehow imprinted on her baby's brain. However tenuous the connection between this mother and child, no matter how much physical distance separated them, there was a bond that would endure.

"Okay, Grace, it's time," Dr. Weston said softly. "You're doing the right thing, and you're going to be fine." Blinking back her own tears, the doctor took the baby from Grace's arms and placed her gently in the Plexiglas bassinet with the small sign that said Baby Girl Miller.

Janet came back in, holding the folder that contained the piece of paper that would dissolve Grace's legal connection to Molly.

Glancing at the living baby doll in the bassinet, her heart weeping just a little bit, she said, “It’s time to sign, Grace. Are you ready?”

Grace nodded quickly, knowing that if she thought about it too long, she would never be able to do it. Her hand shaking, Grace scribbled her signature on the line. It was done.

CHAPTER 22

Dear Baby Girl,

I just said hello and goodbye to you, and it was the hardest thing I've ever had to do, even though I know it's the right thing for both of us. It's only because I love you so much that I can let you go, because I know that you will have a better life with your new mommy and daddy than I could give you right now. I'm not much more than a kid myself, and I'm not able to give you all the wonderful things you deserve. It would be selfish of me to try. Someday I hope you can understand that, and I hope that we can meet so I can explain it to you in person. In the meantime, please forgive me for not being ready for you, for ever giving you a moment of doubt about who you are or where you came from. Just know that you are loved by so many people, most of whom you will probably never meet.

With more love than you could ever imagine,

Grace

Exhausted from the physical and emotional effort of the last twelve hours, Grace dropped the pencil and paper on the thin white blanket. It was over. Her baby was gone, and she was at once relieved and bereft. She wondered if this child would be able to understand what she'd done, would be able to love the mother she might never meet. Grace pictured herself, decades from now, sitting in a coffee shop, waiting to meet her grownup daughter who had decided she was finally ready to see her biological mother.

The door opened slowly, and Charlie's head appeared. He had been sitting in the maternity ward waiting room the entire time, watching people come and go with balloons and flowers, all celebrating the arrival of a new family member.

"I didn't knock in case you were sleeping." Curled up in a tangle of white sheets, Grace looked small and pale, like a sick, frightened child.

Grace shook her head and the waterworks began. Just seeing his forehead wrinkled with worry and hearing his gentle, low voice was enough to set her off. Dr. Weston had warned her that the hormone fluctuations that followed birth would make the emotional rollercoaster of pregnancy look like a kiddie ride. She wasn't joking.

Grace wept for all the things she had lost: her innocence, her self-respect, her old life, and her parents. In spite of the bitter words and the months of silence, Grace still ached to feel her mother's arms around her, and having experienced firsthand how strong a mother's love was for her child, she felt the pain of losing Betsy's love that much more acutely.

Charlie tenderly kissed Grace's forehead. It was finally time to start over. Molly was safely in the arms of her new family, and Grace was once again just Grace. Practically since the day he had met her, Charlie had been waiting for this moment.

Not sure what was the right thing to do, Charlie climbed onto the bed and enfolded her quaking body in his own. A few hours ago Grace had said goodbye to her baby. There were no words to comfort her after such a loss, especially when his entire frame of reference consisted of watching a couple of seasons of *16 and Pregnant* and *Teen Mom* on Netflix, so he just whispered shushing noises in her ear, as if she were a baby herself. There were so many things Charlie wanted to tell her, about how strong and special she was, but Grace was in no condition to listen. What a shame that Mr. and Mrs. Warren weren't here to witness how extraordinary their daughter was. But as Helen said, there would be plenty of time after the big event to help put this jigsaw puzzle of a family back together.

Finally Grace's breathing slowed, and she whispered, "Thank you. I'm okay now." Charlie reluctantly sat up and handed her a box of tissues.

"How do you feel?" That was a stupid question.

"Physically? I feel pretty good, considering. I still don't know how she fit."

Charlie couldn't help cringing at the thought of the actual giving birth part. At his age, he still thought that part of a girl's body was for recreation, not procreation. "Are you in a lot of pain?"

"Not at all. Since I'm not nursing, they drugged me up. By tomorrow I'll be sore, but I'm glad I feel numb all over right now." Grace took a sip of water and leaned back against the pillow. "As hard as it was to give her up, it would have been much worse if my brain weren't so fuzzy from the pain medication."

"Do you wish you'd kept her?" Even as he said it, he realized that it was none of his business. But he was curious. The baby had been a part of Grace for so long that no matter how sure she was that adoption was the right thing to do, she must feel as if she were giving a part of herself away to strangers. Charlie had wondered if there was a chance Grace would change her mind and keep the baby, and what that would mean for him. Without a second's hesitation he knew he would love Grace whether or not she had given up this baby for adoption, and he would love the baby too, as hard as that might be at first.

"No," she said, without hesitation. "How could I compound my stupidity by putting my emotions before my daughter's well-being? Molly didn't do anything wrong, and even though I love her, so much, that's just not enough. She deserves two parents to love her and care for her, and now she has that."

"You're the bravest person I've ever met, besides Aunt Helen." Charlie really meant it. At seventeen, Grace had been through more than many people in their entire lives. "Your parents may have made a lot of mistakes along the way, but they must have done something right for you to turn out the way you did."

"I think you're kind of biased," Grace said, her pale cheeks turning pink.

"Maybe a little bit. Are the Millers going to call her Molly?"

"I didn't tell them about my private name for her. Maybe I'll tell her about her womb name if I ever meet her. Mrs. Olson told me they're calling her Cady, C-A-D-Y. In French *cadeau* means gift, and they said that's what she is. I think it's perfect."

Having said goodbye, maybe forever, to her first child, Grace could feel her sense of normalcy slowly returning, even though she knew her life could never go back to the way it was. With the baby out of the picture, it was time to pick up the pieces of her life, but Grace couldn't believe that she would simply be able to stroll back into the classroom, as if she'd been out for a couple of months with mono.

"It's a beautiful name." *And you're beautiful*, Charlie wanted to say, but as desperate as he was to get close to her and tell her how he really felt, he realized that declaring his undying love, effectively hitting on her a few hours postpartum, was probably bad form. "Can I get you anything? Are you hungry? Thirsty? Do you want something to read?" Helen had said to be there for Grace, however she needed him, and he was determined to do that.

"I'm fine. You look so worried. I'm really fine. The doctor said I can go home tomorrow," Grace said, thinking again how lucky she was to have met this astonishing boy. All by himself, he had managed to restore her faith in the entire male gender.

"What about your parents? Are you going to call them now that things are almost back to normal?" Charlie selfishly didn't want Grace to make up with her parents right away, because that meant she would move out of Helen's house. However, if that was what she wanted, what she needed, he would do anything he could to make it happen.

"I don't know what to do, so I'm not doing anything right now."

"Sounds reasonable. Do you know what the date is today?" Charlie was beyond excited, but he didn't want to show it, just in case Grace's news wasn't as good as his had been.

"It's April first. I may be loaded with painkillers, but I know the date. What perfect irony that I gave birth on April Fools' Day." Would Molly Cady think that was funny when she was older?

"That's not what I was talking about. Besides being April Fools' Day, April first is also the day colleges send out their letters."

"Oh, shit." Between contractions and handing her baby over to a couple of strangers, the last thing Grace had been thinking about was where she would be going to school the following year.

"I got into . . . ." Charlie started to say.

Grace cut him off. "Don't tell me. I don't want to know. We applied to some of the same schools, and I don't think we should tell each other where we got in or where we plan on accepting. We don't want to make a decision for the wrong reasons, do we?"

When she and Charlie were comparing their college lists months earlier, Grace had fantasized about going to the same college, but after they ended up applying to almost all the same places, she started to worry that she might want to follow him because he made her feel safe, and he might want to follow her because she needed taking care of and he was clearly someone who, like his aunt, had a habit of taking care of people, and it all started to feel incredibly co-dependent and psychiatric, rather than heartfelt and romantic, all before a single acceptance letter had been sent. Her greatest fear was that Charlie would come to resent her for compelling him to stay by her side because she was emotionally destitute, a virtual orphan, and not because they were madly in love with each other.

Shutting him out was exactly the opposite of what Charlie had thought Grace would do. Apparently the vibes he thought she'd been sending, especially after that night in her bedroom, were merely his own desperate longings reverberating back onto himself. Whatever had passed between them while she was pregnant must have been nothing more than a happy collision of hormones and romantic lighting. But it had felt like so much more. He would have bet anything that she still cared about him.

Stifling his overwhelming disappointment, Charlie said flatly, "Okay, whatever you want. I brought my laptop if you want to check."

"Thanks."

Surprised and disappointed that Charlie didn't protest her plan to keep it private—if he had put up any fight at all, she would have given in. If Charlie really cared about her, was truly in love with her, as she hoped, wouldn't he insist on knowing what her plans were and sharing his own? Grace needed him to show her how much he wanted to be with her, that he would push and shove his way into her life, even if she seemed determined to keep him at arm's length. It was a test, and tests were stupid, because sometimes people failed them, like now, and Grace was left with information that didn't suit her purposes or expectations. Clearly he wasn't that into her. But it wasn't as if she hadn't misread boy signals before. It was nine short months ago that she actually thought that the coolest kid in school had fallen in love with the co-captain of the math team. Talk about missing the boat. Her people sense had clearly not improved during her pregnancy.

Clicking on each e-mail, Grace bit her lip so that her face wouldn't betray her emotions, which would have been elation, as all six schools had accepted her. Looking up at Charlie, who had been watching her intently, as if he was trying to read the screen's reflection in her eyes, she said, "Okay then."

"That's it?"

"Yeah."

"So you're really not going to tell me what happened?" Still not ready to believe, not wanting to believe, that Grace was pulling away so suddenly and completely, Charlie asked, "And I'm not allowed to tell you where I got in?"

"No. After we send back our acceptances, then we'll tell each other, but don't you think you should decide where to go based on what *you* want, not what *I'm* doing?" Grace wished Charlie would beg her to tell him where she'd gotten in. She wanted him to tell her that he loved her and needed her and couldn't imagine being away from her. She wanted him to be the person she thought he was the moment she met him.

"That's what I'd planned on doing. Did you think I was just going to follow you wherever you went, like a dog?" In truth, he would follow her to the South Pole, in a heartbeat, but that was a revelation better saved for when they'd already been married a few years.

"No, of course not, but you might without even realizing it. I know it would affect *my* decision process if I knew a close friend was going to one of the schools I was considering." As long as she was testing him, she might as well go all the way. If her instincts were right, he was three seconds from throwing his arms around her and shouting out where he was going to college.

Flinching at the word *friend*, Charlie replied, "Well, I'm not like that. I haven't worked so hard for so long to pick a school just because my *friend* is going there."

He could give as good as he got, even though he knew he was being childish, and if he were a real man, he would just tell her how he felt. Well, maybe not everything, but at least the part about wanting to be more than just a supportive friend, now that Grace could go back to being a teenager again. But pride makes people stupid and shortsighted, and Charlie Glass was no exception. This conversation was not going well at all, but he lacked the maturity and nerve to try and steer it out of the ditch it was fast approaching.

"Hey, chica!" Without even knocking, Jennifer bounced into the room, nearly hidden by an enormous vase of flowers. "Sorry I'm late, but I wanted to give you two kids a little time alone together," she said, giving Charlie the evil eye. "So, how's everything?"

Still not certain she had heard what Charlie said, or more to the point, what he hadn't said, Grace turned to Jennifer. "I'm good. Thank you so much for being here. You were a huge help."

"That's what best friends are for, right? Holding your foot so you can push a baby out of your encyclopedia. Truthfully, it was the most amazing experience I've ever had. I should be thanking you for letting me be there." Turning to Charlie, she said, "You don't know what you missed, Chuckles. Next time, maybe she'll let *you* hold her foot."

Turning three shades of crimson, Charlie said nothing, just cleared his throat. His passion for Grace was apparently obvious to everyone but Grace.

Jennifer laughed at Charlie, who was blushing like a virgin bride. "I still don't know how she fit, even though I saw it happen. You must be pretty sore."

"Not so bad. Lots of good drugs." There was a continuous echo inside her head as Grace tried to carry on a conversation with Jennifer while trying to sort out what had just happened with Charlie.

"I never would have believed the human body was so . . . stretchy." Jennifer made a face.

"I don't really need to know all the details," said Grace.

"So the bean's really gone?" Despite seven months of smartass comments, Jennifer understood how traumatic this day had been for Grace.

"Yeah, she's gone. It's hard to believe." Perfect pink Molly, with a tiny dimple in her chin, just like Grace, was on her way to a new life in Philadelphia.

"You're incredibly calm. I'd be freaking out right now," Jennifer said.

"I've done enough freaking out for a lifetime in the last nine months. I'm too tired to get upset." Exhausted in mind and body, Grace was desperate to sleep, but every time she closed her eyes, she could see Molly's rosebud lips and her heart started to race. Sleep would not be easy.

"I'm going to go now," Charlie said casually, putting his laptop in his backpack. The girls were ignoring him anyway. It was clear to him that he wasn't wanted there. "I'll see you tomorrow."

After Charlie left, Jennifer asked, "What's with him?"

"I think I screwed up," Grace replied.

"What are you talking about? There's nothing you could do or say that could change how he feels about you." Not that Jennifer was an expert in matters of the heart, but the way Charlie never stopped staring at Grace, he was either in love with her, or there was something wrong with his eyes.

"I'm not so sure. I didn't tell him where I got in to school, and I wouldn't let him tell me where he got in. I think he was insulted."

"Why would you do that? That was dumb. So where *did* you get in? Am *I* allowed to know?" Jennifer asked.

"I got in everywhere. Apparently getting knocked up your senior year is just the kind of extracurricular activity they're looking for." Grace wondered whether her situation had really helped her, like having an off-the-wall hobby—underwater basketweaving, or skydiving. All that mattered now was that she had so completely misinterpreted Charlie's feelings for her, and she didn't know how she was going to get over him.

"Congrats. That's amazing. And Mrs. T. is footing the bill. It sounds pretty perfect. Not that you care, but I'm going to NYU Stern. They offered me a sweet scholarship," Jennifer said.

"That's a great place for you. I think I'm going to accept at Dartmouth."

"Well, duh. But what about your future husband? Why are you shutting him out? He applied to Dartmouth, too. You could room together."

Grace scowled. "I don't want either of us to decide on a college based on what the other one is doing. What happens if we don't work out in the end?"

Jennifer shook her head. "Full of yourself a little? You're sure he would follow you wherever you went?"

"Maybe," Grace said, realizing the hubris of assuming Charlie's feelings were as intense as hers. Maybe their kisses hadn't meant as much to him as they had to her, or his feelings had faded. When they had been together, it had felt like she was dreaming. Now she wondered if it had all really happened as she remembered it, or was it all just a figment of her desperate imagination?

"And *you* would follow *him*?"

"I'm afraid I might, and I kind of thought he would follow me, but I think I was wrong, from how he acted when he was just here. He didn't seem to care where I got in. He didn't even try to convince me to tell him where I was going," Grace said, her pride bruised by the ease with which Charlie had given up.

"Haven't you ever heard of the male ego? Of course he's going to pretend he doesn't care. Begging you to tell him would be like handing you his balls on a silver platter."

"And she's back. I thought the miracle of childbirth might have cleaned up your language." Grace laughed, relieved that Jennifer was still Jennifer.

"No such luck. Anyway, what are you going to do now?"

"I don't know. Why don't you tell me what to do? I'm too tired to think anymore, and you always have all the answers."

"If I were you, I'd tell him I loved him. But it's none of my business. And it's not like I have any personal experience to work off of."

In Jennifer's world, everything was blissfully simple and straightforward if you were paying attention. Finding someone who could love you no matter how crappy you looked or how stupid you acted was like finding the pot of gold at the end of the rainbow. As risky as it might seem to tell a guy you were in love with him, the payoff was so huge, it was definitely worth taking the chance those feelings might not be reciprocated. If Grace didn't jump on this, she was a moron, but Jennifer had vowed to keep her nose out of this one. Helping her best friend through her pregnancy was one thing, but managing her mixed-up love life was another thing altogether.

"No way, not after the conversation we just had. It's not how I thought it was between us, and now I just have to move on." Besides, now was the time for Grace to work on Grace. Boys, even one as perfect as Charlie, were merely distractions. Determined to rationalize what had happened, Grace had to paint Charlie as the enemy—otherwise she feared sinking into a wicked postpartum depression.

"Fine, do what you want. Hopefully, you two mules can work it out. You know, you're more like your parents than you think," Jennifer said.

"I'm nothing like them," Grace protested. Betsy and Brad were cruel and heartless and unforgiving. The last thing in the world Grace wanted was to be compared to them.

"You're not crazy and spiteful like they are, but you're stubborn like them, that's for sure," Jennifer said. "Remember, like Dr. Phil says, you can be right or you can be happy, but it's hard to be both."

"What does that even mean?" Grace asked.

"Just look at your mom and dad. They think they're right about you being a bad seed. They won't even try to understand your point of view. But what good does it do them? Do you really think they're happy being right about everything . . . and alone?"

"It's a totally different situation," Grace muttered.

"Whatever you say, boss." Jennifer shrugged. "Just remember. You can be right and alone . . . or you can take a minute to think about what Charlie might be feeling. It's totally up to you."

CHAPTER 23

"Welcome home, sweetie," Vera and Ada said together as Grace stepped gingerly over the threshold into the front hall, one arm linked in Helen's, Charlie right behind with her suitcase. Now that all the Percocet had worn off, Grace felt like she'd ridden across the country on horseback. Looking up the spiral staircase, she wondered how she was going to make it up to her room.

"Thank you. It's good to be home." Unconsciously, Grace was starting to consider Helen's house home: a warm, loving, safe place. Catching herself, she corrected, "I mean it's good to be back here."

Helen laughed. "You were right the first time. It's good to have you back home. Just because your bump is gone doesn't mean you have to make any decisions or go anywhere. This is your home for as long as you want it to be."

Tears filled Grace's eyes and she threw her arms around Helen's neck. This must be more of that hormone instability that the doctor was talking about. "I love you, Helen, I really do. You saved me. I wouldn't have made it without you, or you," she continued, turning to Charlie.

Grateful that she still thought he was an important part of her life, even though she had shut him out of the whole college thing, Charlie tried to smile graciously and said, "That's what friends are for, right?"

The last thing he needed was another *friend.* From friend, to more than that, and back again. Hopefully Helen was right—this was just part of the process, and he had to wait until Grace figured it out for herself. But how could that happen if she ended up hundreds or thousands of miles away at college? For the past few months he had held onto this day, the day when she was no longer housing her little boarder and she was free to move on with her life, hopefully with him. Now Charlie, friend and bellhop, stood at the bottom of the stairs, awaiting instructions. What he wanted to do was swoop her up in his arms and carry her up the stairs, but Helen would probably say that was crossing the line, which could jeopardize his move into the *more than friend* area. So instead, he stood like an idiot, watching Grace tentatively mount the first step.

✦

"Where's Grace? I can't find her anywhere." It had been ten days since Grace had given birth, and today was supposed to be her first day back at school. Knowing how much she had been dreading this day, Charlie had made a plan with Jennifer to ensure that Grace wouldn't be on her own for a minute.

"She's gone. She left early this morning," replied Helen softly.

"Gone? Where did she go? She has to go back to school. She didn't even say goodbye." Feeling abandoned and hurt, Charlie appealed to his aunt for an explanation. Trying to do everything right, he had only succeeded in driving her away.

"I know. That was on purpose. Here, read the note she left." Helen sighed and handed Charlie the letter she had already read three times. Although Grace had only been living there for seven months, the house felt empty without her.

Dear Aunt Helen and Charlie,

I feel terrible saying goodbye this way, but if I did it face to face, I would probably chicken out. After everything that's happened to me, I need to get as far away from here as I can, if I ever want to find my way home again. Does that make any sense at all? If not for the two of you, I would have lost myself completely in the last seven months. Helen, I can't even imagine what would've happened to me if you hadn't rescued me that day. You saved two lives. But you can't do everything for me, no matter how wonderful you are, and now I need to figure out who I am, or who I want to be.

I applied to be a junior counselor at a program called No Boundaries. For the next two and a half months I'll be climbing mountains and learning survival skills with a group of young girls in Colorado. All of them have gone through difficult experiences, and I hope that while I help them find their way, I will be able to find mine

I'm not running away from home, from your home. I'll be back. As for my parents, I don't know what to do yet. I know I have to work that out somehow, but like they say in all those recovery programs, one step at a time. If I work on my relationship with myself, maybe all my other relationships will fall into place.

I love you both more than words can say,
Grace

P.S. I took the GED exam, so I have my high school diploma, in case you were worried that I'd forgotten about graduating. Mrs. Evans already knows, and I'm taking the AP exams in Colorado. Don't worry, as crazy as all this sounds, I'm still taking care of business.

"She thinks I don't care. That's why she left. I should've spoken up," Charlie said, more to himself than to Helen. "And she's afraid of heights. She'll get hurt."

"Well perhaps that is exactly why she chose to go to the mountains." Although Helen had not been expecting Grace to run off to the Rockies, now that it had happened, she wasn't surprised.

"But she just had a baby. Climbing mountains can't be a good idea in her condition."

"Grace has a good head on her shoulders. She can take care of herself." Helen said, wishing she could take away some of Charlie's pain. He looked like a lost puppy.

"Do you really think she'll come back?" Desperate for reassurance, Charlie didn't care that he sounded like a love-struck girl. Even though they would probably be leaving for different colleges in September, he had banked on having the whole summer with Grace, and he worried that the perfect days that he had been daydreaming about—water-skiing and hiking and picnics—would never be more than stupid fantasies.

"That's what the letter says."

Quickly scanning the letter again, Charlie said, "Can I fly out to Colorado, just to make sure she's okay? I'll come right back."

"That's ridiculous. She sounds perfectly fine, very determined, and if she had wanted to say goodbye to you, she would have done so. Do you want to spoil any chance you have with her? As I told you a couple of months ago, you're just going to have to be patient."

"Easier said than done."

"Well, only you can decide if she's worth the wait," Helen said, knowing full well that while Charlie might not be happy about this latest development, he was so head over heels in love, he had no choice but to sit back and wait for Grace to find her way back home in her own good time.

"You know the answer to that question," Charlie said.

"It's settled, then. Pick your college, finish out the year, and wait for Grace to come home. The only behavior you can control is your own. You can't make Grace get where she needs to go any sooner than she's able to."

"You sound like a shrink, Aunt Helen."

"After twenty years of therapy, I could probably do a decent job." What would Dr. Needleman think if she had a little competition on the leather couch? "Now go live your life. You're so young. There's plenty of time for this all to work out before you get your first gray hair."

While leaving a goodbye note for Helen and Charlie was necessary under the circumstances, Jennifer had required the personal touch. "Hey, it's me," Grace whispered into the phone.

"Why are you whispering?" Jennifer whispered back.

"It's late, and I don't want to wake anyone."

"So why are you sneaking phone calls after lights out? You want to plan our outfits for tomorrow?" Jennifer asked, stifling a yawn. "Wear jeans, if you can stuff yourself into them. I'll see you in the morning. Do you want me to pick you up, or is your boyfriend, who you refuse to admit is your boyfriend, going to drive you?"

"That's why I called you. I'm not going back to school."

Not drawn in by what was obviously a middle-of-the-night attack of cold feet, Jennifer tried not to laugh. "So you're finally running away with the circus. I've thought about doing that myself. Are you going to be tightrope walker, or are you going to clean up after the elephants?"

"Could you step pretending it's open mic night for five whole minutes? This is important," Grace begged. She was about to regret not leaving a note for Jennifer as well.

"I'm sorry. You're right. It's just a defense mechanism. Speak your piece."

"I'm not going back to school, because I'm going away to this wilderness survival program in Colorado," Grace answered, waiting for the barrage of bad jokes that would surely follow. Sometimes she wondered if she existed solely to feed Jennifer lines.

"But you don't camp, remember? Except at the Hyatt. And what about your shy bladder? How are you going to pee in front of the bears and the mountain lions?"

"I'm *so* sorry I ever told you about that. I'll manage. In the last nine months, half of Connecticut has seen my vag. I think I can pee in the woods."

"You're right. You must be over your stage fright by now. But why are you leaving when the worst part is finally over? You're a skinny kid again. No more baby on board. I thought we'd spend the last couple of months of senior year together."

"I'm sorry, but I just can't go back. I need to figure some stuff out, and I can't do that here, in front of everyone, across the street from my parents. Except for one run-in at the grocery store, I haven't seen them in almost seven and a half months, and I'm not ready to face them yet."

"It's none of my business, but with your fake grandma, who I have to say is the coolest senior citizen I've ever met, who the hell needs parents? Especially your dumbass, narrow-minded, intolerant, provincial—I could go on—parents?"

"But they're still my parents. Doesn't that bond mean anything? I spent two minutes with Molly and I'm irrevocably tied to her, even if I never get to see her again. Holding her in my arms changed me forever. I don't even know how to describe it."

"Not necessarily. Look at Nick. He's Molly's father, but he barely deserves the title of sperm donor. Two minutes of fucking doesn't make people parents."

"But Betsy and Brad were my parents for seventeen years before this happened. We were a happy family. That's not just biology."

"You were a happy family because you were every parent's wet dream . . . up until the moment you weren't. You're beautiful, you're a fucking genius, you have perfect manners, excellent taste in shoes, and you help old people across the street. Until you blacked out and let Private Prick plant his flag in your brave new world, you were like the Hope Diamond."

"How can people feel like that about their child, their own flesh and blood? I can't believe such a thing could be true." That Betsy and Brad could love her only when she was lovable was a notion Grace didn't want to wrap her head around, even though Jennifer's explanation seemed to be the only one left that made any sense after so long.

"You think you're the only kid who ever got kicked out of the house for getting pregnant, or being gay, or breaking some other inviolable house rule? Like I told you a long time ago, parents are just people. Having a baby can't turn pea-brained half-wits into benevolent saints. Betsy and Brad are the perfect example."

"I guess so, but . . . ." Grace didn't have an answer. If what Jennifer was saying wasn't true, then Grace wouldn't be living with Helen and probably wouldn't be fleeing to the Rocky Mountains to conquer her fear of heights and everything else.

"Look, their own parents probably fucked them up and they just never had the chance to unpack their baggage, so they ended up dumping it on you. It's not your fault, and you shouldn't ruin your life trying to figure it out. Take my word, it's not you, it's *them*. Your only job is not to repeat their mistakes. That's all."

Playing psychiatrist at midnight wasn't easy, but Jennifer had spent a lot of time thinking about Grace's relationship with her folks. Not that Jennifer's mom and dad were perfect—far from it—but she knew she was deeply loved. Maybe in the long run that *was* worth more than an American Express Platinum Card.

"Thank you, J. You're crazy, but you're the smartest person I know, and I love you. I'll see you when I get back. I'm not allowed to write or call anyone during the program, so I guess I'll see you when I see you."

“I love you too, biatch. I’m going to miss you at graduation. I guess I’ll have to keep all the awards for myself. Go get sane, and be careful. You’re really important to me. Bye.” Jennifer hung up the phone before her voice broke. If Grace knew she was crying, she’d never hear the end of it.

“Bye,” Grace said to the empty line.

CHAPTER 24

Staring up at thirty feet of fake rock face, Grace was ready to tear off her harness and run back to Connecticut, into the safe, compassionate arms of Helen and Charlie. There was no way she could do this. She could have been standing at the base of Mount Everest.

"Are you ready?" asked Dirk, whose name fit him perfectly. Tall, blond, and ruggedly handsome, he was featured on the cover of the No Boundaries brochure, surrounded by formerly troubled teens who gazed up at him adoringly.

"No, not quite ready." Grace tugged at the nylon straps between her legs. Dr. Weston had examined her and said she was good to go, but it sure didn't feel like it.

"You look good down there," Dr. Weston had said. "You didn't need an episiotomy, so you're all healed."

"So I can go to Colorado?" Grace had explained No Boundaries to her.

"I wouldn't want to go mountain-climbing two weeks postpartum, but you're young, and I know that nothing I say is going to stop you, so just be careful. Your body has been through quite a bit, so try to take it easy. You're going to be tired and sore."

"I'll be fine," Grace said. Tired and sore were nothing after giving birth. It was the pain in her heart and her mind that threatened to do her in.

"You will be," the doctor told her. "Give me a hug, and come back to see me when you get home."

Dirk tugged on his own straps. "The harness is supposed to be tight like that, to hold you in and keep you safe."

"I know."

No one here knew why Grace had joined the program as a junior counselor. In her application she had written about her desire to test her mettle, face new challenges, all while helping young girls who had been through rough times. That was all true, but the reason for her need to do those things was her own special secret. Like Charlie had said, once she left home, no one would ever need to know. If she told, although she was certain everyone would be just as nice, they would see her differently. She would become just like the troubled girls she was helping, and for the first time in a long while, Grace needed to be someone without those kinds of problems.

"Then let's do it, Super G." As appealing as Dirk was visually, that's how annoying he was to listen to. He never called Grace by her given name. It was always some irritating nickname, like G-Woman or Lady G.

"Okay, I'm going." And she did. Managing to avoid looking straight down, Grace clawed her way to the top. Once there, she turned and for the first time looked down at Dirk, who was waving and smiling from what looked like a million miles below. Holding her breath so that she wouldn't hyperventilate, she was at once terrified and ecstatic.

"You did it, Baby G. Now walk down that wall like Spiderman."

Too scared to open her mouth for fear of what might come out, Grace did as she was told. Her arms felt like rubber bands when she got to the bottom; she could barely hang onto the water bottle Dirk handed her, spilling most of it all over herself.

But by the end of that first day, Grace knew she'd made the right decision. She had literally taken one step at a time, and she had conquered the wall. She could feel her power and self-worth returning, like a dead car battery slowly recharging, and as long as she didn't spend too much time looking down, she was okay. Her knees were scraped from the rough concrete wall and her blistered hands ached from gripping the tiny handholds she'd used to pull herself to the top, but in all that throbbing agony was a sense of accomplishment she'd never known. Getting stellar grades had come so easily, and she realized she'd never pushed herself to do things she wasn't already good at. Now she knew she was strong enough to challenge herself physically and emotionally, and the rush she got when she conquered her fears was far better than the thrill she'd experienced when Nick told her she was pretty or the satisfaction she felt when her parents used to pat her on the back for a perfect report card.

On the second day, Dirk made Grace look down every minute or two, and she didn't throw up or faint. Being up high was still scary, but in a thrilling, roller coaster kind of way, because she had learned to trust the rope and Dirk and herself. Strangely, even thirty feet off the ground, she felt safer and more sure of herself than she ever had in her life.

"You're pretty strong for such a munchkin," said Dirk.

Grace shrugged. It wasn't physical strength that was getting her through; it was pure determination. If she failed at this, she knew she would never recover from Nick. Although every muscle in her body was screaming out loud, Grace forced herself to keep going. Like childbirth without anesthesia, the pain was part of her self-inflicted corporal punishment. As nuts as she realized her home-made therapy probably was, it was the only way she was going to be able to forgive herself. Each twinge meant she was another step closer to getting her soul back.

After indoor climbing came outdoor climbing, which was way scarier, but Grace was ready. Then she learned how to build a fire, pitch a tent, kill and cook small animals, catch and gut fish, navigate by the stars, use a compass, gather rainwater, and learn what to do if she ran into a snake or a bear. No Boundaries was for real, and although Grace had read all the paperwork and knew the risks in the abstract, it wasn't until she was dangling off a sheer rock cliff in the second week that she realized she could actually die in the process of trying to rebuild her life. When she first thought about it, still stinging from her crossed signals with Charlie, she became almost fearless, not caring what happened to her. It would serve Charlie right if she never came back—then he would be sorry he hadn't fought for her. But the more she thought about what Jennifer had said right after Molly was born, the more she understood that she shouldn't resent Charlie for lacking cojones when she had been just as much of a chicken. It was the twenty-first century, and there were no laws that said she couldn't tell him first, couldn't put her heart on the line and wait for him to hopefully meet her in the middle. They were both candy-asses, but the time had come for her to cowboy up, which seemed appropriate considering she was learning how to keep body and soul together in the wild, wild West.

After nearly five weeks of training, Grace was ready to meet her team. Under the supervision of a former heroin addict who had first come to No Boundaries as a troubled fourteen-year-old and was now a senior counselor, Grace would help lead four fifteen-year-olds on a two-week program designed to help rebuild broken spirits and shattered self-esteem.

"If you thought the last few weeks were hard, just wait," said Truth. Not her real name, Truth had legally changed it to reflect her new philosophy of life after finding herself at No Boundaries more than a decade earlier.

"I think I'm ready," Grace said, not at all certain she was or ever would be. Although she could start a fire with the tiniest piece of flint and had gotten her fear of heights under control, she wasn't sure she had the emotional strength to help the kind of girls who came to No Boundaries—not just recovering drug addicts, but victims of abuse, runaways, and the occasional anorectic.

"Don't worry about it. No one ever is. I'm still not. These kids are beyond messed up. I ought to know. I used to be one of them. Just remember, no matter how far gone a girl might seem, don't you *ever* write her off as a lost cause." Truth wasn't usually so serious.

"I won't give up," Grace promised.

"I know this is hard for you, having never lived through any of the nightmare shit these girls have experienced, but that doesn't mean you won't get it. When you look them in the eyes, you'll see what I mean."

Several times, Grace had almost told Truth about Molly, but she always stopped herself. Maybe because compared to what Truth and these other girls had experienced, an unplanned pregnancy was like a broken fingernail. Even so, Grace knew it was silly to be so secretive, considering how open Truth was about her own history. More importantly, Grace knew that she needed to own her past if she was ever going to move beyond it, and owning it meant acknowledging it.

"The only thing you have to do is accept them for who they are, and then help them be the best people they can be going forward. That's all we do here," Truth said, putting her hands together in the Namaste pose and bowing slightly.

Grace wanted to cry, because that's all she had ever wanted from her parents—to be accepted for who she truly was, not who they thought she was, not who they wanted her to be.

Truth looked at her watch. "It's time to go meet our girls." She jumped up and held out her hand to help Grace to her feet. A van pulled into base camp and the door opened, but none of the girls got out of their seats. "Sometimes they need a little coaxing. Remember, they're not here by choice."

Grace just nodded. It sounded like they were going to be carrying these girls up the mountain on their backs.

Truth climbed into the van. "Hey ladies, welcome to No Boundaries. My name is Truth, and we are going to do great things together. Please give me your phones as you get off the bus."

No one said a word, but one after another, the girls trudged off the van and stood in a sulky line in front of Grace. Intimidated by their despair, which they each wore like a suit of armor, Grace didn't know what to do next.

"Hi, I'm Grace. I'm your junior counselor," she said, knowing she sounded like a waiter introducing herself as she handed out the menus: *Hi, I'm Grace, and I'll be your server this evening.*

They spent an awkward hour getting to know each other, as much as anyone could get to know four girls who clearly wished they were anyplace else. The girls' silence continued as Truth explained the rules at No Boundaries and went through their duffel bags, confiscating four Fentanyl patches, three joints, two cartons of cigarettes, and a pot pipe that looked like a miniature penis. It was like a druggie Twelve Days of Christmas.

"I get those back after, right?" asked Kat, who had the face of a ten-year-old but the gravelly voice of a veteran smoker.

"You do realize that you were sent here by drug court, and if you use drugs while you're here, you're going to go to jail?" Truth said.

"Whatever. I got that pipe in Tijuana. It's a souvenir, and I'd like it back. Memories," said Kat, staring at a tree behind Truth, not at all fazed by the threat of incarceration. "And the smokes, too."

"We'll see. Hopefully, by the time we're through, you won't want them back."

"We'll see," said Kat, arching one eyebrow.

"Danni, where did you get the Fentanyl patches?"

"My grandma. She has bad arthritis." Danni said, chomping on an enormous wad of pink gum and twirling a lock of hair around her finger.

"Don't you think she's probably missing them right about now?"

"She's got plenty." Danni spit out her gum onto the ground.

"Pick that up right now. This is God's country, and we don't litter."

As Danni bent over she flipped the bird at Truth, ending in a salute as she stood upright. "Thank you. Beth, nice rolling job. Excellent technique, but really? You just got out of rehab two days ago," Truth said, holding up one of the joints.

"I wasn't planning on smoking them," Beth said.

"What were you planning on doing with them?" Rubbing her forehead, which was already throbbing, Truth reminded herself that the first day was always the worst.

"I like to hold them. Like a lucky rabbit's foot, you know?"

Truth shook her head and exhaled slowly. "No, I don't. But you know what, the first rabbit we kill, the foot's yours. How does that sound?"

"Can I have one?" Kat asked, sounding interested for the first time.

"Why not? Tara, thank you for not bringing any contraband. I really appreciate it," Truth said.

"Yes, ma'am," Tara whispered, staring down at her brand new boots.

Dressed for a vacation in Vail, in head-to-toe Patagonia and real Bavarian hiking boots with a thick braid hanging down her back, Tara looked like she was on break from some fancy East Coast boarding school, not carrying out some court-ordered punishment. The other girls were in skinny jeans, Converse sneakers, and about a gallon of black eyeliner. It was going to be a rough trip for Tara. She was clearly the weakest member of the herd.

"Kiss-ass," Danni whispered, making smacking sounds.

"There will be none of that here," Truth said sternly. "Respect."

In spite of their lack of enthusiasm, all four girls were quick learners, and they seemed to enjoy Dirk's silly name-calling. They took pride in their bruises and blisters, and they were all, including Tara, incredibly gutsy. No matter what Dirk asked them to do, none of them backed down. At the end of the first week, Kat Woman, Danni Darkness, the Bethinator, and Terrible Tara were ready to tackle the mountain. They sounded like a roller derby team.

"I'm proud of you, and you should be proud of yourselves for what you've accomplished so far," Truth said, as the six of them sat around the campfire on their first night on the mountain. "Let's each share what the hardest part of your first week was."

Kat, Danni, and Beth all complained about the lack of coffee and cigarettes. Tara said she was afraid of heights. The other girls laughed, and Tara zipped her fleece pullover all the way up to her chin and pulled her hands inside her sleeves. She looked like a turtle withdrawing into her shell.

"Respect," Truth whispered, glaring across the flames at the three rebels who had become fast friends, leaving the debutante on the outside looking in.

"I'm afraid of heights, too," Grace said. "I think you're very brave."

"You too," Tara whispered, her voice barely audible, as if she didn't want anyone to hear what she was saying. Her uncertainty hung in the air around her like a dense fog.

"A few puffs of some good weed, and you'll be ready to jump out of an airplane," said Kat, miming taking a drag on a joint.

Truth reached over and gave her a gentle swat on the side of the head. "You think you're so tough with your penis pipe? When I was your age, I ran away with my twenty-year-old boyfriend. We went on a week-long heroin binge that ended when I got arrested for soliciting an undercover cop. After I got out of rehab, my parents didn't know what else to do with me, so they sent me here. I thought they were full of shit, this place was full of shit, the world was full of shit. But this shitty place saved my life, and it's going to save yours, too. That's the only speech I'm going to make, so I hope you were paying attention."

Kat, Danni, and Beth clapped and whistled. "Awesome story. You rule."

"Make fun. I get it. You're too cool for this place. I only hope you figure it out before it's too late." Just as she'd been when she was their age, these girls, except for Tara, were all bluster and big hair. After a few days without hot water and mascara, they would start to lose their swagger. Adolescent ego was no match for a big mountain.

After everyone was asleep, Grace sat alone in front of the dying fire, thinking about Charlie. As much as she tried to put him out of her mind, she wondered what he was doing, whether he had gone to the senior prom, where he was going to college, and most of all, if he would still want to be her other best friend when she got back.

"Hi." Tara had appeared out of nowhere. Grace hadn't even seen the tent flap open.

"Can't sleep?"

"I can't turn off my brain. When I close my eyes, I see every stupid thing I've ever done," Tara said, grinding her fists into her eyes.

"I know how that is." Grace's nighttime brain was like an autobiographical movie theater showing nightly documentaries of all the low points in her life. Even after an exhausting day on the trail, the movies played on.

"Did Truth tell you why I'm here?"

"No, she never said a word." The other three girls were here at the behest of the court system, but Tara had probably never even jaywalked. "I figured you were like the others, some post-rehab program." She hadn't believed that for a second, but since Grace had her own secrets, she wasn't going to pry.

"I asked her not to say anything, but now I want to tell you. My parents sent me here. A couple of weeks ago, I got accused of cheating at my boarding school. I didn't do it, but this girl lied about it, and the headmaster believed her instead of me."

"Why would she lie?"

Tara fiddled with her braid and stared at the glowing embers. "A boy she liked asked me to a school dance last month. I tried to explain, but nobody cared about the truth. The other girl, Brooke, comes from a really wealthy family that donates a ton of money to my school, so of course they believed *her* story."

"Didn't your parents stand up for you?" Although Grace's parents had not stood up for her, she was still surprised when it happened to someone else.

"No, they didn't even ask me what really happened. All they cared about was how bad it looked. I was so upset when I got sent home that I did something stupid—I ran away." Grace was all too familiar with parents who thought more about how things looked than how they really were. "Half my family went to that school. My parents said that I'd humiliated them and that I needed to see how good I had it before, so here I am. I think it was more because they were about to leave for Europe for three weeks, and they didn't want to leave me home alone. My brothers are both away at college."

Tara's honesty made Grace want to divulge her own sad tale. "Do you want to know why I'm here?"

"Aren't you doing this for college credit or something? That's what the brochure says about junior counselors." Truth still wore the scars of her old addiction, but Grace looked like the self-assured girl Tara wished she could be.

Grace shook her head. "I decided to come here because last year I got pregnant."

Tara gasped but quickly recovered. "I'm sorry. You just don't look like . . . ."

"My parents kicked me out of the house because I wouldn't have an abortion."

"That's horrible." Tara started to cry quietly. Getting sent to boot camp was bad enough, but being disowned—she couldn't imagine it. "Where did you go? Where's your baby?"

"It worked out," Grace said, trying to sound upbeat. "I stayed with my wonderful neighbor, and my baby was adopted by a really nice couple."

"But what about your parents?"

Grace said, "I'm not sure we'll ever be able to work things out, but I'm not going to let that pain make me stupid, which, as you found out, only makes everything worse."

When she was standing in Penn Station in New York City, trying to decide whether to take the train to Washington or Chicago, Tara knew that running away was beyond brainless; it would only make her look like she really was a cheater. But she'd been so hurt and angry that she'd wanted to lash out at her parents. If they worried that she might be gone forever, maybe they would regret how unfair they'd been. "I kind of screwed it up with the running away, didn't I?"

Grace nodded. "But you don't have to do stuff like that anymore. You know better now. Like Truth says: respect . . . for others and for yourself."

Reaching over and squeezing Grace's hand, Tara said, "Thank you. I won't tell anybody about your baby."

"It's okay. You can tell. It's part of who I am. If I'm ashamed of it for the rest of my life, I'll never get anywhere."

"You shouldn't be ashamed. You're amazing," Tara said.

"And so are you. We're not afraid of heights anymore, and we're not going to let anyone, including ourselves, tell us that we're no good." Grace wondered if junior counselors were supposed to be dispensing advice and giving pep talks.

"Thank you, Grace. I think I can go to sleep now."

The two girls stood up and hugged each other tightly, both feeling a little lighter for having shared their secrets.

CHAPTER 25

The Truth squad had broken up and all the girls had gone home, hopefully in a better state than they had been in when they came. After the fireside chat, Tara found her voice, no longer letting the other girls walk all over her. She actually told Kat to fuck off when Kat made fun of the way she talked. And just as Truth had predicted, the other girls had their epiphanies, or at least pretended to. The mountain had worked its magic on the girls, and if they remembered half of what they learned at No Boundaries, they would be well on their way. Right before Kat stepped onto the van, Truth handed her the penis pipe, although she had filled the cavity with some kind of glue so Kat couldn't smoke through it anymore. It was the perfect souvenir.

Now it was Grace's turn. To complete the program, she was required to spend three days alone on the mountain, reflecting on all that she had gone through and demonstrating mastery of her survival skills. Looking down at her sinewy arms and legs—definitely no baby weight hanging around—Grace hardly recognized herself. She'd always been thin, but she'd never been strong. Her skin had turned bronze, not just from the sun, but also from a thin layer of grime that seemed to be embedded in the top layer. After more than seven weeks without a proper shower or a decent meal, Grace was nearly wiped out. It was time to go home. At night she dreamt about taking long, hot baths in Helen's clawfoot tub and eating an entire chocolate cake.

As she waved goodbye to Truth, Dirk, and the others, Grace had to marvel at how far she'd come. Marching off into the wilderness alone, and her heart wasn't even racing. In fact, she was looking forward to it, mostly because the sooner she finished her individual reflection time, the sooner she could take a shower and put on clean clothes. Her whole body itched, and she'd been wearing the same underwear for nearly a week. Grace took one last look at the No Boundaries crew, and set off on her three days of solitude.

That first night, sitting in front of the campfire she had built, next to the tent she had pitched herself, Grace gnawed on a piece of beef jerky and stared out into the darkness. She was supposed to catch and cook her dinner—jerky was only for emergencies—but even though she had seen half a dozen rabbits that afternoon, Grace had read too many Beatrix Potter books to make a meal out of Flopsy Bunny.

To her dismay, Grace discovered that time slowed down when you were all alone in the middle of nowhere. Three days threatened to feel like three weeks. The worst thing about reflection time was the silence. The crickets and the birds were plenty loud, but the absence of human sounds made Grace lonesome. So she sang. She sang all the Beatles songs she knew from the *White Album* and *Sgt. Pepper's Lonely Hearts Club Band.* And she talked to herself. Long rambling conversations with the trees about the last eleven months—all her feelings about Nick and Charlie and her parents—and what she was going to do when she got home.

When Grace woke up the next morning, it had started to snow. She shivered and burrowed down inside her sleeping bag, thinking she should probably just stay there until it was time to go back. No one would know if she'd really climbed all the way to the top, and besides, no one was expecting a snowstorm in June, so she couldn't be faulted for not sticking to the original plan. Grace zipped the bag over her head and went back to sleep.

Dreaming there were mountain lions howling outside her tent, licking their chops while they waited to devour her, Grace woke up in a cold sweat. But it was just the wind. Peeking out through the tent flap, Grace saw that there was nearly a foot of snow outside and it was still coming down. Not equipped for winter hiking, she tried to remember what she'd been taught about avoiding hypothermia and frostbite. She dug in her bag and put on every piece of clothing she had with her. There was nothing else to do but wait for it to stop snowing, so she could hike back down the mountain. But what if it didn't stop? What if she froze to death in the middle of June halfway up a stupid mountain two thousand miles from home? After talking herself out of a full-on panic attack, Grace decided that it wasn't so much the dying part that she feared, but the thought that she would leave so much unfinished business behind, so many things that she had wanted to tell people but had been too much of a coward to say. Taking a pad of paper and a pen from her backpack, Grace decided to finish her business.

Dear Aunt Helen,
There aren't enough words in the world to express my gratitude. I feel blessed to have gotten to know you, and I love you with all my heart.
Grace

Although her letter to Helen was way too short, Grace really felt there was nothing she could say to adequately thank her rescuer and protector. Better to keep it simple. Besides, Helen already knew how much Grace loved her.

Dear Charlie,
This is one of those letters you write when you think you might not get to tell someone everything you wanted to say

in person. I'm sitting in a tent about to be blown off the side of a mountain in the middle of a freak June blizzard. This is supposed to be my moment, the culmination of everything I've learned here—how to dig deep inside myself and find a wellspring of strength to carry me out of harm's way—at least that's what it says in the handbook, which I'm ready to burn if it'll warm up my fingers. But in spite of the fact that I can start a fire with a single twig and survive for a week on one granola bar, I'm not so sure I'm going to make it out, and if I don't, I just want to tell you everything that I didn't have the guts to tell you before I left.

I'll never forget the moment you opened the door to my room the day I moved into Aunt Helen's house. You were wearing a shirt that was exactly the same color as your eyes, and I think I fell in love with you right then. It wasn't how you looked—it was how you looked at me. With a single glance, you seemed to know who I was, to understand me better than anyone I'd ever met, and you liked me in spite of the stupid, self-destructive thing I had done. But I was so afraid that you could never love me because of it. I squandered something precious that I should have saved for someone special, and I'm not sure anyone will ever be able to love me the way I want to be loved, especially not someone as extraordinary as you.

Through all those awful months, when I was wishing I could just disappear into the ground, you held my hand. I'll never be able to repay you for that. And then I screwed it up right at the end, as usual. When you visited me in the hospital after Molly was born I behaved badly, and I am so sorry. I didn't want to tell you where I was accepted for two reasons. First, I didn't want you to feel obligated to go wherever I went so you could take care of me . . . I know, that's incredibly narcissistic. Secondly, I was testing you . . . I know, even more idiotic. I wanted you to stand up to me, to love me enough to bare your soul, even as I was pushing you away. Does that make any sense at all? Did you love me then? I hope a little bit. Anyway, if you're reading this, I'm somewhere at the bottom of a ravine so it doesn't matter, but just know that I would have followed you to the ends of the earth.

That night in the attic when you kissed me, you healed my heart. And then, in my bedroom . . . I feel warmer just remembering how your lips felt on mine. How I wished those had been my very first kisses, because they are the only ones that ever mattered, that ever will matter. You have made me feel special, cherished, and most of all, worthy of love.

I love you, Charlie Glass.

Grace

Hopefully Charlie would never have to read it, and she could tell him everything in person.

Now Grace needed to write to her parents. Even if she survived the snowstorm in one piece, she knew she wouldn't be able to face them head on when she got home and say all the things that needed to be said. Smelling her mother's perfume, watching her father inspect her for some lasting remnant of her public shame—she would be sobbing within seconds and nothing would be resolved. But what to say? Jennifer's speech the night before Grace had left for Colorado had given Grace much food for thought. It was no different from her speech the previous summer when she so accurately predicted how Betsy and Brad would react to the baby news, but since Grace had become a mother herself, albeit for barely a nanosecond, she was privy to an emotion she had never before understood, and she now knew that Jennifer had been right all along. The love of a parent for a child was, or was supposed to be, fundamental. It was irrefutable, like gravity and breathing, and the fact that shit happens and nothing ever stays the same shouldn't destroy a love that powerful.

Dear Mom and Dad,

First I want to say how sorry I am that I disappointed you. I would never do anything to hurt you intentionally, because you are my parents and I have always tried to be the best person I could be, and I almost was. But nobody's perfect, not even your daughter. I still don't have a decent explanation for what happened to me on July second last year, an explanation that would satisfy you. Maybe you can't remember what it's like to be young and confused and staring into the perfect face of a seemingly perfect boy who says that you're perfect too. It's still not a justification for what I did, but I'm hoping that you can appreciate at least a little bit of what I was going through.

Second, as disappointed as you are in my behavior, I am just as disappointed in yours. I know I did a stupid thing, but no matter what I did, I'm still your daughter, not some stranger you can blow off at the first sign of trouble. You chose to have a child, and when you did that, you took on a major responsibility—to take care of me and love me, no matter what. My heart aches knowing that you don't love me without reservation, that you could love me only as long as I played the role of model child to model parents.

I want us to be a family again. I turned eighteen yesterday, and I will always be your daughter, but I am no longer your child. This is me trying to make it right between us. Now it's your turn.

Your daughter,
Grace

Rereading what she'd written, Grace wondered if she would ever have the courage to send this letter to her parents if she actually survived the snowstorm. She had become a totally new person in the last year—the old Grace would never have been able to say those things. In fact, the old Grace would never even have thought those things. But it was all true, and if she and her parents were ever going to salvage some sort of a relationship, they were going to have to hear it.

CHAPTER 26

Standing on the Warrens's front porch, Charlie had no idea what he was going to say, but at this point he had nothing to lose, and his natural sense of order made him want to put Grace's life back together, even if she was two thousand miles away and hadn't texted him a single word in more than seven weeks, and probably wouldn't appreciate him butting into her family business, especially since he was just a friend. Maybe he simply missed her, and talking to her parents was the next best thing to being with her. Helen thought it was a lousy idea.

"You really shouldn't meddle, darling. Grace will deal with her folks when she's good and ready," Helen gently scolded.

"Aunt Helen, really? You're *always* sticking your nose in other people's business, trying to fix things. Remember the green couple?" Of all people, Charlie had thought Helen would understand what he was trying to do and support him.

"I know, Charlie, the pot calling the kettle black and all that, but I'm trying to control those urges myself, and I don't want you to spend your life trying to solve other people's problems when you have plenty of your own issues to work on."

"But I *am* working on mine. If Grace makes up with her parents, she'll be able to focus on her relationship with me . . . maybe." Needing Helen to put her seal of approval on his idea, Charlie argued his case. "Anyway, doing nothing is making me antsy."

"I don't know about that. But if you do decide to go over there, keep your guard up. Those people are nutty as fruitcakes." Feeling responsible for her nephew as long as he was living under her roof, Helen worried that Grace's parents were truly unstable people, capable of real violence, no matter how many charity auctions they participated in.

Now Charlie tried to peek through the gap between the drawn curtains. It didn't look like anyone was at home. Suddenly a rush of footsteps getting louder, and a man threw open the front door. Helen was right—this guy was a lunatic, his hair standing on end, his shirt half-untucked.

"Yes?" Brad instantly regretted opening the door without looking through the peephole. "Whatever you're selling, young man, I'm not interested."

Before Brad could slam the door, Charlie stepped forward to block it. "I'm not selling anything, Mr. Warren."

"Do I know you?" Wondering if this kid was a process server, even though he didn't look old enough and he wasn't holding a manila envelope, Brad stared at Charlie. Brad had gotten back late the night before from DC, and he was too wiped out to think clearly. Spending the last two months in trial and settlement negotiations, he hadn't had a conversation that wasn't work-related since early March. "What do you want?" Not in the mood to waste his precious time playing guessing games with a kid who looked like the photo on the cover of the J. Crew catalog that was sitting on top of the stack of mail, right down to the barefoot loafer look, Brad took a deep breath and waited. This kid had five seconds to state his case.

"I'm a friend of Grace's. I live across the street. I'm Helen Teitelbaum's nephew, Charlie Glass." Wanting to impress this man, whom he imagined he would one day ask for permission to marry his daughter—assuming Grace ever spoke to them again, and assuming he could somehow figure out how to make her fall in love with him—Charlie held out his hand.

Brad just stood there, arms hanging limply at his sides. The fatigue was overwhelming; his brain was struggling to understand what this kid was talking about. "Is she okay? Did something happen?"

So lost in his own little world, and so determined to block out his daughter's inappropriate behavior, he hadn't been keeping track of the calendar. Why wasn't Betsy here to help him with this? The day before he'd left for Washington, Betsy had gone to Chicago to stay with her old college roommate who was recovering from a double knee replacement. She had called the real estate firm she worked for and said she was taking a leave of absence, and that was it. A year ago at this time they were the ideal family, and now they were broken and dysfunctional and scattered, and he had no idea how to fix things.

"She's gone, sir," Charlie answered.

Before Charlie realized that the word *gone* could be interpreted in multiple ways, Brad was on his hands and knees, gasping for air, tears dripping on the wide plank wood floor. "No, Mr. Warren. I'm sorry. I didn't mean . . . Grace is fine. She's not dead. She just went away after the baby was born."

"What, she's alive? Young man, you really should be more precise in your language. I nearly had a heart attack." Only when Brad believed he might have lost his precious daughter did he realize how much he loved her. It was hard to imagine how he had gotten to this wretched place where the only information he had about his only child was being provided by a total stranger. "Is the baby healthy?" Brad lay back on the floor and stared at the ceiling, trying to slow his galloping heart, letting the blood return to his swirling brain.

"Grace is well. She had a little girl. A couple from Philadelphia adopted her, and Grace went to Colorado, to some survival course.

She said she needed to get away from here for a while." Surprised and relieved that not only hadn't Mr. Warren done anything that could be considered insane, but that he seemed truly interested in and concerned about Grace, Charlie waited for the information to sink into Mr. Warren's clearly shocked system.

"Colorado? Survival school?" The one time they had gone camping, Grace had gotten lost, and now she was learning survival skills in the mountains. Clearly he didn't know his daughter very well. Perhaps it was time to get reacquainted. "What about finishing high school? How will she graduate if she's climbing mountains?"

"She already took the GED. She's very responsible." Maybe not totally true, since she *had* gotten pregnant, but except for that single misstep, Grace was the most together girl Charlie had ever met. "Your daughter is an amazing person, Mr. Warren, but you already know that."

Brad grunted. Of course Grace was amazing—she was his daughter. Suddenly it occurred to him that this boy might be more than just a friend. Had Grace sent her new boyfriend over to see which way the wind was blowing? Noting the ten-thousand-dollar diver's watch and the Cole Haan loafers, Brad had to admit this guy seemed far more capable of taking care of her than the teenage Casanova who had talked her out of her virginity in the back of his truck and then disappeared like Houdini.

"Does Grace know you're here—Charlie, did you say your name was?"

"No, sir, she would be furious with me if she knew I was here, but I just thought you would want to know how she was doing. I know this whole situation has been really hard on her, and I imagine it's been the same for you."

Trying to be diplomatic, trying to win this man's trust, Charlie didn't give a shit about Mr. Warren's emotional state. Anybody who could kick his daughter out of the house, and not only not go after her but continue to reject her for the better part of a year, had to be some kind of a sociopath.

Not knowing how to respond to that, Brad said, "Mrs. Warren is out of town. I don't know when she'll be back."

As soon as this boy left, Brad was going to call Betsy. It was time to implement Plan C or D or maybe Plan Z, something to right their capsized ship of a family. Being subtly scolded by a painfully precocious adolescent whom he knew was a hundred percent right was more than he could bear on his own. Today he would call Betsy and tell her to come home. Things were out of hand, and she needed to get back here and get this family back on track.

"Grace is supposed to come home some time in the next couple of weeks." That would give Grace's parents plenty of time to work out a plan to mend the mile-wide rift between them. Mr. Warren's tears spoke volumes, as long as he could hang onto that emotion now that he knew Grace was neither dead nor in danger.

"Her mother will certainly be home by then. By the way," Brad said as he got to his feet, "where did Grace decide to go to college?" How odd it felt to be so uninformed about such an important decision. From the time Grace was old enough to attend her first Yale reunion with him, the two of them had plotted and planned her future. Would she be a Yale bulldog, or a Princeton tiger, or a Cornell bear?

"I don't know. She didn't tell me," Charlie said.

Definitely not the boyfriend, Brad thought. Grace wouldn't keep that information a secret if she loved this guy. "Oh, I see. Well, thank you for stopping by. Is there a way to get in touch with Grace?"

When Betsy got home, maybe they would compose a letter to Grace, explaining their position, proposing a settlement of their differences. He was a lawyer, even as a father, and stating his position in a business letter was the most natural thing for him to do, even if the person he was communicating with was his only child.

"I don't think so. The program is called No Boundaries, and the website says that the participants aren't allowed to send or receive messages." Charlie couldn't believe he'd actually built a bridge with a single conversation.

"Makes sense." Brad opened the front door. "It was nice to meet you, Charlie. Send my regards to your aunt for me."

"Nice to have met you, sir. I'll tell Aunt Helen you said hello." Charlie could barely keep a straight face until he was down the driveway. Sending his regards to the woman he had threatened to charge with trespassing? This guy definitely had a few screws loose, but he seemed pretty harmless, and he sounded like he was ready to repair his broken family. Maybe there could be a happy ending to Grace's story, and to his.

CHAPTER 27

It felt like she'd been gone for a year, but it had only been a little over two months. Sixty-three days, to be exact. When Grace walked around the back of Helen's house, she could hear splashing in the pool. As she stood at one end, waiting for Charlie to reach her, she thought about what she was going to say. Spending weeks wandering around in the mountains, filthy and hungry, had given her plenty of time to think, but now that the moment was at hand, her mind went blank. The love letter she'd tucked in her sleeping bag to be delivered if she froze to death or fell off the side of the mountain was now in her back pocket. She supposed she could use that as a crib sheet, but she didn't want her declaration of love to turn into the delivery of a telegram. After everything she'd put Charlie through, he deserved to hear her whole heart, without notes.

Grabbing the side of the pool, Charlie did a double take, rubbing the water out of his eyes. "Grace, you're back."

Although her note had promised she would come home, Charlie hadn't been sure. He'd been wrong about Grace before. Quickly climbing out of the pool, Charlie wrapped a towel around his waist, but not before Grace gave him a quick up-and-down. It had been a long sixty-three days, and she had forgotten how handsome he was.

"I'm going to Dartmouth," Grace blurted. "And I should have told you before, but I didn't want you to choose, or not choose, a school because of me. And I know that's conceited to think that you would base the most important decision of your life on some stupid pregnant girl your aunt took in like a stray mutt, but I would have followed you to the top of Mount Everest, and you seemed like you liked me a lot, at least for a little while, but I know I was wrong about that, and I'm sorry I acted like an idiot. I understand now that you were just being nice, trying to get me through a really rough patch, and it worked, and I'm grateful. I never would have made it to the end without you. But I behaved like a fool after Molly was born. Maybe it was the hormones, or maybe I was just confused, but now I've got it all straightened out, and I hope we can at least be friends."

If not for the fact that she had run out of air, Grace would probably have kept talking, trying to apologize and make Charlie understand that even if he didn't want her for anything more than a friend, that would be enough, because after more than two months without him, she realized that she couldn't imagine *not* having him in her life. All the stuff about loving him that had flowed so easily from her pen when she thought she was about to cash in her chips was too scary to say out loud when he was standing two inches away and her heart was in her throat. Maybe she would find her backbone when he put some clothes on.

"Are you done yet?" Charlie asked, placing his cool, wet hand on Grace's warm face, her cheeks tan and her nose freckled from so much time spent outdoors. He wanted to save this moment like a snapshot in the photo album of his mind—the moment Grace came back to him.

Grace nodded.

"Okay, then. I'm going to Dartmouth, too." Torn between Princeton and Dartmouth, Helen had tipped the scale. "I had a dream that you were in New Hampshire, and you were happy. Take it for what it's worth," Helen had said, winking. He wondered if Grace had told her what she had decided, or if Helen had a source in the admissions office. But she swore she knew nothing. It was just another one of her feelings.

"Really?" Maybe, just maybe . . . .

"Really, and there's something else, something I should have said before you left, but you were acting weird, which you were totally entitled to do considering what you'd just been through, and I was being pigheaded and stupid. I wasn't just being nice to you all those months. I love you. I think I fell in love with you the day that I met you." Having sixty-three days to think about what he was going to say if and when Grace came back to him, Charlie decided that he loved Grace enough to risk everything, including his self-respect.

Grace's face turned pink under her tan, but she said nothing. Charlie's words hovered in the air between them. For a long minute, they stood, avoiding each other's eyes, Charlie's wet hair dripping on Grace's sneakers.

"Don't you have anything to say about that?" Charlie finally asked. It was so liberating to finally get the words out, even if Grace had fallen for some square-jawed mountain climber while she was away and wasn't interested in the preppy Jewish boy. Whatever happened next, he needed to know how she really felt. "Did you ever feel that way about me, even for a little while?"

Grace nodded, her eyes glassy with tears.

"And now? How do you feel about me right now?" Charlie asked. Before she could answer, he cradled her face in his hands, forcing her to look him directly in the eyes. "Tell me," he whispered. His mouth was inches from hers, and before he could find her lips, Grace reached up and kissed him. Her tears were warm on his cheek, and he could feel her pulse quickening under his hands. Pulling away from her reluctantly, he said, "Does that mean you still . . . ."

"I love you, too. I always have, but I didn't want to ruin your perfect life. I didn't want you to love me because you knew my parents didn't love me anymore and I was all alone, or that I was some lost lamb who couldn't fend for herself." Grace sat down on the grass and Charlie knelt in front of her.

"That's not why I love you, Grace. I know you don't *need* me to take care of you, but I *want* to. There's a huge difference."

"But I *do* need you. You make me feel like *me*, like the person I *want* to be, and when I was away, it just wasn't the same," Grace said. "I don't want to be away from you anymore."

"So don't leave again." Pushing her back into the soft grass, Charlie stretched out next to Grace and kissed her forehead, her nose, both cheeks, her chin, and finally her lips. "It's so short," he said, running his fingers through her close-cropped hair.

"I chopped it off myself. Low maintenance."

"I like it," Charlie whispered into Grace's ear. "I didn't think you were coming back to me, but Helen said I just had to be patient."

"Your aunt is the smartest woman I've ever met." Grace suddenly sat up. "I should tell her I'm back. We have to tell her about Dartmouth. She'll be so excited."

"I have a feeling she already knows." Charlie laughed and kissed Grace again.